HOSTAGE TO LOVE

HOSTAGE TO LOVE

Janet Tanner

This first world edition published in Great Britain 2001 by
SEVERN HOUSE PUBLISHERS LTD of
9–15 High Street, Sutton, Surrey SM1 1DF.
This first world edition published in the USA 2001 by
SEVERN HOUSE PUBLISHERS INC of
595 Madison Avenue, New York, N.Y. 10022.

Copyright © 2001 by Janet Tanner

British Library Cataloguing in Publication Data

Tanner, Janet
    Hostage to love
    1. Love stories
    I.   Title
    823.9'14 [F]

    ISBN 0-7278-5709-6

Except where actual historical events and characters are being
described for the storyline of this novel, all situations in this
publication are fictitious and any resemblance to living persons
is purely coincidental.

Typeset by Palimpsest Book Production Ltd.,
Polmont, Stirlingshire, Scotland.
Printed and bound in Great Britain by
MPG Books Ltd., Bodmin, Cornwall.

Prologue

New South Wales, Australia – 1807

T he boy stood beside the mound of fresh earth, staring intently at the rough wooden cross at its head. A haze of tears misted his eyes and he could scarcely bear to think of the careworn body that lay in the fresh grave, marked only by the cross that he had fashioned with his own hands. But somehow he forced himself to do so.

For these past five years he had watched his beloved mother grow thinner and paler as she worked her fingers to the bone struggling to keep her family together – himself, Rolf, and his younger sisters, Rosalie and Alison. How she had managed it in this wild and unforgiving land he could only guess. What he did know was that she had always been up before dawn, cooking and cleaning and caring for them, and then, when night fell, she would go off to her job at the tavern leaving him in charge of his sisters. It was often the early hours of the morning before he heard her come home and he suspected there was more to her work than serving jugs of ale.

But he did not blame her. He felt only frustration and anger that at fourteen he was unable to do more to help, to save her from the terrible life into which she had been forced.

No, the one he blamed was Andrew Mackenzie.

Andrew Mackenzie had been an officer in the hated New South Wales Corps. It was he who had caused the death of

1

Rolf's father when Rolf was just nine years old; it was he who had been responsible for the family losing their home. And now, just as surely, responsibility for this new grave could be laid at his door. If it had not been for Andrew Mackenzie they would still be a proper family, farming their little grant of land on the banks of the Hawkesbury River. His mother and father would still be alive, not lying in the cold damp ground, and he would be a happy and carefree youth, fishing, riding and – yes – working the long hot days away.

Rolf moved abruptly, dashing his sleeve across his eyes to wipe away the threatening tears, and hatred for the man who had destroyed his family welled up to swamp the grief and harden like stone round his heart.

When Andrew Mackenzie had taken their home and caused his father's death, Rolf had been too young to feel anything but grief and fear. Now he was almost a man, and as he stood there beside his mother's grave all the resentment and frustration of the past five years came together in a wave of pitiless resolution that burned like fire in every nerve of his body and ate its way deep into his very soul.

His eyes fastened once more on the rough wooden cross he had made to mark her final resting place and his hands made fists at his sides.

'He won't get away with this, Mama,' he ground out through gritted teeth. 'I'll give my life to make sure of that. Whatever it takes, and however long, I'll get Mia-Mia back for our family. And I swear, on your grave, that Andrew Mackenzie will pay dearly for what he has done!'

One

1822

A storm was brewing. As she drove the buggy along the rutted road, Regan Mackenzie glanced up towards the distant mountains and saw chain lightning flicker brilliantly along the blue ridges. She could feel it in the air, too. The heat of the day, already oppressive, seemed to have closed in round her, and the deep blue of the sky above the eucalypts and ghost gums had darkened to an ominous purple hue.

'Giddy-up, Lucky!'

Regan flicked her riding whip across the pony's fat rump. Without any need of further encouragement he broke into a canter, and the buggy surged forward until it was bowling along at an almost reckless pace.

Regan laughed out loud with delight as her long red-gold hair swept away from her face and streamed out behind her. She loved nothing better than to drive the buggy at speed, and the coming storm gave her just the excuse she needed to throw caution to the winds. If she made haste, maybe she could be back at Mia-Mia before the storm broke.

Not that the thought of a soaking bothered her much – the cool touch of rain on her face would be a welcome relief after the weeks of scorching drought. But even now her father was likely watching the sky anxiously and working himself up into a fine old rage.

Very little caused concern to Andrew Mackenzie, but the safety and wellbeing of his only daughter certainly did. Ever

3

mindful of the dangers facing a woman alone in this wild country, he was already reluctant to allow her to drive herself to Broken Hill without one of his trusted men to accompany her, and Regan well knew that his fears were not without foundation. Flash floods could rise in no time at all when torrential rains fell on to sunbaked earth, bush fires could begin and spread with perilous speed if lightning hit a dead gum tree in a dry storm. And always there was the danger of escaped convicts, desperate and mad with hunger and resentment, and the renegades who would kill for whatever they could get to enable them to buy their next keg of rum.

Regan was a mistress of winding her father around her little finger to get her own way. But if he was worried enough today then he might well forbid her to drive to Broken Hill again – or even to ride out on the farm as she loved to do – until the danger of summer storms was past. If he confined her to the house for days, or even weeks, she'd go stark, staring mad she thought!

And besides that . . . she cast a glance at the flimsy box on the seat beside her, thinking of its precious contents, her new gown, emerald green silk to match her eyes, which she had just collected from the dressmaker in Broken Hill. If the rain came, it would not be a gentle shower, but a downpour that would soak the box and the tissue wrappings in minutes, and the gown would be ruined.

The thought alarmed her more than any danger to herself, and she flicked the whip across Lucky's rump again. She looked a picture in the new gown, she knew – even Eliza Button, the dressmaker, had said so – and she sewed for all the finest ladies in the district. Why, it was even rumoured she had sewed for the Governor's wife, who had the choice of the best dressmakers in Sydney and Parramatta!

'I've not done a bad job there, Missy,' Eliza had said tartly, but her shrewd little eyes had been shining with pride, and Regan knew that the low neckline of the bodice, exposing her creamy throat and the swell of her firm young breasts, and the tucking which emphasised her small waist, had turned out just as the dressmaker had envisioned it. Regan didn't want the gown to be ruined by rain before she'd even had the chance to wear it. She only wished she felt more enthusiastic about the occasion for which it had been made.

In three days' time David and his parents were coming to Mia-Mia, and she knew the principal reason for the gathering was to discuss arrangements for their wedding. Already she could imagine the way the visit would be – Molly, David's mother, pressing for the sort of grand ceremony that Regan was sure she would hate, whilst her father and David's smiled indulgently and talked over their Madeira wine of the price of wool that would pay for it all.

Not that there was really any concern on that score. Between them Andrew and David's father, Richard Dauntsey, owned most of the farms and the rich pasture land that lined the river banks. But they would pretend there was – just as they had pretended to be surprised as well as delighted that she was to marry David and join their two empires, when each of them knew it was what they had hoped for since the days when she and David had played together as children.

Regan's eyes softened a little as she remembered those days, long and happy, riding their ponies together and fishing in the shallow creeks. She supposed she had known even then that their futures were bound together and she would always be with him. He had been her playmate and her friend, and soon he would be her husband. She only wished, now that she was grown, that he could stir in her some of the excitement that came from galloping her horse through the pastures. David was sweet and kind to her always; she was sure he would make as good a husband as she could ever hope for. But sometimes, when he kissed her gently like a brother, sometimes when she watched his slim fair frame riding away to Glenbarr, his own home, and

5

felt not a whisper of regret, she found herself longing for something more. And the longing was a restless ache deep inside that she barely understood.

It was there now, prickling in her veins as she thought of the meeting to plan their wedding. She should be excited at the prospect, surely? But she was not.

Up ahead the road bent sharply through a patch of thick bush and Regan pulled on the reins to slow Lucky down, but even so the buggy swayed a little and it took all Regan's skill to negotiate the bend. Then, as the road straightened out again, she gasped, reining in hard.

Someone was there in the middle of the road, kneeling over what looked like a bundle of old rags! Lord! She was in danger of running straight into them!

Regan tugged on the reins with all her strength, then, as the buggy slowed, her heart came into her mouth with a jolt. What she had taken for a bundle of rags was in fact a man!

Two horses stood close by. There must have been a terrible accident! Regan thought.

'Can I help?' she started to call, then the words froze in her throat as realisation hit her like an icy wave.

The kneeling man wasn't aiding the one who lay lifeless on the dusty road. He was rifling his victim's pockets for ill-gotten gain! This was no accident she had happened upon. This was a bushwhacking!

Regan gasped with fright. For a moment that seemed to last a lifetime she gazed horrified into the face of the attacker. His eyes were hard and dark in his swarthy face and a livid white scar ran from the corner of one of them down across his cheek. The kerchief he had used for a mask had slipped down around his neck, revealing cruel lips, twisted now into a snarl of fury. It was a face that burned itself into her memory. Then, as she saw him reach for his gun, a rush of adrenalin restored her senses.

Quick as a flash Regan raised her whip and lashed out.

The curling tip caught his bare wrist. He recoiled with an oath, but Regan knew she had bought herself a brief respite only.

'Go, Lucky! Go!' she screamed.

The pony, startled by the unaccustomed assault, plunged forward, almost throwing Regan from the buggy. A pistol shot rang out, whistling past her ear, and then another. Regan screamed, and Lucky, now as startled and terrified as his mistress, broke into a wild gallop. Faster and faster he went, his drumming hooves raising a cloud of thick choking dust.

Regan cast a fearful glance over her shoulder as she heard the thunder of other, faster, hooves, gaining on her. Then, as they drew level, she realised the horse was riderless. Startled by the shots, as Lucky had been, it had bolted and taken off after them.

'Oh, thank God!' Regan sobbed. The bushwhacker could never hope to catch her on foot.

But her relief was short-lived. When she tugged on the reins to slow Lucky's headlong dash there was no response. Lucky had the bit between his teeth. Now he was racing with the big stallion, faster and ever faster along the rutted road whilst the buggy jolted and swayed behind him.

'Lucky! Stop!' Regan screamed, but to no avail. Though he had not the slightest chance of keeping up with the stallion, Lucky plunged wildly on.

The road was rougher now, full of potholes and ruts, but that did nothing to deter the frightened animal either. If anything, the violent lurching of the buggy only served to madden him more. Over a hillock they went, bouncing right into the air as the wheels hit the ground again, and the jolt sent Regan tumbling off balance so that she lost the reins.

With a squeal of fear she landed in the well of the buggy, and the pony chose that very moment to veer off the track. For seemingly endless seconds they careered on, and Regan thought her last moment had come. Then the undergrowth became thicker and gradually the pony's headlong gallop slowed and he stopped beside a tree fern, blowing and sweating.

Shaking from head to foot, Regan pulled herself up and tumbled out of the buggy. Her legs almost gave way beneath her, and she gripped the side for support, working her way round until she reached the pony. Then she stood for a moment, holding his lathered head.

Thank God he had stopped and she was all in one piece! The buggy could have been jerked to flinderjigs and she could have been thrown out and killed! As it was she was more or less unharmed, and Lucky seemed none the worse for his adventure either. But the wheels of the buggy were firmly anchored in undergrowth, and ahead the bush was thick and virgin and she was still a good five miles from home. Walking that far in this relentless heat was not a challenge to be undertaken lightly. And worse than the heat . . .

Somewhere back on the road between Mia-Mia and Broken Hill was an armed and dangerous man who had robbed and killed, and who knew full well she had seen his face.

Regan passed a trembling hand across her moist forehead. Somehow she had to get the buggy back on the road and drive it to safety. But could she do it? And if she did, would she walk straight into the man who would kill her on sight? Shaking with a mixture of fear and determination, Regan caught at Lucky's bridle, trying to turn him, but he stood his ground, unwilling, now that he had stopped, to move again.

'Come on, you beast! Come on!' she urged him, but to no avail.

Helpless tears of fright stung her eyes and she brushed them away angrily with a dust-caked hand. She had no one but herself to blame for her predicament, and there was no one but herself to get her out of it.

With renewed vigour, Regan applied herself to the hopeless task. But the buggy remained as firmly stuck as ever.

Rolf Hannay reined in his mount at the top of the rise and sat for a moment looking down at the valley spread out beneath him.

There, at last, was the road that led to Mia-Mia, following the river through cultivated pasture and virgin scrub. The journey he had sworn to make so many years ago was almost at an end. After all this time he was almost home.

As his eyes, grey as granite in his sun-bronzed face, took in the once familiar landscape, the straitjacket of cold determination that had encased his heart for so long eased for a moment as far-off memories of the boy he had once been came tantalisingly to the surface of his mind. Here, he had once been happy, a carefree lad in a wild and wonderful country. Here, he had been surrounded by a loving family, his father and his mother striving together to build a good life for him and his sisters.

But Andrew Mackenzie had put an end to all that. Andrew Mackenzie had taken their home and their land, and it had been the death of both his father and his mother. Single-handed, Andrew Mackenzie had destroyed them. And now . . .

The icy determination to gain revenge and take back what was rightfully his was back in an instant. Rolf had nursed it for too long to allow himself to weaken now. He did not yet know exactly how he was going to go about it. He'd ridden for more than two days from his own farm in the rich pastureland on the other side of the mountain range without any clear plan in his mind except that somehow he would find Andrew Mackenzie's weak point and exploit it. He must have one. Even a man like him, who had once been an officer in the hated New South Wales Corps, profiteering at the expense of the less fortunate, could not be without his Achilles heel. And Rolf was determined to discover what it

9

was. Then, by God, he would make him pay, and pay dearly, for what he had done.

Rolf was no longer a helpless boy. He was a man who had made his own fortune, and grown harder and more ruthless in the process. He would make Andrew Mackenzie regret his past actions by one means or another. He would make him wish he had never been born!

Rolf shifted his position in the saddle, casting one more glance across the valley beneath him. There were more clearings now than he remembered, more crop fields and more cattle. But beyond them, the bush was still there, as thick and wild as ever.

He stiffened suddenly, his eyes narrowing as his gaze lit upon a flash of scarlet in the midst of unbroken green and brown. What the devil was that?

For a moment the brilliant colour reminded him sharply and painfully of the scarlet coats of the officers of the Corps. But he knew that could not be. The Corps had been withdrawn now, and most of the old Corps officers like Andrew Mackenzie had retired to live on the fat fortunes they had made for themselves during their glory years.

Rolf shrugged his broad shoulders and touched his booted heels to the flanks of his mount. Whoever – whatever – it had nothing to do with him.

He rode down the steep and rutted track to the road below, a tall dark figure, slimly built but well muscled, who sat his horse with the easy grace of long practice. Plenty of women had set their cap at Rolf Hannay, but none had succeeded in winning his heart, or even coming close. Consumed as he was by his desire for revenge, he had had no time for anything but gaining the wherewithal to achieve that end. And now the time was close! Fired up by that thought, Rolf kicked Satan, his jet-black stallion, to a canter the moment he reached the better made-up road through the valley.

He had ridden some half a mile when he noticed some-thing lying in the road on the far side of a hillock. He slowed Satan, gazing at it curiously. It looked for all the world like a dress box. But what was it doing here, in the middle of nowhere? Had it fallen unnoticed from a bullocky's wagon?

Curious, Rolf dismounted, picked it up and lifted the lid. Inside, carefully covered with tissue, lay folds of emerald silk, delicately edged with black lace. A lady's gown, without doubt. Well, he had no use for something like that, though he could well imagine the lady for whom it was intended would be heartbroken at its loss.

A new wave of bitterness consumed him as he remembered the faded prints his mother had been forced to wear. How he would have loved her to own something as fine as this! How *she* would have loved it! The folk who lived hereabouts now certainly had more money to throw away these days than when his family had struggled to farm the land!

About to toss it aside in disgust, he changed his mind abruptly and laid the box down on the scrub at the roadside. Whoever it belonged to might come back in search of it, and he had no quarrel with them. What had happened to his family was the fault of no one but Andrew Mackenzie . . .

Rolf stiffened suddenly as he noticed wheel tracks on the verge and a pathway of trampled brush leading off into the bush. Had the carriage from which the box had fallen gone off the road? Was that the reason it was lying here? In a flash he remembered the glimpse of scarlet he had caught from up on the ridge. Taking his bearings, he realised it might well have been almost at this point.

Leaving the box at the roadside, he took Satan's bridle and led him towards the trampled path. Around him, the bush was silent in the relentless heat of the afternoon.

'Hullo!' he called. 'Is anyone there?'

The stillness and silence remained unbroken.

'Hullo!' he called again.

And then he heard the unmistakable whinny of a horse,

coming from deep in the bush. Leading Satan by the bridle, Rolf set out towards it.

Regan clutched at Lucky's mane, rigid with fear. The moment she had heard the rhythmic beat of hooves on the road she had ceased her efforts to free the buggy. It was the bushwhacker coming after her, she was certain of it! But she was well hidden from the road. If she kept silent perhaps he would ride past and never know she was there.

When the hoofbeats stopped, her heart had come into her mouth with an enormous leap. Dear God, had Lucky's flight into the bush left a trail that the bushwhacker could follow? If he had seen it, it would lead him straight to her! And there was nothing she could do except keep as still as she possibly could – and pray. Flight would achieve nothing, only draw his attention if he didn't already know she was there.

Regan's heart was beating so hard she thought the man must be able to hear it. She crouched against Lucky, scarcely daring to breathe.

And then she heard him call out. Once, twice. Then Lucky whinnied and Regan knew she was undone. Only a deaf man could have failed to hear it.

Undergrowth crunched as someone moved through it and suddenly the wash of cold fear in her veins reawakened her courage.

The man might be going to murder her. Almost certainly that was his intention. And there was nothing she could do about it. But at least he wouldn't find her cowering behind her pony like a frightened child. And she wouldn't beg, either, for mercy which he would surely withhold. If she was about to die, she'd die bravely, damn him!

As the bush parted, Regan stepped forward boldly, glad that the skirts of her scarlet gown hid the trembling of her legs.

'If you dare to touch me,' she ground out, 'my father will

have you hung from the highest gum on the Hawkesbury. . . !'
Her voice tailed away.

It was not the robber, but the finest-looking man she had
ever seen, leading a jet-black stallion.

'Oh!' she whispered faintly.

And as the remaining strength went out of her legs, Regan
found she had to hang on to Lucky for support after all,
contrary to all her best intentions.

Two

L ord, but she was beautiful! Even dishevelled and dirty as she was, there was no disguising it. Her scarlet gown might be torn and muddied, but it still graced a body any red-blooded man would desire. Her red-gold hair, loose and tangled, fell about a heart-shaped face that was streaked with dust and perspiration, but there was still dignity in the emerald-green eyes and the jut of her chin – yes, and defiance too. She stood there facing him with screwed-up courage, and the mix of beauty and vulnerability made his stomach clench with an emotion he had almost forgotten in the years of self-denial.

She swayed suddenly, clutching at her pony for support, and he took a step towards her, instinctively holding out his hand to catch her if she fell. But she steadied herself, drawing a deep trembling breath and looking at him with puzzlement in those emerald eyes.

'I'm sorry. I thought . . .' She gave her head a small shake and laughed tremulously.

'And I'm sorry if I frightened you. I came to see if I could be of assistance.'

She glanced around sharply, and the fear was back in her eyes. 'Are you alone? There's no one with you?'

His eyes narrowed. 'I'm alone, yes. Why?'

She passed the tip of her tongue over dry lips. 'There was a bushwhacking. I came on the scene. The rogue was searching his victim's pockets . . .'

'A bushwhacking?' Rolf repeated sharply. 'Are you sure?'

14

Her eyes flashed with impatience. 'Of course I'm sure! He tried to kill me too.' Her voice wavered at the memory. 'His shots missed, but my pony bolted. That's how I came to be in this mess. I've tried and tried to free the buggy and I just can't do it. It's stuck fast. And even if I do—' She broke off again, biting at her lip, and he read her thoughts. Even if she freed the buggy, the murderer might be waiting for her on the road.

'A dangerous situation,' he agreed, his hand automatically going to his hip to check that the pistol was there, a heartbeat away from his fingertips should he need it. 'And you thought that I . . . ?'

She nodded. 'I thought you were him – coming to do away with me.'

'So that was the reason your father was going to have me hung from the tallest gum on the Hawkesbury?' he asked with a wry smile.

Her chip came up. 'You're laughing at me! I assure you, it was no laughing matter!'

'Certainly it was not! And I assure *you*, I am not laughing at you – far from it,' he said, and it was no more than the truth. He could feel only admiration for the girl.

What courage it must have taken, to stand there and defy the man she believed was about to murder her!

'We'd better see if I can have any more success than you in getting this contraption back on the road,' he said lightly to cover the unaccustomed way he was feeling. 'Whoever may or may not be on the road, you can't stay here forever. There's a storm brewing too.'

'Don't I know it!' Even as she spoke, she could hear the distant rumble of thunder. 'I was trying to get home before the rain came and ruined my new—' She broke off, as if suddenly remembering, and peered anxiously into the well of the buggy.

'Oh no!' she squealed. 'It's gone! It must have fallen out somewhere!'

15

The look of horror on her face was almost the equal of the one she'd expressed when she had thought she was about to be murdered.

This time he did laugh, a great shout of delighted mirth. What a woman!

'Don't worry,' he said when he had stopped laughing. 'Your gown is safe.'

Her eyes snapped. 'How do you know it's a gown I've mislaid?'

He smiled, white teeth flashing in his sun-browned face. 'Because I found it. It's what first attracted my attention, as it happens. I've laid it at the roadside.'

'I must get it!' She made to dash back towards the road, all danger forgotten in her anxiety, and he laid a cautionary hand on her arm.

'Wait! Do you want to get yourself killed for the sake of a gown?' His tone was hard, commanding, and it brought her up short.

'When you venture back on to that road, it will be with my pistol covering you,' he went on, turning to fasten the reins of his great black horse around a sturdy low branch. 'Come here now, take your pony's head and hold him steady while I try to free the buggy.'

Regan did as she was bid and he bent his shoulder to the task, muscles rippling beneath the fine lawn of his shirt and the close-fitting buckskin of his breeches.

For some minutes he heaved and rocked, moving the buggy inch by painful inch until the wheels freed and Lucky, with Regan leading him, was able to pull the buggy back on to the road. Then he straightened, rivers of sweat running down the premature lines that furrowed his handsome face.

'*Now* you can worry about your gown – and other things.' He was looking up and down the deserted road with steel-grey eyes alert for any sign of danger.

Regan dropped the reins and ran to the dress box, still

lying where he had placed it. She picked it up, crushing it protectively to her bosom, before carefully depositing it in the well of the buggy. Then she turned to him, green eyes shining with gratitude.

'Oh, I don't know how to thank you!'

'Thank me when you're safely home,' he said shortly.

'And I don't even know what to call you!' she ran on.

'Rolf – Peterson.' He hesitated only briefly over the unfamiliar name. He had decided upon it before setting out on his mission, knowing that his real name – Hannay – would be instantly recognised by Andrew Mackenzie. Peterson had seemed a good choice, chosen as it was for his dead father. Peterson. Son of Peter. Peter Hannay. But that would never occur to Andrew Mackenzie, and, to Rolf's mind, it was the final superb irony.

'I thank you, Mr Peterson.'

'Rolf, please.'

'Rolf.'

He liked the way it sounded on her lips. 'And you are . . . ?'

A small smile lifted the corners of her soft wide mouth and she lifted a slim hand to push a tangle of red-gold hair away from her face.

'I am Regan Mackenzie.'

Mackenzie.

The despised name hit him like buckshot. He stiffened, standing motionless for a moment as if he were carved from stone. The same stone that had hardened around his heart.

Regan tilted her head slightly to one side so that she resembled nothing more than a small questioning bird.

'You know of my father, perhaps? Andrew Mackenzie.'

He was more prepared this time, yet still to hear the name spoken was to find a chink in his armour. With an effort, he gathered his senses.

'I told you, I'm a stranger hereabouts.'

'You said, yes. But my father was an officer in the New South Wales Corps. Their brief was widespread.'

He bit back the bitter response. Widespread, indeed! And dedicated to their own ends! 'The Rum Corps' had been their nickname, for not only had they controlled all legitimate trade, they had cornered the market in rum also, and ruined many a poor farmer by encouraging him into debts he could never afford to pay from his meagre grant of land. It was not only he, Rolf, who had cause to hate 'The Rum Corps', not by a long chalk.

'Maybe I've heard the name,' he said cautiously. 'If so, I don't remember.'

She frowned slightly, her fine brows knotting. Then she smiled, and it was like sunshine on a dark day.

'And why should you? He's retired from the Corps for many years now, even before it was disbanded. Why, he's been a farmer and landowner for as long as I can remember.'

Rolf passed a hand across his brow, dashing away the fine sheen of sweat.

'You live nearby?'

'A few miles down the road. Mia-Mia is our homestead.'

Mia-Mia. The familiar name hit him like a clenched fist in the gut.

'But we own three other farms too,' she went on, seemingly oblivious to his reaction. 'Two more on the river and another in Cow Pastures. They are run by overseers.'

So, Andrew Mackenzie had done well for himself. Well, it was only to be expected. What – or who – could have stood in his way?

The first spots of rain pattered on the leaves of the eucalypts and, as if they had reminded her of her danger, Regan moved abruptly.

'I must get back there now. The storm is coming – and my father will be worried.'

18

Worried. It wasn't a word Rolf would have associated with Andrew Mackenzie. But then perhaps being a father had changed him. Any father would worry about a daughter as lovely and headstrong as this one, even a heartless swine like Andrew Mackenzie.

In a flash it came to him. He had known that every man must have a weak spot. This lovely girl was, in all likelihood, Andrew Mackenzie's. Rolf had prayed to find a way to get close to him and find a way to make him pay for what he had done. Perhaps a kindly fate had answered his prayers.

'I'll ride with you.' His tone was harsh, for every ounce of tenderness he had felt for this spirited girl had disappeared the moment he had learned who she was.

'Oh, you've done enough already!' she protested. 'I can't impose on you any further.'

'It's no imposition, I assure you. And what would you do if you ran across the bushwhacker alone on the road?'

He saw the fear and uncertainty flicker in her eyes, and knew he was winning.

'I'm going your way in any case,' he said, truthfully, as it happened.

'Well . . .' She hesitated. 'If you are sure I am not inconveniencing you, I'm sure my father would be very grateful.'

Rolf's lip curled slightly. Grateful, Andrew Mackenzie? Not grateful enough to return Mia-Mia to its rightful heir, of that much he was certain. But grateful enough, perhaps, to offer him a job?

It was what Rolf had had in mind – to seek employment as a hand on Andrew Mackenzie's holdings. That would, he had reasoned, give him the chance to get close enough to figure out the way he could gain his revenge.

The rain was falling faster now from a darkened sky and bouncing off the hard sun-baked surface of the road. Regan, still mindful of her precious new gown, tucked the box as far out of harm's way as possible under the seat whilst Rolf made a cursory examination to ensure no great damage had been done to the buggy by the unceremonious dash into the bush.

'It all looks in order,' he said. 'We'd better make haste if you are not to become bogged down again, in mud this time!'

She nodded briefly, taking up the reins, and he mounted Satan.

'Let us go, then.'

He touched Satan's flanks with his booted heels and they set off along the road with the heavens opening above them.

As she handled the buggy with something less than her usual expertise, Regan glanced at the man riding beside her. Lord, but fortune had been smiling on her when he had happened along! But for him she would still be stuck there in the bush, or facing the prospect of a long and perilous walk home. And not only that . . .

Regan's heart skipped a beat as she looked at him, sitting so tall and straight in the saddle. His hat was pulled low now against the torrents of rain but she could still see his face in her mind's eye, that lean sunburned face with the premature lines etched into it, the angular chin, the slate-grey eyes. She remembered too the way his muscles had rippled as he struggled to free the buggy, strong muscles in his shoulders and arms, barely hidden by the fabric of his shirt. Muscles she had wanted, for a crazy moment, to reach out and touch. It was the muscles of his thighs she could see now, rock hard beneath the buckskin of his breeches as he urged his mount along the road, and clipping Lucky's flanks with the whip to make him keep pace, she found herself wanting to touch them too.

Stop it! she told herself sternly. He's a stranger who has helped you out of a pretty pickle, that's all. He's not for

20

you. By tomorrow he'll be gone, out of your life forever.
And even if that wasn't the case . . .

Regan felt a great wave of guilt wash over her. She was
promised to David. Dear, sweet, gentle David. Soon she
would be his wife. She had no business at all entertaining
such notions about another man. But she couldn't help
wishing, all the same, that when she looked at David she
could feel one quarter of the emotion this handsome stranger
was stirring in her. Or that she felt one quarter as safe!

She could see Rolf's pistol hanging comfortingly on his
hip and she knew instinctively that he would be both fast
on the draw and deadly accurate in his aim should the need
arise. No other man besides her father had ever made her
feel quite so protected.

She smiled to herself at the irony of it. She, Regan,
who liked to think she could take good care of herself,
who rode as fearlessly as any man and baulked at the
restrictions her father placed upon her for her own safety,
dependent now upon this stranger's protection and actually
enjoying it! Why, it was almost as if the fright she'd had
earlier had unleashed feelings she hadn't even known she
possessed!

They were travelling through rich pastureland now, where
the cattle stood stoically in groups, steaming in the relentless downpour. One more bend, and home would be in
sight.

Regan experienced a curious mix of relief and regret. It
would be good to get out of her soaking clothes and into
a bath-tub. It would be good to know that, for the time
being, at least, she was safe from the murderous intent of
the bushwhacker. But some small rebellious part of her
wished this ride could go on forever.

'Here we are! There's Mia-Mia! That's my home!' Regan
called out.

Slowing his horse as they approached the driveway, Rolf

felt a great wave of emotion wash over him for which, curiously, he was completely unprepared.

He did not need telling that this was Mia-Mia, and he certainly did not want to hear this girl referring to it as 'her home'. It was *his* home – or it had been! Every stick and stone was his heritage. Or was it? Rolf's eyes narrowed with surprise as it came into view.

His Mia-Mia had been a humble farmhouse, built on the rising ground above the river valley with love and care, but with little money and little time or thought for extravagances. He remembered it as stark and raw, a low, one-storeyed building with a veranda on three sides and a few rickety steps leading to a door that had begun to peel under the fierce sun from lack of painting. Now . . .

Lord, it was almost a mansion! A whole wing had been added, and fine porticos now surrounded the door. It was not only the house that had changed, either. Along the avenue leading to it, mimosa trees had been planted among the native eucalypts. Rolf could only guess at the time and money that had been spent here since he had last seen it, and far from admiring the result he could feel only furious anger at the thought of the other poor souls who had in all likelihood faced ruin to pay for it.

As they turned into the drive the front door of the house was thrown open and a figure emerged. A big man, tall and broad, with a mane of iron-grey hair framing a face tanned to a leathery brown by the sun. A man who had aged twenty years since Rolf had last seen him, but was unmistakable nevertheless.

With a jolt Rolf realised that in this moment he had achieved the first part of his long-laid plan. Once again he was face to face with Andrew Mackenzie.

'Regan! Thank the Lord!'

Andrew Mackenzie took the steps down from the veranda two at a time and raced down the drive towards them.

Within moments his shirt and breeches were soaked, but he paid no heed. Neither did he so much as glance at Rolf. He had eyes only for his daughter.

'You should not have gone to Broken Hill today! I warned you we were due for a summer storm!' His voice was angry but it was the anger born of relief after severe anxiety.

'Well, I'm back now,' Regan retorted. 'Safe and sound – thanks to this gentleman.'

For the first time Andrew seemed to notice Rolf. The eyes he turned on him were heavy with suspicion.

'You'll offer him shelter, I hope?' Regan said swiftly.

Andrew growled something deep in his throat, but he took Lucky's bridle and began to lead him towards the rear of the house.

'This way,' he said to Rolf over his shoulder. 'One of my men will see your horse is rubbed down.'

He led the way around the house. Beyond it, Rolf saw that the few outhouses and the buildings that had accommodated their three convict labourers had also been extended. Lord, nothing had been spared to make Mia-Mia vast – and profitable!

Resentment stirred once more in Rolf's gut, and hardened as a groom emerged into the downpour and led Satan into a stable block where several fine horses stood pawing restlessly in their stalls. Another groom appeared to take charge of Lucky and the buggy, and Rolf followed Andrew and Regan in a dash for the house.

In the kitchen that had once been his mother's, a small round woman wearing a huge wrap-around apron over her print calico gown was kneading pastry.

'Leave that, Ellen,' Andrew Mackenzie ordered. 'See to hot water for baths for Miss Regan and this –' his brow furrowed, '– gentleman.'

She jumped to obey him, wiping floury hands on her apron, though her small eyes were round with curiosity in her pasty face.

Andrew flicked his head, shaking the water out of his iron grey hair as a horse might shake itself after a soaking.

'Now.' He addressed himself to Regan. 'Perhaps you will explain yourself, Miss. Before we go further, I'll know if I may who it is I am forced to offer shelter to, and just how he comes to be riding with you.'

Regan's chin lifted and she met her father's angry gaze with fire of her own.

'He saved my life, Father.'

'Saved your life!' Andrew exclaimed. 'But how?'

'I've had – well, quite an adventure, Father,' Regan said, nervous now at telling him just how close she had been to disaster. 'On the road between here and Broken Hill I came on the scene of a bushwhacking. Oh, it was all over before I got there. The poor man who had been attacked was already dead, and the robber was rifling his body. He fired at me—'

'*Fired* at you! Hell's teeth!' Andrew took a quick protective step towards her. 'A robber *fired* a gun at you? He didn't hit you? You're not hurt?'

'No. I am not hurt. But the shot frightened Lucky.'

'I'll have the countryside scoured for him!' Andrew's face was dark with fury. 'And when I find him, by God he'll pay!'

'He's long gone,' Regan said, with more conviction than she felt. The memory of the ugly scene still had the power to make her quake inwardly. But riding out to hunt the man down would be a vain exercise – as well her father would know once his temper cooled. 'Lucky ran away and the buggy got stuck in the bush. I'd be there now if this gentleman hadn't come along and found me.' She cast a quick glance at Rolf, standing with his hands on his slim, buckskin-covered hips, and felt something as sharp as her fear but a million times sweeter twist within her. 'He rode home with me to make sure I came to no more harm,' she added.

Andrew tore his eyes from his daughter, looking at the man who had been her saviour.

'It seems, then, that I owe you my gratitude.'

Rolf shrugged. 'Any man would have done the same.'

'I think not. In this country, men too often think only of what profit they can gain from another's misfortune,' Andrew said, and the irony of his words was not lost on Rolf. 'My daughter is too often careless of her own safety,' he went on. 'Being raised without a mother has made her wild.'

'Your wife is dead?' Rolf asked before he could stop himself.

For a moment Andrew's face was bleak with an old pain that had never lost its sting. 'She died when Regan was born. I've raised her alone, with only a housekeeper to bring a woman's influence to bear. If she had been a boy . . .'

'But I'm not, Father,' Regan said with spirit. 'I'm afraid you can't choose in these matters. You get what you are given, so you just have to put up with me!'

'I certainly do!' But there was a softness in his voice as he said it, and his pride and love for her was written plainly in his face for all to see. 'It'll be a good thing, Miss, when you're married and become some other man's responsibility. And I only hope he has more success taming you than I have had!'

Again, he raised his eyes to Rolf. 'What do they call you, Sir?'

Rolf stepped forward, out of the puddle of rainwater that had formed at his feet, and held out his hand. As he spoke his voice echoed around the kitchen without a trace of hesitation.

'My name is Rolf Peterson,' he said.

In her room Regan shed her gown and undergarments into a sodden heap and tested the temperature of the water in the bath-tub with her toe.

25

Perfect! Ellen might be surly and sullen, as different to her own dear Kate, who had raised her, as any woman could be, but she was a good housekeeper, and neither Andrew nor Regan had any complaint about her beyond that she often helped herself to wine and Madeira on the sly. Ellen had been a convict, transported for stealing from her employers in the old country, and she had had a hard life. Knowing how charmed her own existence was by comparison, Regan tried always to make allowances for her.

She stepped now into the warm water with a grateful sigh. Her long slender legs were streaked with mud and dirt, and when she lathered them with soap the myriad of tiny cuts and scratches the bush had inflicted burned as if her skin was on fire.

Regan bit her lip, sinking down into the water and laying her head back against the rim of the tub. Her experience had taken more out of her than she had realised. Her limbs felt weak and shaky and when she momentarily closed her eyes, she saw again the body lying on the dust-caked road and the predatory figure bending over it.

Her eyes snapped open before she could see his face.

'Stop it!' she ordered herself fiercely. 'Don't think about it. Think of something nice. Think of . . .'

Think of Rolf. She hadn't meant to do that, either. But suddenly, unbidden, he was there in her mind's eye. Tall, wickedly good-looking, standing there before her in the clearing. She felt again the way her heart had jolted into her mouth and then set up an irregular beating, remembered the way his muscles had rippled as he struggled to free the buggy. Oh, how she had wanted to reach out and touch them! Just thinking of it now started a prickling deep inside her as if nerves she had not known she possessed were tingling to life.

Almost without knowing what she did, Regan's hands slid up her body to her breasts, cupping them with soapy hands, and was surprised to find the nipples firm and erect beneath her palms. For a moment she paused, relishing the sensation, and wondering at the line of sharp sweetness that seemed to join those erect nipples to the trembling core of her like a fine silken cord.

'Rolf,' she murmured, and his name sounded sweet to her ears. 'Rolf . . .'

The sound of the door knob turning made her jump almost out of her skin. Her hands jerked from her breasts as if they had suddenly become red hot, and quick colour flamed in her cheeks. She turned her head towards the door so abruptly that she cricked her neck, and for a crazy moment she imagined she would see Rolf standing there as he had stood before her in the clearing.

'Who's there?' she called sharply.

There was no reply. She could see no one.

'Who is it?' she called again, reaching for a towel to cover herself.

The door creaked and she heard a footstep on the bare polished boards.

'Don't be cross, Regan. It's only me.'

At the sound of the childish voice, Regan let her breath out on a sharp sigh. 'Elizabeth Greenstreet! You little minx!'

A round freckled face beneath a mop of brown curls appeared cautiously round the door frame. The blue eyes were wide and innocent, but the rosebud lip was caught firmly between small even white teeth in a gesture of guilt.

'Well, come in if you're coming!' Regan said, and added, mindful of the fact that the guest room which had been allocated to Rolf Peterson was just along the corridor and he might at any moment walk past, 'And shut the door, whatever you do! Quickly, now!'

The child came in, shutting the door after her as Regan had bid, and stood, thumb thrust into her mouth, regarding Regan solemnly.

'You frightened the life out of me, do you know that?' Regan said sternly.

27

'I'm sorry.' Dimples puckered her plump cheeks.
'I should think so too!' Regan scolded. But as always her heart lifted at the sight of the little girl.

Elizabeth was the daughter of Andrew's overseer, Jud Greenstreet, and she reminded Regan so much of herself when she, too, had been seven years old. Like Regan, she was motherless – Mary Greenstreet had caught a fever and died from it three summers ago. Like Regan, Elizabeth had the run of Mia-Mia from dawn till dusk while her father went about his work. And like Regan she was mischievous, wild and a little precocious. Remembering her own lack of female company, Regan never minded when the little girl followed her like a shadow, and she knew that she would miss Elizabeth when she married David and went to live with him at Glenbarr.

She stepped out of the tub, wrapping herself in the big soft towel. Elizabeth regarded her solemnly.

'Why are you having a bath in the middle of the afternoon, Regan?' she asked.

'I got caught in the storm. I was wet through and muddy,' Regan told her.

'Oh yes. I saw you from the window.'

Elizabeth wandered across the room to Regan's dressing chest, picking up a necklace and fingering the blue glass beads with loving care. Then she glanced slyly over her shoulder at Regan. 'There was a man with you.'

'Yes. He brought me safely home.'

'Why? You don't need a man, Regan. You don't need anyone.'

She was thinking of David, Regan knew. When David visited she always clung closer to Regan than ever. Sometimes David became irritated with her – one of the few things that disturbed his usual good nature. 'Can't we ever be alone without that child?' he would ask, and Regan, quite relieved that Elizabeth's presence was a bar to him trying to kiss her, would reply shortly: 'She's doing no harm. And we'll have all the time in the world to be alone together when we are married.'

She smiled now at the little girl. 'I couldn't have managed without him this afternoon, Elizabeth. Lucky ran away with me and the buggy got stuck in the bush. He rescued me.'

'Oh! Like the knights in my story book?' Elizabeth asked.

'Not exactly,' Regan said. 'He didn't have to fight any dragons. But he did get the buggy back on the road. I wasn't strong enough to do that on my own.'

'He's strong then?' Elizabeth asked. There was a reluctant admiration in her voice.

Regan laughed, remembering the effect those muscles had had on *her*. Lord, in ten years' time some man would rouse just the same response in Elizabeth! The thought was a disturbing one; suddenly she was overwhelmed with a desire to protect that sweet youthful innocence.

'He's strong, yes. But that isn't all. He's kind, too. That's why he saw me safely home. Because he was afraid some harm might befall me. And now he's as wet and muddy as I was, so he's having a bath too. And afterwards, I hope he'll stay for supper.'

'Oh, can I stay for supper too?' Elizabeth asked eagerly.

'You usually do, Miss.'

'Yes. Unless I've been very bad.' She bit her lip. 'I haven't been bad today. Well not very.'

Regan took a clean chemisette and drawers from the linen chest, wrinkling her nose in pleasure at the fresh scent of lavender that rose from them.

'And what have you been up to today that was ever so slightly bad?'

'I put a big spider in Ellen's mixing bowl,' the child admitted.

'Elizabeth!' Regan said sharply. 'You shouldn't touch spiders! You know very well that some of them are poisonous.'

'I know which ones are poisonous,' Elizabeth retorted disdainfully. 'This one wasn't. It's Ellen who doesn't know the difference.' Her cheeks dimpled and she giggled. 'She screamed and screamed,' she added.

'I expect she did!' Regan slipped into her undergarments and a cotton wrapper. 'You'll have no one but yourself to blame, Elizabeth, if your father makes you miss supper.'

'I don't *think* he will,' Elizabeth said solemnly, handing Regan her hairbrush from the chest. 'I swore I didn't know anything about it.'

'So you have been telling untruths too!' Regan tugged the brush through her tangled locks, regarding Elizabeth sternly.

The rosebud lips puckered in mock regret, but there was still a wicked sparkle in her blue eyes. 'Mm. You won't tell though, will you?'

'We'll have to see about that!'

'You won't. You're my friend.' She paused, head going to one side like a sparrow in contemplation. 'He's very handsome,' she added thoughtfully.

Regan smiled. In the mirror above the dressing chest her own eyes sparkled like emeralds and a faint rosy colour tinged her cheeks.

'Yes, he is,' she said, and thought there was no way that fact could be denied.

Rolf was certainly handsome – and also dangerously attractive. The fact that she couldn't stop thinking about him was proof of that!

Three

In the big flagstoned kitchen supper was in progress. Seated around the supper table were Andrew and Regan, Rolf, Jud Greenstreet and Elizabeth. The little girl had been allowed to stay after a severe ticking-off from her father. Jud was dubious about her denials that she had had anything to do with the spider in Ellen's mixing bowl, but powerless to prove otherwise.

It was an informal meal, the fare simple but good – salt pork and pickles, with fresh-baked crusty bread. So far the conversation had centred around the bushwhacking

''Twas an escaped convict or a returnee, no doubt,' Jud had opined – returnees were convicts who had served out their sentence. 'There are too many of them without a proper living, mad with hunger and crazy for a noggin of rum.'

'They should be shot!' Andrew stated bluntly. 'And if I get my hands on this one I'll see to it that he is.'

'I wonder who the pour soul was that he murdered?' Jud said.

'I don't know.' Regan shook her head. 'He looked just like a bundle of rags to me. But the robber – I saw *his* face. I'll never forget it as long as I live.'

Andrew swore. 'The devil you did! Was he not masked?'

'His mask had slipped – or maybe he had pushed it down because of the heat, not expecting anyone to come by.'

'You were lucky to escape, Regan!' Andrew exclaimed. Beads of sweat had broken out on his forehead as he thought of the mortal danger his beloved daughter had faced. 'He

31

would have killed you too without a second thought. Still might, knowing you can testify against him, if he can find you. You must not ride out alone again until this devil is caught and dealt with.'

'But he'll be miles from here by now!' Regan protested. 'Surely I'd be safe enough?'

'Under my roof, you'll do as I say, my lady!' Andrew roared. 'You are a sight too rash for your own good. Do you want to end up like the man you saw today, a bundle of rags in the road? Fortune took care of you today and no mistake. But you cannot always expect to be so lucky. If anything happened to you . . .' His voice cracked and he broke off . . .

'But it didn't, Father. I'm home, safe and sound – thanks to Rolf.' She glanced at him across the table and felt her pulses begin to race and the colour rise in her cheeks as their eyes met. Swiftly, she looked away.

'He was her knight in shining armour,' Elizabeth piped up. 'She told me so.'

'I told you nothing of the sort!' Regan said, her voice sharp with embarrassment.

'You did! You said—'

'No, *you* said, Elizabeth. And I told you that at least he had not had any dragons to fight.'

'But he would have! He'd have fought a dragon for you if he'd had to.'

Her piping voice was so insistent, her admiration for Rolf so crystal clear, they all burst out laughing. All but Regan. In her confusion the best she could manage was a smile.

As the laughter died away, Andrew turned to Rolf.

'It certainly was fortunate you were on that road today. May I ask what brings you to this part of the river valley?'

Rolf speared a pickle casually with his fork. 'I'm looking for work.'

Andrew frowned. From the cut of his clothes and the

thoroughbred horse he had been riding, Andrew had envisaged that Rolf was in the neighbourhood on some kind of business.

'What kind of work?' he enquired.

'Whatever I can get,' Rolf replied easily. 'I know about stock and farming. I've lived all my life on the land.'

'Then why—?' Andrew broke off, realising he was breaking one of the unwritten rules of this wild country. Here, almost every man had secrets in his past, of one sort or another. It was not the done thing to ask too many questions.

'I have nothing to hide, never fear,' Rolf assured him. 'Well, nothing but a family quarrel with my brother. We farmed together, but strong though a blood tie might be, it is not always possible to agree with one's kith and kin. I judged it was time for me to move on.'

'I'm surprised you chose the Hawkesbury,' Andrew said thoughtfully. 'Most of the land here is already claimed. There is rich land now on the other side of the mountain range, and plenty of it, or so I'm told.'

'That's true. In fact, it's where I've come from.' Rolf's response was swift. 'But I wished to put some distance between me and my brother until I have the capital to set up a place of my own. At present I am penniless. I left his employ with nothing but the few belongings I could carry with me. I need to start over and the only way I know to do that is to earn a living honestly, doing what I know best.'

He paused, then added with deliberate casualness, 'You are not looking for hands, I suppose, Captain Mackenzie?'

The moment the words were out, he could have bitten off his tongue. This man was no longer *Captain* Mackenzie, and had not been these last twenty years. How could he, a supposed stranger, have known his host's rank in the New South Wales Corps? But to his relief no one seemed to notice the slip and Rolf breathed a sigh of relief, vowing that he would be more careful in future.

'I have all the hands I need,' Andrew said. 'An overseer

33

here and on each of my farms, and plenty of convict labour. I'm sorry, Peterson.'

'Father!' Regan exclaimed. 'How can you be so ungrateful?'

Andrew turned sharply, taken aback by her outburst and she rushed on: 'When he brought me home safe – at great inconvenience to himself – you said you could never do enough to repay him. Now, the first thing he asks you, you refuse! For what reason? We can never have enough labour – I've heard you say often enough the convicts are unreliable. Here you have the offer of an honest man. Surely there must be work that he could do?'

'Regan, you know nothing of the economics of the farms,' Andrew blustered, annoyed to be taken to task so by his daughter.

'Fiddle-de-dee! I know almost as much as you! Who kept the books when you were sick last winter? Why, me! I know very well we could afford to pay another wage. And besides have you not just forbidden me to ride out alone? Who will take my place looking out for broken fences and sick animals if I am to be confined to the house, I'd like to know?'

'It's true enough,' Jud interposed warily. For all his standing with Andrew Mackenzie he was apprehensive of interfering in this unexpected battle between father and daughter. He had witnessed too many of their spats, and knew that to take sides was not helpful to his position when they made up their differences – as they always did – and soon. Andrew and Regan were as close as two buds on a bough – in the end the friend to one was the friend to the other – and the enemy of the one despised by the other.

Andrew ignored him now. 'Regan—'

'Father, please!' The anger in her voice was replaced by a soft pleading urgency. 'This man saved my life. Surely, in return, you could offer him work, for a little while at least. Until you feel it is safe for me to ride out again.'

Andrew looked at her small determined face and knew

34

he was about to weaken. When had he ever been able to refuse his Regan anything? And it was true, her life had been saved by this stranger. If harm had befallen her . . . Andrew shuddered inwardly.

She was right. He owed this man a debt of gratitude he could never repay. Yet his gut instinct had been to tell him no. For some reason he could not explain he felt that, hero of the hour or not, Rolf Peterson spelled trouble.

'Father?' Regan said again.

Her eyes, so like her mother's, held his levelly. He sighed. Just so had his Anne wound him round her little finger, he who could be as hard and ruthless as any man living.

He nodded abruptly, acknowledging defeat, and turned again to the man to whom his daughter owed her life.

'Very well,' he said. 'There's work here if you want it.'

Regan cast a glance across the table and felt her heartbeat quicken. Rolf was not looking at her, but the spell he cast over her was none the less potent for that.

'I thank you, Sir,' he said. 'It seems that fate has played a hand. I'm glad not to have to journey further. I accept your offer of work in the spirit that it was made.'

His lip curled slightly at the irony of the statement.

'And I hope you won't live to regret it,' he added, in what everyone around the table took to be nothing more or less than a joke.

When the meal was over Jud and Elizabeth left for their own quarters in the new wing. Rolf remained for a while, talking with Andrew and Regan, before excusing himself. For all that he had given in to Regan's pleading to give Rolf a job, Rolf felt that the older man still had reservations. His manner, though polite, was less than cordial, and Rolf did not want to impose himself on their privacy for too long, too soon. He had the perfect excuse – that he had been riding since dawn – and when he made it, Andrew accepted it readily.

'You must be tired, yes. I hope you sleep well.'

'I'm sure I will,' Rolf replied, but he was sure of nothing of the kind.

The blood was racing in his veins and every nerve was alive and singing. He could scarcely believe his luck in gaining entry to the Mackenzie household with such ease, and as he went upstairs to the guest room which he had been allocated, it was all he could do to keep from punching the air in triumph.

Then, as the door closed after him, it came to him that he was spending his first night under the roof of Mia-Mia since he had been a boy, and the memories came crowding in, dampening his mood and strengthening his resolution.

This would not be his room after tonight, he realised. Now that he had been taken on as a farm-hand more suitable accommodation would be found for him away from the main house. But for tonight he was here, sleeping in the house his father had built – and died for.

He looked around the room, savouring the moment. The furnishings were all much grander than his parents could ever have hoped to afford, the big brass bed, festooned with shining knobs and covered with a blue silk throw, the heavy oak dressing chest, the marble-topped washstand. Most of it must have been shipped out at enormous expense. The bare board floor had been polished to a high sheen and the bright rugs scattered on it were warm and inviting. The wet clothes he had discarded into a heap in a corner had been removed, he noticed – presumably taken away by the housekeeper for drying. Again his lips twisted with satisfaction as he thought of it – Andrew Mackenzie's housekeeper waiting on him, Rolf Hannay. Well, she may not be doing that again, but once was enough. The first small step of his revenge. And how furious Andrew Mackenzie would be when he knew the truth!

Rolf crossed to the window, looking out. The rain had stopped now, but the sweet scent of it on the leaves of the eucalypts rose fragrantly and wafted in through the open casement. It was not quite dark – now that the heavy clouds had passed, the moon was bright enough to light the lines of mimosa and gums along each side of the drive and suddenly, like a ghost, Rolf seemed to see his father there, riding along the drive like a madman as he had ridden on the day he died.

There had been no upper storey to the house in those days to give an elevated view. Instead, Rolf had watched him go from the veranda, with his little sisters Rosalie and Alison clutching one another and crying, and his mother running vainly after the horse as his father kicked Bess to a gallop.

It was always the same when Peter Hannay was angry or upset. First he would gulp down far more rum than was good for him – or than they could afford – then he would take Bess and ride her, wild as the wind, until the fury left him. Then he would return, sobered and sheepish, like a naughty child creeping home after a tantrum. But that fateful day it had been much, much worse than usual, and the sense of impending disaster had been heavy in the air like the oppressive threat of an impending storm.

And it had begun with Andrew Mackenzie coming to Mia-Mia.

Rolf had seen him ride up the drive, seen, too, the looks that passed between his mother and father, and been afraid. Things had been bad – and getting worse – for some time, he knew. The Hannay family had always struggled against the odds to make the farm pay, and there had never been any money for even the smallest luxury. More often than not, in the summer months, Rolf and his sisters went barefoot, and the only gown his mother owned was faded and threadbare. But there was always food on the table and he and his sisters had been happy enough. Until the great flood came in the autumn when Rolf was nine years old.

For weeks on end the rain had fallen relentlessly, and as the Hawkesbury rose alarmingly, pastures disappeared beneath flood water, livestock drowned and haystacks were swept away. Unlike some of the little farms along the river, Mia-Mia was built on high enough ground to escape the flood, but the crops were destroyed and a good many cattle perished. Poor and struggling as they were, the Hannays could not stand the losses. By the time the water receded it was clear they would be ruined unless Andrew Mackenzie extended his credit – as one of the Trading Ring, the Hannays owed him a great deal of money. To make matters worse, Peter Hannay had begun drinking heavily to drown his sorrows, and since Andrew Mackenzie controlled the supply of rum also it was not long before they were even deeper in debt.

Though Rolf had been too young to be aware of all the details he saw his father's drunken rages and the way his mother's eyes were often red-rimmed from crying and knew something was seriously wrong. And later his mother had explained what had occurred at that dreadful time.

Andrew Mackenzie had wanted Mia-Mia for himself, to add to the other grants of land he was amassing along the river bank in readiness for his retirement from the New South Wales Corps. He had seen that the easiest way to come by it was to force Peter Hannay deeper and deeper into debt to him, and then foreclose on the loan.

That was the reason he had come to Mia-Mia that fateful day. Rolf and his sisters had been turned out of the kitchen where the confrontation had taken place, but they had lurked within earshot on the veranda. They had heard their mother weeping and pleading, and to their horror they had heard their father reduced to tears too. Rolf would never forget the shock he had felt – his father, his strong, lusty father, his voice breaking with helpless emotion. And they had heard Andrew Mackenzie coldly turn down every plea. If the Hannays could not repay him in full by the end of the month, he would take possession of their home and their land.

When he had gone away, stomping stony-faced and ruthless past the frightened children without sparing them so much as a glance, and riding away down the drive, they had crept back into the kitchen where the atmosphere of despair hung heavy in the air.

Jessica, Rolf's mother, had sat at the kitchen table weeping, Peter, his father, stood, head bowed. For a while he had not spoken. Then he had turned, and the expression on his face had frightened the children still more, if such a thing were possible.

'We are ruined,' he said. Those three words, nothing more, but they were burned into Rolf's memory.

And then Peter had begun drinking.

Desperately, Jessica had tried to stop him. 'What good will drinking do?' she had cried. 'Has not the rum already made things a thousand times worse?'

'It's all I have left, woman!' Peter had roared. 'Don't deny me this one last comfort! At least when Mackenzie takes our house and land he won't get his hands on the rum as well!'

The tears were gone now, replaced by furious anger. The children huddled out of his reach – when the drink was in him, there was no telling what Peter Hannay would do.

At last, roaring drunk, he had grabbed his coat and buckled on his gun.

'What are you doing?' Jessica had screamed at him.

'Never mind! Look after your children, woman, and leave men's business to men!'

Rolf's heart had almost stopped beating. Could his father really be going after Andrew Mackenzie to pick a fight with him? He was not even sober enough to sit his horse, surely! But nothing they could say or do could stop him. Rolf and his sisters had watched Peter gallop wildly away, and trembled.

They had never seen him alive again.

Rolf remembered with a heavy heart the long hours of

waiting, the growing certainty that something terrible had happened. Late that night there were horses' hooves on the drive, and they all ran out expectantly. But it was not Peter. It was a group of men from down river bringing his body home. Riding like a madman, driven on by anger, despair – and liquor – he had been thrown from his horse. Bess came back next day unharmed. But Peter was dead, his neck broken.

After the burial, the family had left Mia-Mia. Andrew Mackenzie had got what he wanted. From that day to this, Rolf had never set eyes on his old home again.

Now he stood at the window remembering, and the pain was there, sharp as it had ever been, sending piercing arrows through the stony determination that encased his heart.

Damn Andrew Mackenzie and all his kind! Revenge would be sweet indeed.

A movement on the veranda steps beneath the window caught Rolf's eye and he peered down. Andrew Mackenzie and his daughter were sitting there talking. The bright moonlight had turned the man's hair to silver, and shone on the pale skin of the girl.

Lord, but she was a beauty – and spirited too. Rolf's mouth curved upward suddenly as he remembered his first sight of her in the clearing and the way his gut had clenched just looking at her. That sweep of tangled red-gold hair, the jut of her small courageous chin, the flash of her emerald eyes – those things alone were enough to make a strong man weak. Add to that her luscious body, to which the thin sodden fabric of her gown had clung revealingly, and the potent mix of courage and vulnerability, and for a moment he had almost believed he might at last have found a woman who could melt the ice about his heart.

But that had been before he had known who she was. The moment she had spoken her name he had forgotten all else but that she was Andrew Mackenzie's daughter.

How in Heaven's name did a man like him come to sire

such a delectable woman? It was almost beyond belief. But there was little doubt his blood ran in her veins. From his ruthless nature came her own fierce spirit. And the protective love he felt for her was clear in every word he spoke, every move he made. Andrew Mackenzie worshipped his daughter. And because of her Rolf was now in the position for which he had long planned.

As he watched them, Regan leaned across and touched her father's sleeve. He turned towards her, and the bright moonlight illuminated his face, confirming Rolf's thoughts.

She was his weakness, without doubt.

In that moment the idea came to him. What better way to exact revenge against Andrew Mackenzie than to woo and win his daughter?

The blood began to pump furiously in Rolf's veins as he thought of it. With Regan in love with him, Andrew Mackenzie would be putty in his hands. Why, he might even marry her! Regan was sole heiress to Mia-Mia, and if she were his wife, Mia-Mia would return to him without the need for further plotting or even violence. He would take it back by stealth, as Andrew Mackenzie had taken it from his father.

And when he knew the truth – oh, how sweet that would be! The daughter he worshipped wed to Rolf Hannay, the child he had not deigned to acknowledge that long-ago day on this very veranda! And if Regan was hurt, well, Rolf was sorry, but being hurt was part of living.

He glanced down again at the pair as they talked, heads close together, the silver and the red-gold, and his mouth curved again.

Wooing her wouldn't be the most unpleasant thing he had ever done. It would be a good deal *more* pleasant than most of the plans for revenge that had passed through his mind these past years. But, by Jove, it would be every bit as effective!

*   *   *

'Thank you, Father,' Regan said. She reached over and touched Andrew's sleeve and he turned to her, smiling.

'What for? What have I done, my Regan?'

She smiled back, her cheeks dimpling. 'As if you didn't know!'

'You mean taking on that young man as an extra hand when I have no need for one, I suppose,' he said.

She looked him straight in the eye. 'You owed him that much, Father. He saved my life, remember?'

'And are you quite sure that was the only reason for your insistence?' he asked, holding her gaze.

Colour flamed in her cheeks; he saw it clearly in the bright moonlight and felt his earlier misgivings stir once more.

'Because if there *was* something other than gratitude behind your pleadings, you would do well to remember you are promised to David Dauntsey,' he went on sternly.

'I know, I know.' She was covering her momentary lapse with a show of impatience now. 'And I know too how much the match means to you, Father.'

'It's not just for me,' he pointed out. 'It's for you too. David is a good man. He will make you a wonderful husband.'

'I *know*! I had no reason to ask you to take Rolf on but common gratitude. And you *will* need an extra hand if I'm not allowed to ride out.'

'That's true enough,' he agreed. 'Just as long as you remember that he is hired help, and you are my daughter.'

'Of course.' She dimpled again. 'You can be so fearsome sometimes, Father. You always told me it took Mama to sweeten and tame you. Well, I intend to carry on the good work she began. Heaven knows what you were like before you came under the influence of a good woman! You were a monster, I've heard tell!'

He shrugged, smiling slightly. 'You may be right. They were hard times, Regan.'

He was silent for a moment, remembering. He and his

42

fellow officers in the New South Wales Corps had certainly had the whip hand, with their choice grants of land and their control of trade – and rum. But this hard new world had bred hard men. Andrew was not altogether proud of the way he had built his empire, but he had not had that many regrets either. In those early days it had been every man for himself – survive and prosper, or sink and drown. Andrew had used his advantage to the full. He had never allowed himself to stop and feel pity for those he trod underfoot. Perhaps, as Regan said, he had been something of a monster, but he had been no different to a hundred others.

And his Anne had softened him, without a doubt. Lord, how he had loved her! But she was gone, dead now for close on twenty years. And in her place was this lovely girl.

At first, when Anne had died bearing her he had not been able to bring himself to so much as look at the baby, much less touch her. This bawling scrap had cost his Anne her life and he hated her for it. But before long he had begun to weaken, and as she grew he found himself transferring all the love he had borne for Anne on to her daughter. Soon she had become his reason for living. And as she turned from child to woman, growing more like her mother by the day, he could not imagine what he would do without her, and he thought constantly of her safety.

Dear God, today he had been out of his mind with anxiety when the storm came and she had failed to return home! And he had been right to be worried. The dangers were so many in this wild land. And she had brushed with one as perilous as any.

His gut clenched. He reached out and touched a red-gold curl, full of wonder that he could have fathered such a lovely creature, full of gratitude that she had come home safe to him – thanks to the man sleeping upstairs.

'God keep you, Regan,' he said softly. 'For if any harm ever befell you, there's little doubt but that I would become a monster again.'

'Don't worry, Father. Nothing is going to happen to me.' Her voice was full of the confidence of youth. It tugged at his heartstrings.

'I hope not, Regan,' he said, 'for believe me, I would kill the man who hurt you with my bare hands.'

The moonlight shone on her small smiling face.

'Nothing is going to happen to me,' she repeated.

Andrew found himself thinking suddenly of the man upstairs, and wished that he could be so sure.

Four

'I'd like the fences checked on the down river borders today, Jud,' Andrew Mackenzie told his overseer. 'Last time I was out there, they looked as if they might be becoming insecure in one or two places.'

Breakfast was just finished, but they were lingering over another cup of strong coffee before beginning work for the day. Rolf was there too. It had been decided that for the time being he should remain in the house and take his meals with them. As a free man it was not right for him to have to share the convicts' quarters, which were always locked at night and the only other room in the outer buildings was not habitable at present.

Jud glanced in his direction.

'Rolf is the only man I can spare – and the only one I'd trust so far from my sight, apart from Dickon Stokes, and he's got a full day at work here in the stables. It's why you hired him, after all. Trouble is, he don't know the lie of the land.'

'I can find my way, I'm sure.' Rolf spoke quickly. If he was deemed to be of little use, Andrew might yet decide there was no point in hiring him, and so far he had had no chance to begin to put his plans into operation. Besides, little did they know he knew the land hereabouts as well as the back of his own hand – or had done, once.

Regan set down her cup with a clatter. Bright spots of eagerness had risen in her cheeks. For two whole days she had been confined to the house and its close surroundings,

45

and she had thought she would go mad with boredom. But not only that . . .

She cast a glance at Rolf, sitting on the other side of the table, and felt her heart miss a beat. Two whole days and she hadn't had a single chance to be alone with him either, when all she could think about was how good it had felt to have him riding at her side. Two whole days with this unfamiliar but very pleasant emotion prickling like fever rash under her skin.

She shouldn't feel this way, she knew. She was promised to David, and before long she would be married to him. But where was the harm? Once she was married there would be precious little freedom – or fun.

'Why don't I go with him?' she said now. 'I could show him where the boundaries lie. No harm will come to me if I'm with Rolf.'

Andrew hesitated. Refusing Regan anything when she looked at him in that way was not easy, but he was still doubtful of the wisdom of what she was suggesting.

'She's right,' Jud said bluntly. 'The sooner Rolf is familiar with the land, the more use he'll be. And there's no one better than Regan to show him.'

Andrew sighed. 'Very well,' he agreed reluctantly. 'I don't want my stock wandering. That's the only reason for my change of heart, Regan.' He turned to Rolf. 'Make sure you take good care of her, do you hear? If any harm comes to her, you'll have me to reckon with.'

Rolf nodded. 'Don't worry, Sir. I'll protect her with my life,' he said.

Regan set Betsy, her beautiful roan mare, to a gallop across the wide unbroken pasture. Her hair streamed out behind her, and she laughed aloud with delight.

Oh, but this was sheer bliss! Since the storm had passed the skies had been clear cloudless blue, and against it the trees, refreshed by the rain, were green again. The sun was warm on her skin, the breeze was cool on her face and tangling in her hair, and Betsy's galloping hooves seemed to keep time with the beating of her heart. She was free again – free! And even better . . .

She cast a glance over her shoulder as she heard Satan come galloping up behind her. Rolf sat the great horse with easy grace, his back straight, his legs hard and muscled in the long stirrups. The sight of them stirred a chord deep inside her and set her heart beating even faster.

'Steady up!' Rolf called to her.

'Why?' she shouted back, touching Betsy's flanks with her heels once more.

'Steady up,' he ordered again, and reaching out, took Betsy's reins with an athletic, fluid movement, slowing them both to a canter and then a trot.

'Why did you do that?' Regan demanded, breathless and affronted.

'You heard me promise your father no harm would come to you,' Rolf told her. 'He may have been thinking of the bushwhacker, but there are other dangers besides him. How would I go back and break the news if you went over your horse's head and broke your neck?'

'Oh, don't be so stuffy!' Regan retorted. 'I can handle Betsy! I've been riding since I was big enough to sit in the saddle.'

'Maybe. That's no guarantee against a fall if your mare catches her foot and stumbles. What you do, Regan, when you are alone, is no concern of mine. But whilst I am responsible for your safety, I'll see to it that you ride at a reasonable pace.'

Regan's eyes sparked emerald fire. 'I take orders from no one!'

A corner of his mouth curved upward. What a picture she made, with defiance in every line of her pretty face and her hair tangled about it in a red-gold cloud! And the boy's shirt and breeches she wore left little to the imagination, either. He felt a pang of desire twist hot within him.

'You take orders from your father,' he said sternly, suppressing the unwanted reaction. 'If you did not, you would not have been confined to the house these last two days. And at this moment, I am acting in his place. At his request. If you refuse to do as I tell you, then we'll return to the farm immediately.'

'You can't make me go with you,' Regan argued.

'Perhaps not. But if I return without you and tell your father the reason for it, then he'll likely confine you for weeks, not days. The choice is yours, Regan.'

She bit her lip, admitting defeat. He was right, of course. If he returned without her, Andrew would be furious.

'Am I allowed to trot?' she asked sarcastically to cover the humiliation of having him beat her. 'If not, we shall not reach the boundaries until a week and a day!'

He smiled at her spirit.

'You are allowed to canter. It's this headlong gallop I intend to put a stop to.'

'Well, thank you indeed!' She touched her heels to Betsy's sides, and as the horse lengthened her stride, Regan felt the exhilaration begin again, a bubble of excitement deep within her.

And this time, she acknowledged, it was not just from the freedom of seeing the grass flash past beneath the flying hooves. It had to do with her spat with Rolf – and the fact that in the end she had lost the argument. David would never have stood up to her like that. With David, she did as she pleased. But Rolf had got his way. She should feel angry with him – and perhaps she did, a little. But at the same time she was aware that his mastery had aroused some deep answering emotion she could ever remember experiencing before.

Regan had met her match, and she only respected and liked him the better for it.

* * *

As the sun rose higher they rode side by side, Regan pointing out features of the land whilst Rolf pretended it was all new to him. And of course much of it was. There had been many changes since his days on the Hawkesbury, pastures extended, land cleared and cultivated, homesteads and farms improved as more money became available to spend on them.

At last Regan reined in. 'This is the boundary of our land. Beyond lies Glenbarr, the home of the Dauntseys. It will be my home, too, when I marry David.'

She heard the swift involuntary intake of breath, and glanced round at him. For a crazy moment she almost imagined that the expression she caught on his handsome face was one of dismay, then it was gone, replaced by his usual impenetrable look.

'You are betrothed, then?' he said.

She nodded. 'David Dauntsey and I have known one another since we were children, and as you can see, our fathers' lands adjoin. It's only natural we should wed.'

'Do you love him?' Her eyes snapped up to meet his, and he shifted in the saddle. 'My apologies. I had no right to ask that question.'

'No, you didn't,' she said. 'But I'll answer it, nevertheless. Of course I love David. He is like a brother to me.'

One eyebrow lifted slightly at her answer, but Rolf made no reply, only touched Satan with his heels to stir him once more. 'If this is the boundary, we'll check the fences then.'

Regan rode alongside him, ruffled by his directness but determined to hide it. Did she love David? Yes – of course she did! As a brother, as she had said. What right had she to expect more? She would be safe and happy with him. He would be a kind and gentle husband to her. And with the union, most of the lands on the Hawkesbury would be owned jointly by their two families. So why this restlessness within her every time she glanced at the man riding beside her? Rolf Peterson was a stranger. He had come into her life without warning and he would leave it as suddenly. To allow herself to think otherwise, for even a moment, was sheer folly. Worse than folly, it was madness.

The sun was directly overhead now, its heat merciless. Regan tilted her hat to shade her face. But there was no such protection for the horses.

'There's a creek over there,' she said. 'We can rest awhile, and the horses can drink.'

She headed towards it, no longer forcing a fast pace, and Rolf followed.

After the pitiless heat of the noonday sun the creek was a refuge, cool and shady. They rode right down to the water's edge and dismounted, leading the horses into the shallows. When they had drunk their fill, Regan and Rolf looped the reins around the branches of a tree and knelt at the water's edge, cupping their hands and drinking deeply themselves. The water tasted cool and sweet and Regan splashed some on to her hot face and neck. A little trickled down into the furrow between her breasts and she shivered with pleasure.

She raised her head to see Rolf watching her, and as their eyes met he moved abruptly, indicating a fallen log.

'We'll sit here.' There was a rough edge to his voice. Sharp sweetness twisted deep inside her as she heard it.

'Is that another order?' she asked teasingly to cover her momentary confusion.

He laughed out loud. 'Yes, it is. This heat is too much for man or beast. We'll rest here until it is a little less fierce.'

She sat beside him, obedient now, stretching out her small booted feet and sighing with contentment. 'You're afraid I might get sunstroke now, is that it? One more thing you would have to explain to my father!'

'Sunstroke, Regan – you? No, I am beginning to believe that you are truly a child of this wild country.'

50

'And so I am! I've known nothing else.' She cast him a quick, curious glance. 'And you? Were you born here also?'

'No.' His face had darkened, grown shut-in.

'So – where were *you* born?' she persisted.

'In England.'

'Your parents came here – all the way from England – bringing you with them?' Regan could sense Rolf's reluctance to answer, yet could not stop herself. She wanted desperately to know something of this man.

'They thought they would find a better life here. They were wrong.' This time the finality of his tone deterred even Regan from questioning him further.

'I've been lucky, I suppose.' She plucked at a blade of grass. 'But at least you *had* a mother. I never knew mine. She died when I was born. All I had was a portrait and some of her things that Father saved for me. Some jewels, a wrap, a pair of slippers . . . I used to put them on, you know. Fasten the necklace around my throat and toss the wrap around my shoulders, and fancy that I could still smell her scent on it. I don't suppose I could. Not really. She had been dead for too long. But I liked to think so, all the same.'

Her eyes were faraway; for a moment neither spoke. Then Regan pulled herself together.

'You see? I'm just a silly, sentimental girl at heart.' She ended with a little self-deprecating laugh which caught in her throat as she felt his hand on hers.

She wheeled round, startled out of her reverie, both by his touch and the warmth that seemed to spread from it, creeping up her veins and sending a prickling through the whole of her body. His eyes were on her, not steely now, but deep as river pools after the rains.

'I don't think that you are in the least silly,' he said. 'I think that you are . . .' His voice tailed away, his eyes completing the sentence that his words had not.

He was moving closer and she knew that she should

51

pull away, but, mesmerised by those deep grey eyes, she could not. Then his lips were on hers, gentle at first, then harder, more demanding. Beneath them she felt her own lips move in response and the prickling in her veins spread again with the speed of a bush fire so that she seemed to be alight with it.

He slipped an arm about her waist, pulling her towards him. His chest was broad and hard against her soft yielding breasts; she slid her own arm around him and felt the rippling muscles of his back beneath her fingers.

Oh, but it was sweet! The touch of him, the smell of him, the taste of him! Those lips, probing hers, that firm muscled arm around her waist, were evoking in her all manner of responses beyond anything she had ever dreamed of. She felt she was drowning in him; reason was lost, time standing still.

'Regan,' he murmured, and the sound of his voice broke the spell. Though her body was still aflame, her conscious mind registered just what it was she was doing, and with an enormous effort of will she wrenched herself free.

'No!' She put both hands on that hard chest wall, levering herself away. She was trembling now, both with the unfamiliar sensations and disgust with herself for what she was allowing – not just allowing but welcoming! 'Stop it this instant, do you hear me?' she gasped, breathless from his kisses. 'I think you forget yourself!'

'And you?' Rolf's eyes challenged her. 'Did you forget yourself, too, Regan?'

'Yes!' she retorted. The flame was still there, whether she wanted it or not, and it made her burn now with a frustration that came out as anger. 'Yes, I did forget myself. I told you – I am promised to David Dauntsey. If he – if anyone – knew what we had just done . . . If my father knew . . . !'

'They won't know, I promise.' He held her gaze. 'But you and I, we both know, don't we, Regan? I know I shall not forget. Will you?'

Her mouth puckered. How could she forget? Suddenly she was close to tears.

'Damn you!' she whispered.

He stood up abruptly. 'I think perhaps we had better be on our way, don't you?'

But as she watched him stride to the tree, unhooking Satan's reins, a terrible sense of loss and of business unfinished overwhelmed her.

As he helped her up into Betsy's saddle the light touch, no more personal now than any groom's, was almost more than she could bear, and though the words 'Damn you!' hovered on her lips again, they found no answering echo in her heart.

They rode in silence. It was all Regan could do to restrain herself from kicking Betsy to another wild gallop. It was the only thing, she felt, which would release the tension inside her, the sharp tingling of sensitised nerve endings, the aching, bubbling frustration – the guilt! But she knew she must not. In the scorching heat of the early afternoon sun it would be worse than folly. And besides, if she disobeyed Rolf and he told her father, Andrew might confine her to the farm again.

Regan cast a sidelong glance at Rolf, riding beside her, and felt her heartbeats quicken once more. It was madness to want to be free to ride with him again, especially after what had just happened between them, but she did – she did! There could be no more kisses, of course. There must not be. The way she had responded had been not just improper, but downright dangerous. But just to be in his company would be enough. It would have to be!

She turned her gaze towards Dauntsey land. Soon enough this would be her home, yet at present the boundary fence marked a step into foreign territory. Would she ever come to feel about it as she felt about Mia-Mia? She couldn't imagine so. She loved every stick and stone, every blade of grass on Mia-Mia with a fierce protective love. Mia-Mia was her roots, her heritage. Mia-Mia was in her blood. But soon she would have to get used to calling Glenbarr home, just as she must get used to being David's wife.

A horseman was coming towards them on the Dauntsey side of the boundary.

'David!' Regan cried in surprise. 'It's David!'

Rolf stiffened in the saddle, but she did not notice as she turned Betsy closer to the boundary fence.

David Dauntsey drew alongside and reined in his mount.

'Regan! What are you doing out here?' His voice held surprise, but there was no mistaking the pleasure on his fine, almost girlish, face.

Regan laughed. 'The same as you, I imagine – checking fences.'

'Well, yes! It's a pleasant surprise, anyway.' His eyes, clear blue behind a fringing of dark lashes, went to Rolf, who was waiting some little way off. 'I'm glad you're not alone, though. Sometimes I fear for your safety with the freedom your father allows you. There was a bushwhacking not far from here three days ago. Francis Duncan from Rourke Farm was set upon and killed and robbed.'

'Oh, was it Francis Duncan!' Regan said, horrified. She had known the farmer all her life.

'You've heard about it then?' David asked.

Regan bit her lip. She didn't want to have to go over the whole story again.

'We heard about it, yes. A terrible thing. But as you can see, I'm escorted today, so you have no need to worry about me.'

David's gentle mouth softened. 'I shall always worry about you, Regan.'

'Oh, David!' She should be grateful for his devotion, she knew. But somehow it just made her impatient.

David glanced again at Rolf. 'Who is it riding with you anyway, Regan? I don't think I know him, do I?'

'No, he's a stranger in these parts.' Regan turned in the saddle. 'Rolf, come and meet my fiancé, David Dauntsey. David, this is Rolf Peterson.'

Rolf rode over to them and David extended his hand.

'You are staying with Andrew Mackenzie?'

'Working for him.' Rolf's hands were still firmly on the reins and for a moment Regan thought he was going to reject David's gesture of friendship. Then he reached across, stretching out his own hand to take David's proffered one briefly.

Watching, Regan felt her heart miss a beat. The man she was to marry and the one who seemed to invade her every thought since he had ridden into her life, shaking hands over a boundary fence! And how different they were! The one dark, muscled and undeniably all man, the other slight and fair with the classically handsome features of a young Adonis. And it wasn't just physically that they were so different, she knew, or because Rolf must be at least ten years older than David. Ten years on and David would still be a sweet-natured dreamer, whilst Rolf . . .

Rolf, she knew instinctively, had never had time for dreams. He was a man of action, as hard and uncompromising as the land to which his parents had brought him as a child. Perhaps he was a little dangerous too. Yes, without doubt there was something dangerous about him. The trouble was, it only made him the more attractive.

'So how do you come to be working for Andrew Mackenzie now?' David was asking him, and Regan could see from the set of his body that Rolf was reluctant to reply.

'It's a long story,' he said shortly, and Regan thanked her stars. She didn't want David knowing the full details of her brush with danger.

'Yes, it is,' she put in swiftly, 'and we should be heading back to Mia-Mia.'

David smiled, that sweet smile that held no trace of jealousy or suspicion.

55

'I shall look forward to hearing it nevertheless. Perhaps the opportunity will come on Sunday.'

Regan caught Rolf's puzzled look, and smiled herself.

'David and his parents are coming to Mia-Mia for dinner on Sunday,' she explained.

'To discuss the details of our wedding.' David leaned across the fence, touching Regan's arm, his face lighting up as he said it.

Was it her imagination, or did Regan sense a sudden tension in the hot still air? She glanced quickly at Rolf, but his features, set in stone, gave nothing away.

Satan blew suddenly, flicking his head against a fly that was worrying him, and Rolf looked at Regan.

'I think it's time we were getting back,' he said with decision.

Something that he might have thought was jealousy if he hadn't known better was burning in his veins. It was *not* jealousy, dammit! It was annoyance that he had less time than he had thought to put his plan into action. And just when he had thought he might be getting somewhere too! He'd known, of course, that Regan was promised to this David Dauntsey – she had told him as much – but he had not realised the marriage was so imminent.

And what a milksop, Rolf thought bad-temperedly, staring towards the distant mountains, a dark blur in the heat haze. A woman with Regan's fire would make mincemeat of him. And he would never satisfy her. Never! There was passion beneath that fire. He'd tasted it when he kissed her.

The memory of it sent a hot spark through his loins just as the kiss itself had done.

Strange. He had planned for just such a moment, as coldly and with the same ruthless determination that had driven him all these years and finally brought him back to Mia-Mia. Yet when it had come, it had taken him by surprise. He had touched her because he had wanted to touch her, and when he had taken her in his arms he had thought, for those moments stolen in time, of nothing but the sweet vulnerability of her, the lonely child that still lurked hidden somewhere within her woman's body. And how desirable a body it was! The fire sparked once more, unbidden and unwanted, in his loins.

When she said he had forgotten himself, she had been right – though not for the reason she meant. He *had* forgotten himself – forgotten all his bitterness, all his burning desire for revenge, all the pain and hatred that had made him the man he was – in a moment of tenderness that had flamed into desire.

He could not afford to forget himself so again. If he was to achieve his end and win Regan's heart he must concentrate all his energies on maintaining the ruthless determination that had brought him thus far.

And he must work fast, or the chance would be gone forever.

Rolf glanced at her and suppressed that treacherous flickering desire with a supreme effort of will. 'I suppose after today you won't want to ride with me again?' he said, purposely reminding her of what had passed between them.

She tossed her head. 'You know as well as I do you are my only hope of escape from the prison of the house! I'll ride with you again, as often as Father will let me. Just so long as you promise to behave yourself.'

'I'm not sure I can promise that,' he said teasingly, and saw the hot colour flood her cheeks.

'You must! Otherwise . . .'

He laughed. 'Very well, then. I agree.'

But even as he said it, he knew it was a promise he would not keep.

Five

There was no chance for riding out together the next day. Regan was fully occupied in helping with preparations for the visit of the Dauntseys, and Rolf burned with frustration. But he counselled himself to be patient. He must not allow himself to be pushed into acting too rashly. If he did, he might frighten Regan off and lose his chance altogether. As it was, he had her interest, he was certain of it. It was there in her eyes every time they were together, even though others were always present.

On Sunday morning, after a whole day's domesticity, Regan was restless again. The preparations for the evening were all in place and the day stretched ahead long and – to her mind – tedious.

She would not even have Elizabeth to distract her today. Jud's dead wife and Elizabeth's mother had been a devout Christian, and Jud always insisted on taking the little girl to the chapel in Broken Hill on Sunday mornings as he felt her mother would have done if she had been alive.

'It wouldn't hurt, surely, Father, if I went out for a few hours?' Regan said when breakfast was done.

He looked doubtful. 'Don't forget tonight.'

'As if I could! The Dauntseys are coming. Yesterday I did nothing but help Ellen with baking and washing all the best china and glassware.' Regan tossed her head in disgust at the memory. 'But it's all done now, and they won't be arriving until late this afternoon, will they?'

Andrew hesitated. 'I still think you should stay around the house today.'

He broke off at the sound of footsteps on the bare board floor of the hallway, and Jud entered the kitchen. His big, good-natured face was anxious. 'Is Elizabeth with you?'

'No, she's not here,' Andrew returned. 'She left with you half an hour ago to get ready for chapel.'

'Well, I don't know where the little minx can be.' Jud sighed with exasperation. 'She was in her room, supposed to be changing into her Sunday best, but when I went to tell her it was time to go, there was neither hide nor hair of her.'

Regan bit back a smile. Elizabeth hated the enforced weekly visit to chapel, she knew. And she could hardly blame her. Parson Meredith's sermons could go on for a full hour and a half.

'She's hiding somewhere, I expect,' Regan said. 'You want me to help you look for her, Jud?'

He ran a hand through his thinning hair in exasperation. 'I wish you would, Regan. She could be anywhere. I'll tan her hide for her when I do find her.'

But Regan knew it was only an idle threat. Jud had never laid so much as a finger on Elizabeth, nor would he. The child was the light of his life, and his indulgence of her was one of the causes of Elizabeth's wild ways.

'I'll help too, Jud,' Rolf offered. 'Unless there's anything more pressing you want me to do?'

'There's nothing more pressing than finding my daughter!' Jud returned.

They split up, Regan to search the house, Rolf and Jud to take the outhouses, barns and stables, and their close surrounds. As she went from room to room calling Elizabeth's name, Regan was still smiling to herself. She could remember pulling much the same trick herself when boring visitors had been due to call – and remember, too, her father's anger when he had eventually found her. But it had been worth it not to have to sit through the tedious conversations, and even that, she thought, paled into insignificance compared with an hour and a half of Parson Meredith's solemn preaching!

In every room she checked the likely hiding places – beneath the beds, behind the curtain drapes, inside the heavy oak chests. Outside's Rolf's room she hesitated. Surely Elizabeth would not choose this one to hide in? But one never knew. She was very taken with Rolf. Better check it out and be sure.

Regan pushed open the door and went inside, instantly realising it wasn't just diligence that had made her do so. There was something tantalisingly intimate about the room in which someone slept, and when that room was the one where Rolf was alone with his privacy . . . Warmth prickled in Regan's veins, and she was enveloped by a feeling of closeness to the man she found so irresistibly attractive.

The shirt and breeches he had worn yesterday were lying discarded in a heap on the floor, presumably waiting for Ellen to collect them for laundering. The bed, as yet unmade, was turned back to reveal the sheets on which he had lain, and the pillows still bore the imprint of his head. Regan resisted the desire to touch them, simply jerking up the counterpane and peering beneath the bed. No Elizabeth there!

She crossed to the wardrobe. Rolf's coat was hanging on the door and she caught the scent of him, faint, but very male. For a moment she buried her face in the cloth, drinking it in. Then she caught herself up short, jerking the door open. No Elizabeth there either, just the few clothes he had brought with him hanging on the metal hooks.

Again she hesitated, fascinated by the magic that seemed to emanate from those simple garments – but garments that he had chosen, garments that clothed that glorious body.

With a snap she closed the door again and was about to leave the room when her eye fell on a few small personal items deposited on the dressing chest. A handkerchief, his pocket watch – and a lady's locket. Curiosity overcoming her creeping sense of guilt, Regan picked it up. It was cheap, she could see that at once, and well-worn, the base metal faded and dull. But when she pressed on the clasp it came open to her touch, and she saw that it contained a lock of faded brown hair.

For a moment she was pricked by insane jealousy. Who was this woman, the memento of whom meant so much to Rolf that he carried it with him wherever he went? Then realisation dawned. The age of the locket, the faded colour of the lock of hair – it must have belonged to his mother.

Regan snapped the locket shut, ashamed of the way she was prying uninvited into something which was obviously precious to the point of being sacred. But she held the locket for a moment longer anyway, wondering about the woman who had given birth to such a man. Then she replaced it on the dressing chest, took one last longing look around the room and went out, closing the door behind her.

A quick search of the remaining rooms proved just as fruitless. Regan went back downstairs and out of the house. Jud was emerging from the stables.

'Have you found her?' she called.

'No – and her pony's gone!' Anxiety made his voice rough now. 'She knows she's not allowed to go off on her own.'

'Oh, Elizabeth!' Regan sighed.

'I'll have to find her,' Jud went on. 'I can't have her off God-knows-where alone.'

Regan was beginning to feel anxious now. 'We'll help you, Jud.' She turned to Rolf, who had appeared around the corner of one of the outbuildings. 'Will you ride with me?'

He nodded at once. 'We'll saddle the horses. Where do you think she might have gone, Jud?'

The big man shrugged helplessly. 'Who can tell? Up river to find the Molloy children, maybe. She plays with them sometimes. Or she might be hiding out somewhere on her own.'

'We'll find her, never fear,' Rolf said reassuringly.

But the anxiety hung heavy over them all the same as Jud went off to summon two of the most reliable of the men to help with the search, and Rolf and Regan went into the stable to saddle the horses. By the time they were ready Jud was back with Dickon Stokes and John Bray, two convicts who had almost worked out their sentence. Both men looked worried – every last one at Mia-Mia thought the world of Elizabeth.

'We'll spread out,' Jud said. 'That's the best way of finding the little madam.'

'Which way do you want us to go?' Rolf asked.

'We'll go down river, you take the other way,' Jud replied.

Rolf held Betsy's bridle whilst Regan climbed up on the block and mounted her, then he vaulted into the saddle himself. Just a few minutes ago Regan would have been weak with admiration at his athletic grace, now she was too worried about Elizabeth even to think of it.

They rode, their eyes ceaselessly scanning the horizon as well as every possible hiding place, calling Elizabeth's name, but there was no answering sound from the bush. As they passed beneath a ghost gum a kookaburra perched in the branches set up its wild unearthly laughter and the sudden sound made Regan jump, taut with nerves as she was.

'I've heard that laugh since I was a little boy, but I never quite get used to it,' Rolf said. 'I'll never forget the first time. I thought it was a banshee!'

Regan said nothing. Usually she couldn't help laughing along with the kookaburra, but today she was too worried even to smile.

For an hour or more they searched without success.

'Do you think the others have found her?' Regan asked.

'Should we go back and see? She wouldn't have come further from home than this, surely?'

Rolf was silent, bending over the boundary fence to pluck at a small knot of hair that had caught there.

'Elizabeth's pony is a chestnut, isn't it?'

Regan nodded. 'Yes. That's the reason she calls him Blue. But why?'

Rolf held out his hand. In the palm lay a small knot of chestnut hair.

'She may have jumped this fence. It could be nothing, of course, but . . .'

Regan strained her eyes into the distance. 'There's no sign of her.'

'There might not be.' Rolf sat silent for a moment, getting his bearings, though Regan did not realise it. Then he turned Satan. 'Let's try this way.'

He backed Satan up and galloped him at the fence, clearing it easily. Regan followed, puzzled. It was almost as if Rolf knew where he was going . . .

They cantered across the pasture, then slowed as they approached a big clump of bush that followed a sharp bend in the river. Rolf led the way into it. The ground was rocky here, the thick cool bush strewn with boulders. Rolf picked his way carefully up the rise.

It wasn't a place Regan knew at all; for all her intimacy with the land she couldn't ever remember having explored this territory.

'Rolf, she wouldn't . . .' she began, then broke off, her heart giving a gigantic leap.

Blue was standing quietly amidst the trees, cropping lazily at some fresh growth.

'It's her pony!' Regan cried. 'It's Blue!'

She urged Betsy forward. Blue raised his head, regarding them with mild interest. He and Betsy were, after all, stablemates.

'Elizabeth!' Regan called out urgently. 'Are you there?'

And this time, to her enormous relief, there was a reply. 'Regan?'

Elizabeth's voice! But where was she? Regan could still see no sign of her.

'Over here.' Rolf dismounted, throwing Satan's reins around the trunk of a gum and scrambling up a rocky incline. Regan followed.

'Careful!' he warned her. 'Take the track I've taken.'

She did so and a moment later gasped in surprise. The rocky incline fell away suddenly into a small gorge, and Regan saw the mouth of a small natural cave, half hidden by undergrowth. Rolf scrambled down to it and Regan picked her way after him.

'Regan!' she heard Elizabeth call again. Her voice came from within the cave.

Regan rounded a boulder and saw her sitting there in the gloom.

'Elizabeth Greenstreet!' she burst out. 'Do you know how worried we've all been about you? What do you think you are doing? Half Mia-Mia is out looking for you, and all because you didn't want to go to chapel!'

'Don't be cross with me, Regan!' The small voice was tearful and Elizabeth made no attempt to get up.

'Never mind me being cross! Your father is going to be furious! Now come out this instant, do you hear me?'

'I've hurt my foot, Regan.'

Now that her eyes were beginning to grow accustomed to the dim light, Regan could see that indeed Elizabeth's leg was twisted at an awkward angle. She dropped to her haunches beside the little girl and examining her leg. Elizabeth squealed with pain as Regan touched her ankle, which bulged uncomfortably over the lip of her boot.

'I twisted it on the rocks,' Elizabeth said miserably. 'I knew I'd never be able to climb back in the saddle. I can't even stand up on it! I didn't know what to do! I crept back in here to think. But the more I thought, the more frightened

I got.' Her voice cracked tearfully. 'I didn't think anyone would ever find me!'

'You're very lucky we did!' Regan scolded, but more gently. 'You could have been here for days and days if it hadn't been for Rolf. Well, now we have found you, we'd better get you home. Your father will be half out of his mind with worry.'

'But I can't . . .' Elizabeth wailed. All the usual fight seemed to have gone out of her.

'Come on Elizabeth, where's your spirit of adventure?' Rolf bent over her, lifting her easily into his arms as if she weighed no more than a feather. Then, carrying her, he picked his way back up the gorge and down the rise to where the horses were tied, and Blue was still cropping quietly.

The pony whinnied softly to see his young mistress. Perhaps in his own way he had been worried too, Regan thought. Rolf deposited Elizabeth in the saddle.

'You can still hold on, I take it?' he said.

'Of course I can!' She was indignant at such a suggestion. It wouldn't take her long to recover and become her usual mischievous self, Regan thought.

Rolf unhooked Satan's reins, and Regan did likewise with Betsy. Between them they led the three horses out of the bush and back to the track.

'Come on then,' Rolf said, and his gentleness with the child stirred Regan strangely. 'Let's get you home and set your father's mind at rest.'

'And from the look of that ankle it will be at least a week before you go worrying us to death again!' Regan added tartly.

'Elizabeth – thank God!'

Jud had seen them coming and came running down the drive to meet them.

Regan was reminded of her own father rushing out to

65

meet her on the day of the storm. She might be a grown woman, but she supposed that to Andrew she was still his little girl.

'Where did you find her?' Jud asked Regan.

'In a cave of all places. Up river, near Larry's Rock. But it wasn't my doing. It's Rolf you have to thank for finding her. I was all for turning back when he . . .'

She realised Jud was scarcely listening. He lifted Elizabeth out of the saddle, hugging her to his broad chest. As yet he was too relieved to be angry with her, but as he took her into the house to put a cold compress and bandages on her swollen ankle, Regan heard him saying sternly: 'I expect it does hurt, my lady! Well, you've no one but yourself to blame. That's what you get for not going to chapel!'

'We'd better stable the horses ourselves,' she said to Rolf, for the men were nowhere to be seen. No doubt they were still out searching for Elizabeth.

After the heat of the sun outside it was dim and refreshingly cool in the stable and Regan wrinkled her nose in pleasure at the familiar smell of horses and hay.

As she hung Betsy's saddle on its hook, a thought occurred to Regan.

'How in the world did you know where to look for her?' she asked.

There was a moment's silence, though Regan did not appreciate its significance.

Then: 'Intuition, I guess,' Rolf replied roughly. 'All these years in the bush. And I was a child once myself, remember. Though it may be hard to believe that now,' he added with a short laugh.

'But all I've lived here all my life and I never even knew that place existed . . .'

Regan broke off suddenly as his arms went round her. For a moment she leaned back against his hard chest, her heart beating a crazy tattoo. His hands were about her waist, holding her firmly, and she could feel his mouth, warm and gentle, on the soft skin of her neck just behind her ear. She stood motionless, her pulses racing and that crazy spark of desire stirring deep within her.

Oh, but it felt so right! And it was so exciting! Forbidden – and the more full of magic because of it! She held her breath, wanting it to go on forever. Then, gently, he turned her towards him. His hands seemed to burn through the thin fabric of her shirt as if he were branding her with his fingers and she slid her hands around his broad back, feeling the ripple of muscle and sinew, and lifting her chin for his kiss.

As his lips touched hers their pressure intoxicated her. The tip of his tongue probed her mouth and she parted her lips willingly, instinctively. Never – never! – had she kissed, or been kissed, like this before, but she needed no teaching! She flicked her own tongue to meet his, delighting in the taste and the sensation.

'Regan,' he whispered. 'You are the most beautiful woman I have ever laid eyes on.' The words were unexpected, yet they were everything she had ever wanted to hear. 'And I want you,' he added roughly.

His hands were on the fastenings of her shirt, tweaking them open with urgent insistence. She should stop him, she knew. But she was powerless to object. Every nerve ending in her body was sensitised to sharp awareness; her legs felt weak and trembling, yet she pressed herself against him, her flesh drawn like a magnet to his.

His fingers, long and strong, slid inside her shirt, toyed for a moment with the fastening of her chemisette, then rasped over the soft skin of her breast. Instantly her nipple rose hard and erect to his touch and he plied it gently between finger and thumb. The sharp sweet cord that seemed to join her nipple to the deepest, most secret parts of her tingled to life and as she pressed her hips close to his she almost cried out at the sensation she experienced. How could anything be so sweet, so urgent, when there were yet layers of clothing to keep their hotly aroused flesh from touching? Lord, but the delight of it was almost more than she could bear!

He bent his head, pressing his mouth to the sweet curve of her breast, but delicious as it was, the movement meant that his hips had moved away from hers, and that snug excitement was what she wanted most of all. She threw her head back, wriggling closer again, desperate to experience once more that all-consuming sensation. A small voice within was nagging at her, telling her 'no', but she could not, would not, heed it. Nothing mattered in the whole wide world but the need to be closer, ever closer, and the longing for this to go on and on forever . . .

'Oh, Regan, Regan . . .' She could hear the answering desire in his voice, low, throaty and urgent.

And then the clatter of hooves in the yard outside impinged on her wondrous trance, and the sound of men's voices, loud and rough. They snatched her away from the brink of ecstasy with a jolt so sharp she gasped.

The men were back! At any second they might come bursting into the stable!

All the lovely dreamlike sensations disappeared in a burst of panic.

'Rolf!' she squeaked. 'Rolf – the men . . .'

The stable door opened and a shaft of sunlight speared into the gloom. Regan turned her back on it, pretending to be settling the saddle on its hook.

'Who's there?'

It was the voice of John Bray, one of the convicts. His eyes had not yet become accustomed to the dimness in the stable, Regan realised, and her knees went weak at the narrowness of their escape.

'It's me – Rolf – and Regan.' Rolf's voice was throaty. She could hear in it the frustration of interrupted desire. Pray God the convict could not!

'Rolf! You found her, we hear.'

'We found her. Not too much the worse for wear.'

Rolf was in control of himself again. Regan experienced a stab of admiration – and gratitude. What a man he was! So strong, so gentle, so . . .

And you very nearly disgraced yourself for him! she reminded herself.

The colour heightened in her cheeks. What must he think of her, allowing such intimacies, welcoming them? The shame was hot as the fires of hell. And yet . . .

Beneath the shame and confusion were other unfamiliar emotions. An aching sense of loss. The prickling edge of frustration. And above all the longing to experience it all again, and this time to be able to follow it through to its uninterrupted conclusion.

As they walked back to the house Rolf stretched out a hand towards her.

Regan jerked away. 'No! Don't dare touch me!'

A wry smile twisted his mouth. 'Very well. If you don't mind your father seeing you with straw in your hair.'

'Oh landsakes! Have I?' She ran her fingers through her hair. 'Is it all gone now?'

'But for this one.' He removed another strand, smiling, and the touch, so light now, so platonic, made her knees tremble once more.

'Rolf – you won't . . . ?'

'Tell anyone? And have myself hung from the highest gum on Mia-Mia for my pains?' He grinned. 'Your secret is safe with me, my sweet.'

They were in the shadow of the veranda now. He turned to her, his face no longer smiling. 'You can't marry him, Regan,' he said. 'You must not waste your life on a man you don't love.'

'I *do* love him – I've told you,' she protested without much conviction.

His eyes met hers, steely grey in his sunburned face. 'You call what you feel for Dauntsey love? Well, in the end, it's your word – and your choice. Just remember when you marry him it will be for a very long time. And you will never, ever, experience with him one quarter of what we just shared. Remember how it was, Regan? Remember what you felt?'

'How do you know what I felt?' Her face was burning again.

'Because I felt it too,' he said with soft urgency.

'*You!*' she said, startled. '*You* felt . . . ?'

'It does not come often, that special spark between a man and a woman,' he said. 'When it does, it is to be prized as a treasure, not cast aside for anything less. You think you might find it yet with David Dauntsey? You are wrong. Think on that, Regan!'

With that he turned on his heel and strode away from her up the veranda steps.

Regan stared after him, all her doubts and anxieties resurrected. She never had felt that way about David, and instinctively she knew she never would.

But how could she jilt him now and break his heart – and her father's?

Oh, dear God, what could she do?

Six

The dinner was in full swing. The big oak dining table which Andrew Mackenzie had had shipped out from England twenty years earlier was set with the best china and glassware, and candles burned brightly in the silver candelabra at each end.

Andrew himself sat at the head, beaming at his guests as he tucked into the finest rare roast beef from his own herds, with David on his right-hand side. Opposite him were David's parents, Molly and Richard, dressed in their best for the occasion and glowing with pride. And beside him sat Rolf. When he had heard that it had been Rolf who had found Elizabeth, Andrew had extended the invitation – indeed, insisted that Rolf should join them.

'It seems we have cause to be grateful to you once again,' he had said, and if the reserve he instinctively felt was still there, he took pains not to let it show. 'You must dine with us this evening as a token of my thanks.'

Regan, still flushed and guilty, had wondered what her father would have said if he had known what had taken place in the stables when they had returned. Andrew's gratitude would most certainly have been quite overtaken by a paroxysm of rage. At best, Rolf would have been given his marching orders. But at least she would not have had to sit in his presence for hours, her body remembering the excitement of his touch every time she looked at him, her mind racing in circles as the blunt words he had spoken to her afterwards came back to haunt her again and again.

When she had come down to greet the guests, dressed in her new emerald-green gown, she had passed him in the passageway and she had almost thought he was going to kiss her again as his hand lightly touched the shining silk.

'So the rain did not get to your gown, Regan,' he said softly. 'It becomes you.'

'Thank you,' she murmured stiffly.

'But then, you look beautiful even in a boy's shirt and breeches,' he went on. 'And even more beautiful without them, I warrant.'

If it had not been for the well-hidden desire she glimpsed in his eyes she might almost have thought he was laughing at her.

'Don't say such things!' she had hissed, but his words and his touch had once more stirred up the turmoil that had bubbled in her ceaselessly since the morning's encounter.

She glanced at him now and felt her pulses begin to race giddily. How could he do this to her? How could she feel such things when it was dear, gentle David she was to marry? She would never experience one quarter the delight with David as with him, Rolf had said.

Her eyes turned to David, to his handsome face above the ruffles of his shirt, to his hands, narrow and long-fingered, and knew deep inside that it was so. Those gentle lips would never start in her the fire that Rolf's could, those hands never stir her body as Rolf's had. And the knowledge was a sickness in the pit of her stomach that made each mouthful of food taste like sawdust.

'So, we are agreed that the wedding should take place early next spring,' Molly said. 'Oh, I am so looking forward to it!' She laid down her fork, pressing her plump little hands together. 'It will be here, of course, at Mia-Mia?'

'Where else?' Andrew returned, beaming proudly.

'Oh yes! It's a splendid house, and when it is decked with flowers . . . May I oversee the arrangement of them, Andrew? You know how I love flowers, and since dear

Anne . . .' Molly bit her lip. She knew how Andrew still
grieved for his lost wife.

'I think that would please Anne very much if she knew,'
Andrew said gravely.

'How proud she would be!' Molly went on after a
moment.

'She would indeed,' Andrew agreed. 'And happy, too, to
know that Regan was to wed your son and our families be
joined.'

I can't bear this! Regan thought wildly. *I simply cannot
bear it!*

Molly turned to her, quite unaware of the thoughts spin-
ning round inside her head.

'What about attendants, my dear? You have no sisters and
we, alas, have no daughters – though that will be remedied,
of course, when you become the daughter I have always
longed for.'

'Regan thought to ask Elizabeth to attend her,' Andrew
said. 'She is very fond of the child, are you not, Regan?'

Regan nodded but could not reply. A knot of desperation
had risen in her throat, choking her. She scraped back her
chair and rose abruptly. Every eye turned to her and the
heat of the room seemed to close in on her suddenly.

'I'm sorry,' she whispered faintly. 'Please excuse me.'

As she fled from the room the assembled company gazed
after her in stunned silence, then Andrew scraped back his
own chair.

'She was badly frightened by Elizabeth's disappearance
this morning,' he said. 'The shock is doubtless catching up
with her. Pass me the brandy, Richard. A little of that will
soon revive her.'

David rose. 'Please allow me to go after her, Captain
Mackenzie. I am, after all, soon to be her husband. She will
be my responsibility then, and I'd like to comfort her now. If
she is indeed ill, be assured I will let you know at once.'

Andrew nodded his reluctant agreement and David took

the glass of brandy his father had poured and made for the door.

David found Regan in the small formal garden that lay beyond the veranda. She was leaning against the trunk of a flowering cherry, her head bowed, her arms wrapped around herself as if, in spite of the warmth of the evening, she was cold.

He set the glass of brandy down on a flagstone and went towards her warily. In all the years he had know her, he had never seen Regan behave this way before.

'Regan?' He spoke her name hesitantly. 'Sweetheart – what is wrong?'

She lifted her head, staring up at the black velvety sky studded with a million stars. By the light of the moon he could see that her face was wet with tears.

'Was it talk of your mother that upset you?' he asked gently. 'Your father thinks it is because you were so worried about Elizabeth this morning, but I know you better than that. You cast your worries aside, Regan, as I can never do. You're too strong and brave to be still fretting over something that turned out well in the end. But I know you still grieve for the loss of your mother, though you never knew her.'

Regan was silent, and emboldened, he put his arms around her, drawing her into his embrace. But she did not respond and though her folded arms were still between them he could feel the tension in every line of her body.

'I will be your family soon, Regan,' he whispered. 'I can never replace her, I know, but you will never lack for love, I swear. And we'll have children, boys for me and a girl for you, and they will fill those empty spaces your father and I can never fill, no matter how we love you. Our children, Regan – think of it! A house overflowing with laughter and joy, and you and I building a home, raising a family, growing old together . . .'

Her strangled sob startled him and a violent tremor ran through the whole of her body.

'Regan, whatever is it, my love?' he cried, alarmed. 'You can tell me.'

Regan unfolded her arms with a sharp movement, pushing him away. His hands dropped woodenly to his sides and she ran a few steps blindly, stumbling into the forgotten brandy glass and overturning it.

Frightened, he followed her. 'Regan, please . . .'

She swung round, her eyes meeting his for the first time and the look in them frightened him still more. 'I can't marry you, David!' she burst out.

He froze, and his voice rose, high and tremulous with shock. 'What are you talking about?'

She bit her lip, rocking slightly. 'I can't marry you, David,' she said more softly. 'It wouldn't be fair – to either of us.'

'I don't understand! What do you mean, not fair?' He felt dazed, numb almost.

'I don't love you . . . in that way,' she said, choosing her words now with care. 'I love you like a brother, just as I always have. But it's not the way a wife should love her husband. There's more to marriage than tender regard, much, much more.'

She was afraid! David thought. Afraid of physical intimacy! Tenderness suffused him.

'There's nothing to fear, my love,' he said gently. 'I'd never hurt you. And I won't rush you either, until you are ready. God knows, I've waited patiently all these years, I can wait a little longer. But I think you'll find that what is begun in gentleness can very soon become pleasurable, for both of us.' Another thought occurred to him. 'And if it's having children that frightens you, then we need not rush into that either. We're young yet. We have all our lives before us. There's no need for us to rush into anything.'

Regan shook her head. 'You don't understand. It's not

that I'm afraid. Well, maybe a little. But I know that women have babies every day without dying, as my mother did. It's not that, truly. It's just that . . .' She broke off, wondering how she could explain without hurting him unbearably, and realising she could not. 'I'm sorry,' she said humbly.

David shook his head in bewilderment. 'But we decided long ago. I thought you were happy.'

'I thought so too,' she returned, but she knew it was a lie. Why, even before Rolf had come into her life she had begun to have doubts. And now . . . 'It would be wrong,' she said carefully. 'I had to tell you how I feel before it's too late.'

'Dear God!' David turned away from her, his hands balling into fists. 'I can't believe what you are saying, Regan. I *won't* believe it! You're my world, you're every-thing to me!'

To her horror, Regan realised he was weeping. Her stomach clenched. Men didn't weep. Never had she seen her father allow his emotions to get the better of him. Her mother's death had broken his heart, she knew. Sometimes when he spoke of her his eyes misted and the gruffness of his tone betrayed a lump in his throat. But never had he weakened to the point of tears. Yet here was David, losing control of his dignity, his very manhood, and it was all her fault.

She reached out to touch him and he shrank away. 'Don't! I can't bear it! Not if I'm to lose you, Regan. Oh, how can you do this? To me, to your father, to my parents. They'll all be devastated. Do you know how they long for us to be wed? Do you?'

'Yes,' she whispered. 'I know.'

'Then think of them if not of me! Marry me, Regan, for God's sake! If you don't, I swear . . .' He broke off, struggling with his tears. 'If you don't, I swear I'll end my life!'

'David, don't say such a thing!' Regan cried, horrified.

'I mean it!' His hands were gripping hers like vices of iron. 'Without you, Regan, it wouldn't be worth living.'

'Oh, dear God!' she breathed. This was much worse than she could ever have imagined it would be.

'David, my dear . . .' she tried again.

'Don't "my dear" me if you don't mean it!' he snapped, then resorted once more to pleading. 'Without you, Regan, nothing would have meaning any more. *You* are my life. And that's the way it will end. I'll kill myself, and you will be free. I'll do it now, quickly . . .'

'Stop it!' she screamed. 'Stop it this instant!'

'Then say you'll still marry me, Regan!'

The breath left her lungs in a gasp. Tears of shame sprang to her own eyes. If he did this terrible thing she would have killed him as surely as if she had put the pistol to his head herself and pulled the trigger. What future would there be then for her – with Rolf, or any man?

'Very well,' she whispered. 'I suppose I must keep my promise.'

'Oh, Regan!' He began to sob again, this time from relief.

The sickness was a weight around her heart. She had to do it. He had left her no choice. But she couldn't endure the months of waiting for spring to come, couldn't bear the thought of the doubts that would torment her until the final commitment was made.

'Just one thing,' she said. 'I think we should be married sooner than we planned. If we are going to have this new life together, then let's make a start on it without delay.'

'Oh, my darling!'

He took her in his arms and she allowed him to do so. But the touch, which had never excited her, now actually repelled her. She stood stiffly in his embrace. Somehow she must put aside all the restless yearnings and learn once more to succumb to his gentle loving. But she had not the slightest idea how she was going to manage it.

*   *   *

All eyes turned to them as they went back into the dining room.

'Regan?' Andrew said anxiously. 'Are you all right?'

She couldn't bring herself to speak, though she forced a smile to her lips.

David took her hand. His eyes were bright now, if a little puffy.

'We have something to tell you all,' he said excitedly. 'Regan and I have decided to bring the date of our wedding day forward. We want to be married as soon as possible.'

For a moment they stared in surprise, then they all spoke at once, Richard and Molly enthusing and congratulating, Andrew still concerned. Only Rolf said nothing, but Regan felt his eyes on her, cold and steely. She could not look in his direction.

'Can it be arranged, do you think?' David asked. He sounded a little light-headed.

'Anything is possible,' Andrew said. 'Though I thought spring was what we had agreed upon.'

'But if your eager young lovers cannot wait . . .' Richard squeezed Regan's hand and beamed at his son.

'I'll have to visit the dressmaker!' Molly bubbled. 'I haven't even thought of ordering my gown yet!' A thought struck her. 'What about your gown, Regan? And Elizabeth's? There will be so much to do, and so little time to do it!'

'I'll go into Broken Hill next week, and take Elizabeth with me,' Regan said.

'Oh, the child is going to be so excited!' Molly gabbled. 'Heavens above, I'm excited myself! What a day this has turned out to be!'

'It's wonderful news, certainly,' Richard said. 'Now, sit down and finish your dinner, both of you. You've hardly begun! And there's nothing like the night air – and a little ardour – to give a person an appetite, is there?' His eyes were twinkling.

They took their places at the table and David set about his meal, even though it had now grown cold, with an eagerness which suggested he had not eaten for a week.

But Regan thought that so much as a mouthful would choke her. The very suggestion of eating was making her stomach turn. She picked up her fork and put it down again.

'I'm really not hungry,' she said, forcing a smile to her stiff lips.

'Too much excitement, I wouldn't be surprised!' Molly beamed.

Richard rose to his feet. 'A toast, I think. To our son and your daughter, Andrew. And our two families, soon to be one. A great deal sooner than we expected!' he added.

They all rose. Regan risked a glance at Rolf. His expression was quite unreadable. But as he raised his glass his eyes reproached her for a moment, and his smile became sardonic.

'To the happy couple,' he said. 'A lifetime's happiness.'

Regan's heart fluttered like a trapped bird.

She alone knew he did not mean a single word of it.

'Regan, are you quite sure this is what you want?' Andrew asked.

The guests had gone, Rolf had retired to his room, and they were alone.

'Why do you ask, Father?' Regan stalled.

'Something is wrong.' His eyes were searching her face with anxious paternal eyes. 'You were upset when you ran from the room, and when you returned you did not, to me at any rate, have the look of an eager bride. David's delight was plain to see. But not you.'

'I didn't feel well, Father,' Regan said carefully. 'I think I had too much sun this morning.'

'Codswallop!' Andrew said roundly. 'I know you better than that. Too much sun? It's never bothered you before.

Why are you bringing the wedding forward, Regan? And why are you less than happy about it? There's not something you are not telling me, is there? Something I ought to know?'

Her face flamed as she read his mind. 'Of course not, Father! How could you suggest such a thing?'

'Because these things happen,' he said roughly. 'I must confess I would be disappointed in you if you have allowed David liberties before you are his wife, but I'm a man of the world. I know the temptations that beset you when you are young and in love.'

In love. The words made her want to laugh hysterically. Perhaps she was in love. But not with David. She recalled the way she had recoiled from his embrace this night, and shuddered inwardly. But she certainly couldn't admit that to her father.

'I just think there's no sense waiting,' she said woodenly.

'I'm glad of that at least.' Andrew crossed to the chiffonier and poured himself a brandy. 'But I'm still not satisfied with your behaviour – or your excuses for it.' He swirled the golden liquid round the glass and sipped it thoughtfully.

'This wouldn't have anything to do with the other young man present, I suppose?'

Regan felt the colour flood her cheeks and fade again. 'What do you mean?' she whispered.

'You haven't designs on him, I hope,' Andrew said sternly.

'Oh don't be so foolish, Father!' she managed. 'He's never so much as looked at me!'

'Maybe not,' Andrew said. 'But perhaps you'd like him to. This hasty marriage is not meant to goad him to interest, I hope?'

'Why, of course not!'

'Because if it is,' he went on as if she had not spoken, 'that would be a bad mistake, Regan. He's a stranger, and

80

a farm-hand at that. He is not for you, and you would do well to remember it.'

'I know it, Father,' she said stiffly.

He downed his brandy in one gulp. 'You know your happiness is my greatest concern, Regan,' he said, wiping his mouth with the back of his hand. 'God knows, you have been my reason for living since your mother died, and I could not bear it if I thought you were making a marriage against the dictates of your heart. A good marriage can be a wonderful thing. I only wish that Anne had been spared so we could have enjoyed a little more time together as man and wife. And it's what I want for you, my Regan.'

Her heart was full. 'Yes, I know that too, Father.'

For a brief second or two she forgot that it was she who had insisted on bringing the marriage forward. She felt a tiny irrational dart of hope that all might yet be well. Then he spoke again and hope died, crushed out like a ripe walnut underfoot.

'David will be a good husband to you, Regan, I know. He will take care of you and you will want for nothing. Be patient for just a little while with him and you will have your reward. He loves you so much.'

She bent her head to hide the tears sparkling in her eyes. For all his fine words, what her father wanted for her was what *he* wanted, what *he* thought best. And perhaps he was right. But in her heart she knew he was not.

Rolf paced his room restlessly. He knew he would never sleep and he did not want to. He drew a flask of rum from the pocket of his coat and took a healthy swig, his senses churning.

When Regan had run from the room earlier he had thought he had won the game. Not so. If anything, things were worse than before. He had less time than he had thought to bring his plans to fruition, if such a thing were still possible.

She wanted him, he knew. Just as he wanted her. But

there was a big difference between the wanting of a man for a woman. It was his body that yearned for her. When he had seen her distress he had felt a sharp pang of protectiveness, yes, but he had been able to stifle it quickly. However lovely, however desirable, she was Andrew Mackenzie's daughter. He could never allow himself to forget that. But for Regan . . .

When a woman responded as she responded to him, it was not just the desires of the flesh – unless of course she was a trollop. And Regan was no trollop whatever else she might be.

Rolf swore softly. By rights he should have won the game already. But somehow Dauntsey had appealed to her finer nature and not only succeeded in his entreaties but actually managed to persuade her to bring the wedding forward. Somehow Rolf had to find a way of getting to her – and quickly!

He tilted the flask once more and as the warmth ran through his veins the wanting her became a fire once more. Lord, what a woman she was! In different circumstances he would give David a run for his money and for quite a different reason than the one that drove him now. Why, if he didn't know better he might almost believe it was jealousy that was hardening his determination to win her away from that milksop.

Rolf swigged at the rum again, knowing he was drinking more than he should, and not giving a damn.

What he wanted to do right now, he acknowledged, was to go to her room, tear that gown of emerald green silk from her lovely body and ravage her. But it was too dangerous. Andrew Mackenzie might yet be awake – the slightest sound and he would hear it. And that would be the end of it.

A thought occurred to him and his eyes narrowed.

So far he had failed to persuade her to jilt Dauntsey, but perhaps there was another way.

If she bore his child, then Mia-Mia would return to his family, no matter who her husband was.

An heir with Hannay blood in his veins may yet have to suffice!

Rolf's hands tightened around his hip-flask, and he stared unseeingly out into the night.

Seven

'I think I should go to Broken Hill today, Father,' Regan said. 'I need to see the dressmaker without delay.'

She was very pale this morning and the dark shadows beneath her lovely green eyes spoke of sleepless hours spent tossing and turning. But there was a determined jut to her chin and her firm tone gave away none of her innermost feelings.

Rolf looked up quickly from his mug of tea. Was this another chance, and so soon, to be alone with her? But a moment later his hopes were dashed.

'I suppose I should go there to visit the tailor myself,' Andrew said. 'As you know, Richard and I thought to wear our old regimental uniforms for the ceremony. The scarlet jackets of the Corps are a sight cheerier than black frock-coats, and smarter, to boot. But when I tried mine on last night I found it a little tight around the midriff. I'll escort you to Broken Hill myself.'

Rolf turned his head away, anger suddenly swamping his disappointment. Lord, if he saw Andrew dressed in that hated red coat it would be all he could do to keep his hands off him!

'We must take Elizabeth with us,' Regan was saying. 'She'll need a new gown too.'

'Oh yes, yes!' Elizabeth clapped her hands together with excitement. 'Can it be pink, Regan? With ribbons and bows?'

Regan laughed. Once again she thought how much the

child reminded her of herself. Wilful and mischievous she might be, a tomboy of the first order, but still full of excitement at the thought of a new gown!

'We'll see,' she said. 'It will all depend on what we can find in the store.'

'Blue, then. I wouldn't mind blue . . .' Elizabeth leaped to her feet, quite forgetting her injured ankle, and cried out as the weight went on to it.

'Careful now!' Regan warned. 'There will be no running about and skipping for you for a day or two if you want that ankle to heal in time for the wedding.'

'I'm an invalid, then, am I?' Elizabeth asked slyly. She got up from her chair, more carefully this time, and hobbled over to Rolf. 'Will you carry me to the buggy, Rolf, like you did yesterday?'

'Come on, Miss,' Regan said sharply, not wanting to be reminded of the events of yesterday. 'Go and wash your face and get yourself ready. And no, you don't need to be carried to your room, if you were thinking of asking.'

'I don't need to go to my room either!' Elizabeth retorted. 'I shall wear what I've got on. And I could always wash my face in *your* room.'

Regan clucked, but she was smiling. 'I don't know what I am going to do with you, Elizabeth Greenstreet! All right, you can come up to my room, if you like. Come on, now!'

Whilst Regan changed into a sprigged gown fit to be seen in Broken Hill, Elizabeth sat on the edge of the bed watching her.

'Rolf's nice, isn't he?' she said thoughtfully. 'Don't you think so, Regan?'

Regan concentrated on the fastenings of her gown. 'Yes, he is nice,' she said, glad that her face was hidden from Elizabeth.

'And he's handsome too. And brave,' Elizabeth went on.

In spite of herself, Regan couldn't help laughing. 'How do you know he's brave?'

'I just know. I can tell,' Elizabeth said with confidence. 'But he's really kind, as well, and that's the most important thing, isn't it?'

'And how do you know he's kind, pray?' Regan found that she wanted to go on talking about Rolf – and talking about him with Elizabeth was, after all, perfectly safe.

'I know that too.' Elizabeth swung her undamaged foot against the folds of the counterpane. 'He was kind to me yesterday. Not cross at all. Just, well, *kind*.'

Remembering the gentle way he had cradled the child in his arms, Regan felt forced to agree.

'Do you think, Regan . . .' Elizabeth's voice interrupted her thoughts.

'Do I think what?' Regan fastened the last ribbon and looked up at the little girl.

'That one day, when I'm grown up, he might marry me?' Elizabeth's small face had gone very pink.

'*Marry* you!' Regan couldn't keep from laughing in amusement.

'Don't laugh!' Elizabeth protested defensively. 'I'm serious. I mean, you don't want to marry him, do you? You are going to marry David. And he's nice too,' she added dutifully. 'But I really would like to marry Rolf. If you think he might wait for me.'

'I think you are much too young to be thinking about getting married, Elizabeth,' Regan said firmly. 'But when the time comes I'm sure you'll find someone just as nice as Rolf to marry.' Regan reached for a cameo brooch which had once been her mother's and fastened it at the neck of her gown.

'And as handsome? And as brave? And as kind?'

'I'm sure so.'

But she couldn't help thinking, all the same, that if Elizabeth was able to find a man with one quarter of

86

Rolf's attributes, she would be a very fortunate young lady.

As they were harnessing Lucky to the buggy, Dickon Stokes came riding into the stable yard. He was red in the face and his horse was lathered.

'What ails you, man?' Andrew asked.

'You're needed, Captain Mackenzie. Out on the farm. One of the cattle got herself stuck in a ditch. We've managed to free her, but her leg is in a bad way. Jud sent me to fetch you. He thinks you should take a look at it.'

Andrew frowned. 'I was about to ride into Broken Hill with Regan and Elizabeth.'

'Jud did say . . . But if the cow has to be destroyed . . .' The convict shifted in his saddle, clearly not relishing having to report back to Jud that the boss would not come.

'I know, I know,' Andrew said impatiently. 'Just give me time to change into my working gear.' He swung round to Rolf, who was checking the buckles on Lucky's girths. 'You'll have to take the girls to town, Rolf. And my visit to the tailor will have to wait for another day.'

He strode off towards the house.

'Rolf is going to take us!' Elizabeth whispered excitedly to Regan. 'Isn't that grand?'

Regan nodded and patted the child's arm.

She wasn't sure that 'grand' was quite the word she would have used. But her pulses had begun their relentless drumming at the prospect of it anyway.

On the road to Broken Hill Rolf rode alongside the buggy on Satan as he had on that first day.

As they approached the place where the bushwhacking had taken place, Regan felt the nerves knot in her throat, and as if he understood her feelings, Rolf glanced at her.

'It's long gone,' he said reassuringly.

'What is?' Elizabeth piped up.

87

'Nothing,' Regan said shortly.

Elizabeth looked hurt, and Rolf winked at her. 'You don't want to know, young lady.'

'I do! I do!'

He raised an eyebrow, teasing her. 'Would you believe . . . a ghost?'

'A ghost!' Elizabeth squeaked, looking around in delicious terror. 'Is there a ghost on this road?'

'Did I say that? I just asked if you would believe it.'

And so there might be! Regan thought with a shiver. The ghost of poor murdered Francis Duncan! But at least Rolf had managed to divert Elizabeth's attention. There were some things that were too terrible for Elizabeth's young ears, even though she had been born and raised in this wild and lawless land.

It was almost midday and the sun was high overhead in the sky when they reached the outskirts of Broken Hill. As they passed the first wooden shacks an old woman sitting in the shade of her veranda called out to them.

'Hullo there, Regan!'

Regan waved out to her. 'Hullo, Mistress Robinson!'

But she did not stop the buggy to converse. Mistress Robinson might be old now, and harmless, but Regan could remember when she had been the owner of the tavern where the men of the hamlet had gathered for their nip of rum and, she now knew, other pleasures besides. For all her air of faded respectability, Mistress Robinson was not the kind of woman an innocent young girl like Elizabeth should be acquainted with.

Into the main street of the hamlet they rode, and Regan experienced her customary excitement at the hustle and bustle. She loved the farm, loved the open countryside, but it was also good to see human beings other than their convicts and hands going about their business. Past the Commercial Hotel they went, past the shack that served as a chapel and where Elizabeth should yesterday have sat with Jud to listen to Parson Meredith's interminable sermon. Then, as they approached the General Store, she slowed Lucky.

'Here we are!' she called to Rolf. 'Here's the store!'

'So I see,' Rolf returned, but he had needed no telling.

Memories were rushing in. The place had changed little since he was a boy; in his mind's eye he could see himself climbing the wooden steps with his mother and going into the dim cluttered interior to buy candles and flour. The place had always seemed to him an Aladdin's cave, and it was no different now.

As they passed through the doorway, hung with cooking pots for sale, the same old smell tickled his nostrils, and he let his eye rove for a moment over the sacks of flour and kegs of molasses, the shelves piled high with cooking utensils and the rolls of fabrics stacked against the walls.

Regan was making for them eagerly, Elizabeth in tow. It was almost as if she had forgotten the purpose of their errand in her excitement at seeing the enticing array – brightly coloured silks from the East piled alongside delicate muslins and floral chintz, and the inevitable calicos and worsteds.

'Regan! What can I do for you this fine day?' Perry Mullins, the store owner, came bustling towards them from the rear of the store, wiping his hands on the big baize apron he wore tied around his skinny frame.

'I'm looking for fabric, Mr Mullins,' Regan returned.

'Then you're in luck! I had a new shipment in just this week.' He indicated the overflowing shelves. 'You'll be spoiled for choice, as you can see. There's a green striped taffeta that would suit your colouring. Or the spotted muslin . . .'

'I'm looking for fabric for a wedding gown,' Regan told him.

'Oh, a happy occasion indeed!' The store owner glanced at Rolf, slightly bemused at seeing Regan with this stranger, but not wanting to show his surprise. 'You are a lucky man, my friend.'

Elizabeth giggled and high spots of colour rose in Regan's cheeks. 'Oh no, you've got it wrong . . .' she began.

'I'm afraid I am not the fortunate bridegroom,' Rolf said. 'Would that I were!'

His eyes slid, challenging, to Regan's, and her flush deepened.

'Have you anything suitable, Mr Mullins?' she asked, hoping the moment would pass quickly.

'I have indeed!' The little man was flustered now too and he covered his embarrassment with a great show of bustle. 'Just wait here and I'll fetch it for you. I have it in the back room.'

He scuttled off and Regan stood with her back firmly turned towards Rolf, ignoring him. A moment later Perry Mullins was back with a roll of ivory figured silk.

'Now this is just the thing.' He unwound a yard or so, holding it out for her to see. 'This end here took a little water damage on the voyage, but once that's cut off . . .'

'It's perfect,' Regan said. 'I'll take a length of that. And now I need something for Elizabeth. She is to attend me. Which do you like, Elizabeth?'

Elizabeth was round-eyed at the display. 'Oh I don't know! They're all so lovely!'

Together they chose a pale green taffeta and some ecru lace trimmings.

'Fancy, the man thought you were to marry me!' Rolf murmured in Regan's ear as Perry left to package the purchases. 'He must have thought we made a likely couple.'

'Well he was wrong, wasn't he?' Regan flashed. 'It's a good thing I put him right and quickly, or the gossip would have been all over Broken Hill before you could say Jack Knife! Everyone knows I'm betrothed to David.'

She whirled away from him, looking for Elizabeth. The child had lost interest now in the fabrics and was rooting about amongst the other assorted items that filled every inch of the store.

'Oh Regan, look!' she cried suddenly, picking up a doll. 'Isn't she beautiful!'

Regan had to agree; the doll was as fine as any she had ever seen, with a china face and yellow hair. She was beautifully dressed in a tiny gown of ivory and around her neck was a little choker of minute seed pearls.

'Oh Regan, I want her!' Elizabeth breathed. 'I've never had a proper doll. Never!'

It was true; to Regan's knowledge, she never had.

'You'll have to tell your father about her, Elizabeth,' she said. 'Perhaps if you are extra specially good he'll come into Broken Hill and buy her for you.'

'But she could be sold by then!' Elizabeth was clutching the doll as if she would never let her go.

Rolf stepped forward. There was a curious expression on his face. Surprised, Regan recognised it as tenderness. 'I'd like to buy the doll for you, Elizabeth.'

Regan's eyes went round with surprise, but before she could say a word, Elizabeth had run to him, throwing her arms around him.

'Really? You'll really truly buy her for me?'

'Rolf, you can't! I'm sure she'll cost a great deal of money,' Regan protested, and she was startled still further when Rolf drew out his pocketbook and extracted a wad of notes.

'Allow me to buy the child a present,' he said, smiling at her. 'We are friends, aren't we, Elizabeth?'

'I'm sure you are, when you spoil her so!' Regan said and instantly regretted it. Rolf was making a truly generous gesture and she must not spoil it. But she couldn't help wondering how an itinerant farm-hand came to have so much money on his person.

Of course, he wasn't just a farm-hand, she reminded herself. He'd said that he and his brother had farmed land on the other side of the mountains. Perhaps the brother had paid him off handsomely to be rid of him. But all the same . . .

91

It was strange, Regan thought. Elizabeth had said he was kind. Clearly her child's instincts had been correct.

When their purchases were wrapped and paid for they left the store, Elizabeth clutching the doll.

'What am I going to call you?' she asked, touching the china face with loving fingers.

'Why don't you call her Jessica?' Rolf suggested. There was a faraway look on his face, and, without needing to be told, Regan knew it had been his mother's name.

'Jessica! Yes! That just suits her!' Elizabeth said, delighted. 'I shall call her Jessica.'

A faint smile touched Rolf's lips.

'I think so too,' he said.

The dressmaker, Eliza Button, had her premises a little further along the main street. Leaving the horses tethered at the hitching post, they walked the short distance. Then, whilst Regan and Elizabeth went in to place their order, Rolf walked back and forth outside, drinking in the sights and sounds of the little hamlet he had once known so well.

It was a strange feeling, he conceded, to return after so long as a grown man. The hamlet had seemed so big to him then; now it was just that, a bustling hamlet, even though he could see new buildings where once there had been gaps of waste land.

But the store, at least, had changed little. Rolf could remember how he had ferreted, fascinated, amongst the items for sale whilst his mother shopped, just as Elizabeth had done. And one day, again like Elizabeth, he had spied something he had wanted very much.

A toy horse. He could see it now, carved from wood and brightly painted, its legs supported on curved rockers. Oh, what he would have given to have been able to take that horse home with him! But of course there had been no money to spare for such frivolities. There was scarcely enough to buy the bare necessities.

Across the years, the remembered ache of longing had been sharp when he had seen how Elizabeth coveted the doll, and suddenly he had wanted to buy it for her so that she, at least, would not have to leave it behind in the shop and yearn for it all the way home. In a strange way it had been as if he had been buying it for himself, for the little boy he had once been, as well as wanting to make Elizabeth happy.

He should not have done it, of course. He'd seen the way Regan had looked when he'd pulled out the wad of money. He could well have aroused her suspicions. But what did that matter now? She was going to marry David Dauntsey.

The pleasure he had gained from buying the doll for Elizabeth left him all of a rush. He turned on his heel and walked back to the dressmaker's to wait for Regan and Elizabeth.

When Regan emerged once more from Eliza Button's premises, Elizabeth skipping excitedly at her side, she saw Rolf standing on the other side of the street at the entrance to the forge. His back was turned towards her, but the sight of his broad shoulders and long muscled legs encased in buckskin breeches made her heart turn over.

Oh, if only it *was* him she was to marry! Being measured for her wedding gown, choosing the design and attempting all the while to sound happy and excited as a bride should be had been sheer torture. Now her throat ached with unshed tears.

Elizabeth spotted Rolf at the same moment as Regan did.

'There he is!' she cried and raced across the street towards him. Regan followed more slowly. She wanted time to compose herself before she had to face him.

By the time she reached them they were standing side by side looking through the open door of the forge. Rolf's hand lay on Elizabeth's shoulder and he was explaining to her the work of the blacksmith, whose swarthy, leather-aproned figure bent over his anvil. Before him, the fire glowed red-hot in the dim light, and iron rang on iron as he hammered the horse shoe he was fashioning into shape.

'How can he stand it?' Elizabeth was asking. 'All day long in the dark and heat?'

'He's used to it,' Rolf replied. He turned and saw Regan. 'All done?' he asked her. 'Your wedding gown ordered?'

Regan heard the hard edge in his voice and swallowed hard at the lump in her throat.

'All done. And Elizabeth's too. Now, shouldn't we be making for home?'

'Oh, can't we stay just a little longer, Regan? Please?' Elizabeth begged. 'It's so exciting here in Broken Hill – and the smithy is the most exciting place of all.' She stared once more into the dark depths. 'Frightening, too, though. Do you know what it reminds me of? It's like one of the pictures in our Family Bible!'

Rolf laughed aloud. 'Fire and brimstone, you mean?'

'Yes. Parson Meredith says I'll go to a place like that if I don't behave myself.' She wrinkled her nose in disgust. 'I don't believe him, though,' she added. 'I don't think I've ever done anything *that* bad.'

'I should hope not!' Rolf returned.

Elizabeth looked up at him. 'Do you have a Family Bible, Rolf?'

'No, Elizabeth, I don't. My mother and father could never afford such luxuries.'

'It isn't a luxury!' Elizabeth said, shocked. 'You have to have a Bible! Parson Meredith says . . .'

'That you really will go to hell if you don't read it every day?' Rolf finished for her. 'There's no hope for me then, I'm afraid.'

'Oh, *you* won't go to hell, Rolf!' Elizabeth assured him quickly. 'You're much too nice for that. No one who bought me a doll like Jessica could ever go to hell!'

Rolf made no reply but gazed into the dark smithy, and

neither Elizabeth nor Regan had any way of knowing what he was thinking. Hell did not have to be some mysterious subterranean bonfire. Hell could be right here on earth. And he had been there already.

'I'm sorry, Elizabeth, but we really do have to go home now,' Regan said firmly. 'But it won't be long before we're back again. We have to have a final fitting for our gowns – they are much too important to leave anything to chance. And my father has to visit the tailor to get his scarlet coat altered. So there will be lots of opportunities for you to come to Broken Hill again.'

'She's right, Moppet,' Rolf said, ruffling her hair. 'We don't want Captain Mackenzie thinking we've all run off together, do we?'

Over Elizabeth's head his eyes met Regan's. The challenge in them was unmistakable. Her cheeks flamed scarlet and she turned quickly away, setting a brisk pace along the dusty street.

The horses were waiting patiently where they had left them at the hitching post. Rolf lifted Elizabeth up into the buggy – a quite unnecessary chivalry since the child seemed to have forgotten all about her injured ankle. Then he handed Regan up too, his touch on her arm burning as if his hand were one of the blacksmith's branding irons, and unhitched Satan.

'We'll give the horses a drink before we set off,' he said, heading for the low trough set in a block of stone a little further down the street.

Another man was watering his horse at the trough, a bow-legged, bent figure Regan recognised as Will Targett. Once, long ago, Will had been pot-boy for Mistress Robinson at her tavern, and Regan had no more desire to speak to him than to his erstwhile employer.

The man glanced up as they approached. A grubby hat was jammed on his head and his eyes were pale and rheumy. They fastened for a moment on Regan and she

95

nodded curtly. Then he turned them to Rolf, staring as if he had seen a ghost.

'Peter Hannay?' The cracked voice held astonishment and disbelief. 'Is it you?'

Regan looked at Rolf and saw that his face had gone stony and shut-in.

'I beg your pardon, old timer?' There was something in his voice, too, that she had never heard before.

Will Targett shook his head, as if trying to clear it of the mists that came from too much rum, taken too often.

'No. No – it couldn't be, of course. Peter Hannay has been dead these twenty years. I beg your pardon, sir. I'm addled as a bad egg these days. But for a moment there I thought . . . well, I thought you were somebody else. Somebody I knew a long time ago.'

'I assure you I am not!' Rolf laughed shortly. 'I'm a stranger in these parts.'

'Well you look like him and no mistake!' The old man shook his head again. 'Forgive me, Sir. I meant no offence.'

'Granted,' Rolf said. Then he turned Satan, as if to avoid further conversation. 'As you said, Regan, it's time we were making for home.'

To Regan he sounded angry and a little impatient.

Dear God, what a close shave! Rolf thought as they cantered along the road back to Mia-Mia. He didn't know who the man was – as a child he'd never known him, as far as he was aware – but the man had certainly recognised Rolf!

I hadn't realised I was that much like my father! he thought.

But then, he had been only nine years old when his father had died. The memory of his face was clouded by the mists of time. How could Rolf have ever realised that the face which looked back at him from his shaving glass bore such a family likeness?

Had Andrew Mackenzie recognised him too? A cold sweat broke out across his back at the thought. But no, surely not. If he had he would never have taken Rolf on, no matter how deep his gratitude for rescuing Regan. But if the old-timer had seen the likeness, addled as he was by his own admission, then why had Andrew Mackenzie not seen it too?

There could be only one explanation. Peter Hannay had been of so little importance to Andrew Mackenzie that he had quite simply forgotten all about him.

A fresh wave of cold hatred washed over Rolf. Andrew Mackenzie had ruined his father and given him no more thought than he would give a beetle he had crushed underfoot.

Rolf glanced at Regan, and once again his treacherous desire for her was swamped by ice-cold determination. One way or another he would have his revenge. And no power on heaven or on earth would stop him. No power – and his weakness for a lovely, spirited girl either. In silence, with the sun beating down and the dust flying beneath his horse's hooves, Rolf repeated the vow he had made so many years ago at the graveside of his beloved mother.

'He won't get away with it. I'll give my life to make sure of that. Whatever it takes, I'll get Mia-Mia back for the Hannays. And I swear Andrew Mackenzie will pay dearly for what he has done!'

Eight

As she turned the buggy into the stable yard, Regan saw that a strange carriage had been drawn up in a shady corner and a driver she did not know was watering the horses.

'It looks as if we have visitors,' she said to Elizabeth. 'Who can it be, I wonder?'

She climbed down and, leaving John Bray to unharness Lucky, hurried into the house.

After the white-hot heat of the day it was cool and dim within. Regan could hear voices. She followed them through to the drawing room. Then, in the doorway she stopped, staring in pleased surprise.

'Sara! Uncle Alistair! I don't believe it! What are you doing here?'

A girl of about Regan's age got up from the chaise. Her fair, fine-boned face was flushed with pleasure.

'Why, we've come to visit you, of course! Aren't you pleased to see us?'

'Oh, how can you say such a thing!' Regan ran forward, hugging her. 'It's such a surprise, that's all! Goodness, I thought you never left Sydney these days!'

The man, tall and handsome still, though Regan knew him to be much of an age with her own father, was leaning elegantly against the mantleshelf. He laughed now.

'You make it sound as if we are rooted there, Regan!'

'Well, aren't you, Alistair?' Andrew Mackenzie asked good-humouredly. 'When did you last leave civilisation to come calling out on the river? It's two years if it's a day!'

'Yes, I suppose it is,' Alistair was forced to agree. 'Well, we're here now, Regan. We're staying with the Hillyards over at Cow Pastures whilst I conduct a bit of business with Hillyard, and we thought you'd be offended if you learned we'd been in the district and not paid you a visit.'

'We certainly would!' Andrew said heartily, and Regan echoed the sentiment, holding Sara's hand tightly between her own.

Oh, but it was so good to see her, the cousin who had come out from the old country with her parents when she was twelve years old! Her father, Alistair, was Andrew's younger brother, and he had been enticed by Andrew's letters to try his own luck in the wild new land. Until he had found somewhere for the family to live they had stayed at Mia-Mia, and for a time Regan and Sara had grown close. But Alistair had decided farming was not for him. His strength lay in trading. He had opened a store in Sydney and bought himself two clippers, which had brought him a fortune. The family had moved to a fine house he built for them in the hills overlooking the bay, and from that time forward, Regan had seen little of them.

Yet she and Sara had never lost the warm affection that had grown between them in those days, though they could scarcely have been more different. Where Regan was wild and daring, Sara was gentle and sweet; where Regan was bold she was timid, and overawed by the strangeness of the country she found herself in. With her fair colouring she had suffered dreadfully at first from the heat, and she had never been at home on a horse, as Regan was. Regan could clearly remember the terror on Sara's pretty face when Regan had one day encouraged their ponies to race one another across the open pastureland.

All in all, Regan had thought that life in Sydney would be much better suited to Sara's ladylike ways, but she had

missed her all the same – the only real girl-friend she had
ever had in her years of growing up in a man's world.

And she had been right, Regan thought, looking at
her now. In her muslin gown and magenta silk spencer,
demurely frilled at the neck, Sara looked every inch the
fashionable town-dweller. Her fine blonde hair was covered
with a straw bonnet trimmed with magenta ribbons, and a
matching reticule dangled from her wrist.

'Oh, let's go somewhere where we can have a good
gossip!' she said now to Sara.

The two brothers smiled indulgently and Regan led the
way up to her bedroom, which had once been the scene
of so many shared confidences as the girls had chatted far
into the night – and long after they were supposed to have
been asleep!

'So tell me all about Sydney,' Regan said, flopping down
on the edge of the bed and patting it to invite Sara to join
her. 'Have you been to any grand receptions lately?'

'Well, we did go to a ball at the Governor's residence,'
Sara offered.

Regan clapped her hands together. 'And did you meet the
Governor himself?'

'Well, of course!' Sara said, amused. 'And his wife.'

'Oh, how exciting!' Regan was scarcely able to contain
herself.

'Not half as exciting as your news, Regan. You're going
to marry David, I hear.'

Regan frowned. She had forgotten all about her forthcoming nuptials in the pleasure of seeing Sara.

'Oh, you are so lucky, Regan!' Sara's tone was wistful.
'I shouldn't say it, I suppose, since he's to be your husband.
But . . . well, I always thought David was wonderful. Do
you remember, when we lived with you, and he used to come
over from Glenbarr? I used to almost faint with excitement
at the thought of seeing him!'

Regan smiled. Sara coming close to fainting had been a

common occurrence. She did recall Sara saying something on one or two occasions about liking David, but Regan had thought nothing of it. In those days David was just a friend, someone to ride with and have fun with. Now she was startled to discover that the girl she had thought she knew so well had all these years been harbouring dreams of David.

'Anyway that's all a long time ago,' Sara said quickly. 'Tell me about the plans for the wedding. You've just been to the dressmaker to discuss your gown, Uncle Andrew said.'

Regan wished they didn't have to talk about David and the wedding. She would much rather have stayed on a less painful subject.

'Do you think you'll be able to be here for the ceremony?' she asked. 'It would be wonderful if you could attend me. I have Elizabeth, of course, but I could do with the support of another woman – especially one I love like a sister.'

'You'd really like me to attend you?' Sara's face shone with sudden pleasure.

'I'd like nothing better! Will you be able to stay that long, do you think?'

'I'm not sure what Father's plans are.' Sara bit her lip thoughtfully. 'Once his business at Cow Pastures is completed I think he'll want to get straight back to Sydney. One of the clippers – the *White Swan*, I think – is due home, and he'll want to be there to see her in and safely unloaded. Though he does plan to call at Glenbarr to visit the Dauntseys,' she added, a little flush returning to her cheeks.

'Oh, that is a shame,' Regan said, disappointed.

'But I shall implore him to let me come back for the wedding,' Sara ran on. 'It wasn't nearly as long a journey as I remembered – the roads are so much better than they used to be. And I'm sure dear Mama would like to be here to see you wed, too. Between us we'll persuade Father, and even if he can't spare the time to come himself he'll assign one of his employees to travel with us. Or maybe even two. It's lawless out here on the river, isn't it? You had a narrow escape the other day, Regan, I understand.'

'Yes.' Regan didn't want to talk about that either. She still woke sometimes in the night with the horrid face of the bushwhacker floating before her eyes. 'But that's all over now. I'm safe – so long as that murderous swine doesn't get to learn who I am or where I live. There are far more pressing things to talk about than that – and nicer too! What you will wear to attend me, for one thing.'

'I can get a dressmaker in Sydney to make a gown for me if you'll tell me what colour you'd like it to be,' Sara said. She also was glad to turn the subject away from the things that frightened her. 'I'll have first choice of all the lovely new rolls of fabric when the *White Swan* comes home, remember.'

'I'm sure you'll look lovely whatever you wear,' Regan said. 'The fact that you're going to be there beside me is what matters to me, Sara, not the colour of your gown.'

The two girls hugged again. It was so good to have female company! Regan thought.

'Now, what about you, Sara?' she asked. 'Do you have a sweetheart?'

Sara shook her head.

'But you must meet many young men in Sydney,' Regan said, surprised.

'Oh I do!' Sara laughed lightly. 'Officers of the military, businessmen, captains of sailing boats . . . I'm not without offers.'

'I'm sure you're not!' Regan exclaimed. 'You're as pretty as a picture, Sara. I'd have thought you'd have married long before me, not the other way about. Is there no one at all?'

'No one I care for,' Sara said. 'That's the crux of the matter. I've never met anyone I could care for . . . in that way. And I don't want to marry just because it's expected of me. I can't think of anything worse than having to spend the rest of my life with a man I didn't love. I'd rather die an old maid than that, wouldn't you?' She smiled faintly. 'But then of course you don't have to worry about such a thing. You are so lucky, Regan.'

If only she knew! Regan thought wretchedly. *And if only things were different! If David loved Sara instead of me, everyone would be happy!*

But he didn't. For some reason it was herself David had fastened his sights upon. And he had threatened to take his own life if he lost her.

As they chatted on, Regan's cheeks ached from the effort of keeping a smile on her face, and her heart felt like stone in her breast.

When the girls came downstairs some time later Andrew and Alistair were deep in conversation. Andrew turned towards them as they entered the drawing room.

'Regan, I am very interested in the business proposition Alistair is discussing with Colm Hillyard. I'd like to ride over to Cow Pastures with him and be party to it. Would you mind if I left you alone here for one night at least? Rolf will be in the house, and Jud won't be far away should you need him.'

'Of course I don't mind, Father,' Regan said. From an early age she had been used to Andrew having to absent himself on business from time to time.

'That's settled then.' Andrew nodded, satisfied. 'Perhaps Sara would like to stay here and keep you company,' he added.

'Oh, I'd have loved to, yes,' Sara said. 'But I haven't come prepared. I've nothing but the clothes I stand up in. If only I'd known . . .'

'Pity.' But Andrew's thoughts were now firmly centred on what he saw as a good business opportunity. It was how he had managed to make himself a small fortune, by always being ready to seize the moment. Just as Alistair had done. The Mackenzies were a formidable family when it came to building their own empires.

'Doubtless the Hillyards can provide me with a bed,' Andrew said. 'But they won't be expecting an extra mouth to feed. I'll dine here first and then follow you. Riding Tolliver I should be able to reach Cow Pastures by nightfall.'

Regan heaved a silent sigh of relief. The thought of sharing her own evening meal alone with Rolf was a daunting one.

'I'll hasten it on,' Andrew said. 'It shouldn't inconvenience Ellen too much. And I'll see the pair of your later at the Hillyards' place.'

An hour later Regan bade Sara farewell with hugs and kisses and promises to see one another soon. Another hour, and with the evening meal over, she stood on the veranda steps to watch her father ride away down the drive between the eucalypts and mimosa.

She couldn't help feeling a little anxious for his safety; the sun was already slipping towards the horizon, and the ride before him would take him through much wild country. But worrying did no good. Andrew was well able to take care of himself, and she had other things on her mind.

Already, without him, the house seemed silent and empty. Rolf was in the kitchen, Regan knew – or at least that was where he had been when she had gone outside to wave her father off. In a deliberate attempt to avoid him, Regan made for the drawing room, but a few minutes later she heard his footsteps on the polished boards of the hallway and her heart fluttered painfully in her breast.

'So.' His voice came from the doorway. 'How shall we spend our evening, Regan?'

She wheeled round. His eyes were, she felt, mocking her.

'I don't know how you intend to spend it,' she said defiantly, 'but I am going to play the piano.'

She flounced across and plumped herself down on the brocaded stool.

'What could be nicer?' Again the amused tone of his voice made her think he was mocking her. 'I shall enjoy listening to you, Regan.'

'I'm not very good,' she said defensively, knowing that her trembling fingers would very likely falter on the keys. 'Mistress Kate, who taught me, despaired of me many times.' Her heart contracted with sudden tenderness at the memory of the woman who had been like a mother to her. 'Kate's father had been a music master in the old country, and she played like an angel. But she was sadly disappointed by my lack of talent, I'm afraid.'

'I'm sure you won't disappoint me, Regan.' He flung himself down on the chaise, spreading his long legs out comfortably before him. 'I can't believe there is a single way in which you could disappoint me!'

Her cheeks flamed and she bent determinedly over the keys. For all that her fingers were clumsy with nervousness, Kate had taught her well. The music flowed out, filling the room with its sweetness, and as she gained confidence Regan began to enjoy herself.

There was something magical about sitting here playing for Rolf, something warm and satisfying and curiously right. When at last she stopped he applauded her, and this time it did not occur to her that he might be mocking her.

'Bravo, Regan! I think you are more talented than you know – either that, or more modest than I realised.'

He got up and came over to stand beside her, lightly touching one of the keys with a long brown finger.

'Do you play?' she asked him.

'Me? Lord, no!' He laughed aloud. 'I like to sing, though. Do you know *Drink to Me Only*?'

Tentatively she picked out a few notes and he began to sing along with her.

'Drink to me only with thine eyes
And I will pledge with mine
Nor leave a kiss within the cup
And I'll not ask for wine . . .'

To her surprise he had a fine baritone voice. The richness
of it plucked at a chord deep within her. When the song was
finished it was her turn to applaud. 'That was wonderful!'

'What a team we make!' he said lightly. 'Do you not think
so, Regan?'

Instantly the colour flamed in her face again. She closed
the cover of the piano and stood up. 'It's beginning to get
dark. I must light the candles . . .'

'No, don't do that.' He stopped her, one hand on each
arm. His touch set her on fire, and with the wanting came
a tide of panic.

'Why ever not?' she retorted breathlessly.

'Because I like the twilight, don't you?' His voice was
low; his fingers tightened on the soft flesh of her arms.

Breath caught in her throat; she could neither move nor
speak. Gently but firmly he drew her towards him, his head
bending to hers, and she felt his lips on her forehead. She
stood motionless, and his mouth moved down the side of
her face, kissing the hollow beside her eye, moving down
to the lobe of her ear.

Regan felt her knees go weak; if it had not been for
his hands still gripping her arms and supporting her, she
thought she would have collapsed like a rag doll in a heap
on the floor.

Oh, the delicious sensations that flowed from wherever
his mouth touched! So sweet, so sharp, she could hardly
bear it! Involuntarily she parted her lips, but still he avoided
them, running a line of kisses down her neck instead, and
burying his face in the swell of her breasts above the low-cut
neckline of her bodice.

She should stop him, she knew. But oh, not before she

106

had tasted his lips, not before her tongue had touched his as it had done in the stables, not before that, please!

'Oh, Regan!' His voice was rough; her name was almost a groan.

His hands slipped around her waist, drawing her closer so that the whole length of their bodies touched, and she felt the swell of him, deliciously hard, in the hollow between her legs. Scarcely knowing what she did, she pressed against it and felt her own body throb with tingling awareness as if each nerve ending, every inch of flesh, was rising to meet him. It was wrong to take such pleasure in the nearness of a man who was not her fiancé, she knew, wrong to glory in her own response . . . the guilt nagged at her and yet still she ignored it.

It wasn't just the way he touched her that set her on fire. It was more, much more than that. From the first moment she had set eyes on him her heart had called out to him – she knew that now – in a way it had never called to David and never could. This man was, she felt, her other half, her soul mate. Until now, she would have deemed such a sentiment fanciful; with him it was a reality she could no longer deny. And she was powerless to stop his kisses, powerless to draw away from his caressing hands and his aroused body. The strength of her emotions made her weak. She couldn't give him up, not yet!

At last – at last! – his mouth was on hers, and she parted her lips, drinking him in.

Oh, the sweetness of it! Yet the aching longing at the core of her being told her it was but a staging post on the road to unimagined delights.

His fingers found the ribbons at the neck of her gown and loosened them, pushing down her bodice and betsie to expose her breasts. The nipples were already erect and tingling; beneath the gentle friction of his fingers they grew hard too.

She tilted her head backwards, arching her neck so that he

could kiss those erect rosy tips, and as he tugged gently with his teeth on one of them the sharp delight twisted and ran through her like chain lightning along the mountain ridges to settle in a glowing warmth deep within her loins.

He straightened and in the half-light she could see the desire etched into every line of his face. His hands were on the fastenings at the waist of her skirt now, and she could find no murmur of protest as they came loose and the folds of fabric slipped away to rustle gently to her ankles. Nor could she feel shame, standing there in her corset and drawers – no, nothing but delight and desire and a sense that this – this! – was how it was meant to be.

He lifted her then in his arms, carrying her to the chaise and laying her down upon it. She watched, her heart thudding in her throat, as he removed his own clothing and towered over her for a moment in all his glorious male nakedness. Then he knelt beside her, slipping a hand between her thighs and probing her most secret places with gentle, yet unyielding fingers. She squirmed in ecstasy as they slid easily into the already moist orifices, parting them like the petals of a flower to probe even deeper.

'My love.' The words, softly yet urgently spoken, seemed to come from his heart. She could not deny him, no, not if her life depended on it.

He moved to climb on to the chaise beside her and she wriggled until her spine pressed against its curved back to make room for him. Lying close together she could feel the hot swell of his manhood between her thighs where his fingers had lately been, and now there was no clothing between them to mute the sensation. Burning flesh touched burning flesh.

'You are mine!' he whispered against her cheek.

'I am yours,' she whispered back.

He moved decisively then, so that she lay flat on the chaise, her head pillowed against the cushions, and she felt his weight upon her. Instinctively she parted her legs and he slid between them and into her.

There was no pain as she had been led to expect – perhaps many hours in the saddle had long ago claimed her virginity – only a sensation of fullness and unbearable sweetness. As he moved within her the sweetness grew to almost frightening intensity; Regan wanted to cry out in her need of him, as if even now, as close to him as she could ever be, it was not enough.

As he worked within her she moved to the rhythm of his body, raising her hips to his thrusting manhood. She heard him cry out, felt his hot seed spill into her, and still she moved against him, not wanting the glory of the moment to pass, knowing that even yet there were new heights to be reached.

Her whole being was centred upon attaining it; She had no thought beyond the pressing urgency of her body's demands. And then, quite suddenly, it was as if she were being borne upward on the crest of a wave, riding it, riding it, higher and higher, gasping his name with every breath, until the wave broke, casting her up into searingly bright sunlight and she screamed with wild abandon. The wave had lost its ferocity now; it rocked her and carried her gently towards shore where she lay passive for a few moments, bathed still in its ripples.

Rolf rolled away from her, kneeling now beside the chaise, and she rolled with him, her arms still about his neck, her fingers caressing the long hard tendons.

'Oh Rolf, my love,' she murmured.

'I've wanted to do that from the first moment I set eyes on you,' he said.

'I know, I know. I've wanted it too . . .'

And suddenly the guilt was creeping in. She tried to push it away and could not. It was growing in strength with every moment, spoiling her memory of the glory, marring her delight in touching his bare flesh. And with it came a dawning sense of horror at what they had done. 'Oh, dear God!' she whispered.

A tremor ran through her body, and this time it was a tremor not of desire but of disgust for herself that she had allowed this, welcomed it.

She released him abruptly, pushed him aside with a strength born of despair, and leaped to her feet. Her nakedness shamed her now; she wanted to hide it from his eyes.

She ran to the pile of petticoats that lay where they had fallen, scooping them up and holding them protectively in front of her.

'Oh Rolf!' Her voice was a tortured sob. 'Oh Rolf, what have we done?'

Then she ran from the drawing room and up the stairs to her own room as if all the demons of hell were on her heels.

'Regan!' Rolf took a step after her. She ignored him and ran on.

His face darkened. He'd done what he'd set out to do and seduced her. He'd had his way with her, and she had welcomed it, just as he had known she would. But now . . .

He felt no sense of triumph. There was a hollowness in his victory that made him ache with some emotion that was foreign to him.

The sweetness of her kisses, the eager yielding of her soft body, had fired him so that he had quite forgotten his purpose. All he wanted to do now was gentle her, pet her, comfort and protect her and kiss away the tortured guilt he had seen in her face.

It wasn't enough that he had taken her – Andrew Mackenzie's beloved daughter. It wasn't enough that he may have impregnated her with his seed. He wanted to possess her again and again, and the wanting had nothing to do with revenge.

Rolf brought his balled fist down with a thud on to his bare thigh, hating himself for the unwanted emotions that were coursing through him.

He'd known he was desperately attracted to her, in spite of everything, but he had thought he could control his feelings. Well, he still could. He must! He could not allow his weakness for this lovely girl to come between him and the vow he had sworn so long ago.

Maybe now it would be at cost to himself, as well as Andrew Mackenzie. So be it.

Rolf struggled into his breeches and shirt and made for the stairs. This night might be the last chance he would have to finish what he had started. He must not waste it.

Nine

Reaching the haven of her room, Regan stood for a moment still clutching the bundle of clothes to her, as if by hiding her nude body she could somehow deny what had happened.

She was still trembling from head to foot. How could she have allowed him to make love to her? And not only allowed it, but gloried in it? What must he think of her? Well, whatever, it could be no worse than what she thought of herself. Bad enough for any decent girl to give herself so completely outside of the marriage bed, but when the man was not even the one who was to be her husband . . . Regan closed her eyes momentarily, hot colour flooding her cheeks.

She was no better than a whore. No better than Mistress Robinson, who disgusted Regan so much she could barely bring herself to speak to her! Well, perhaps not quite as bad as that. At least she had not sold herself for money. But she was disgraced, all the same. Disgraced and sullied. And yet . . .

For all her shame, some small treacherous part of her could not regret it. The touch of his lips and his hands, the wonder of his glorious body, the rapture of her own unexpected response to it, remained still something to be cherished. It warmed her still in a corner of her being that the shame could not touch.

That was the way it could be with a man when the heart led the way. She'd known it instinctively even before Rolf had

112

come into her life, and the knowing had made her restless and reluctant to commit herself to dear, sweet David, whom she loved only as a brother.

And then Rolf had come, and he was every dream she had ever dreamed made real.

Slowly, wonderingly, she lowered the bundle of clothes, staring all the while at her reflection in the looking-glass, expecting it somehow to look different than before.

It didn't – not really. Her nipples were still erect and dark in their shell-pink aureolas, her skin glowed with a bloom of perspiration, and there was a faint rosy patch just above one breast where his chin, slightly rough with a day's bristle, had grazed. Otherwise it looked just the same. But that was an illusion. For one thing, she was no longer a virgin. She could no longer take her maidenhead as her wedding gift to David. But more importantly, perhaps, that body now knew the glory of lovemaking when real passion – real love – was there. How could it ever now be satisfied with less?

A board on the stairs creaked. Regan jumped as if she had been shot, covering herself again. As he appeared in the doorway her heart leaped into her throat.

'Regan . . .' There was tenderness in his voice.

All she wanted to do was to run to him and throw herself into his arms, forget all her shame and misery with her face laid against the strong wall of his chest, beg him to make the world go away. Instead she flared at him.

'Can't you see I'm wearing no clothes?'

A corner of his mouth quirked. 'I can see that, yes.'

'Then have you no sense of decency?' she blazed. 'At least allow me to put something on before you come bursting in!'

The quirk blossomed to a smile. 'Believe me, you have no need to be ashamed of your body, Regan.'

'I think I have every reason!' To her annoyance she felt tears pricking at her eyes. 'Turn your back, if you please, while I cover myself.'

'Very well. If that's what you want.' He turned around, but even so she kept the bundled garments protectively in front of her whilst she crossed the room to the wardrobe and picked out a silk wrap. Only then, safely hidden by the wardrobe door, did she let her gown and petticoats fall to the floor whilst she slipped the wrap on and tied the sash securely around her waist.

'May I come in now?' he asked humbly.

'If you must. But don't think you are going to begin all over again.'

'Regan, why are you talking this way?' he remonstrated with her.

She bit her lip. 'You know very well why! Oh Rolf, we shouldn't have done what we did! It was terribly wrong!'

'Why?'

The bald question shocked her. 'Surely you don't need me to tell you that!' she snapped.

He came into the room, silhouetted tall and dark in the dim light. 'There was nothing wrong in what we did. It's only natural when a man and a woman . . .'

He reached for her hand; she snatched it away.

'Of course it was wrong! I'm betrothed, Rolf! To David!'

'And *that* is what is wrong,' he said quietly. 'You don't love him, Regan. You must not waste your life on him. Surely you know that now, if you did not know it before.'

Her lashes fell on to her cheeks like damp butterfly wings and she realised they were wet with tears.

'So you made love to me to save me, did you?' she asked sarcastically. 'You did it to show me the error of my ways, not for any other reason?'

'Partly, yes,' he admitted.

'Well, how very noble of you!' Why was she speaking to him like this – as if she hated him – when everything in her was crying out for him? 'It wasn't because you wanted to satisfy your male lust at all, I suppose?'

'Regan, will you stop this?' He reached for her again and

114

this time there was no escape. His fingers bit into her upper arms through the thin silk of her wrap. 'I wanted you, of course I did. I've wanted you every time I've looked at you from the first moment I set eyes on you. But it isn't just male lust, though heaven knows, you are lovely enough to drive any man mad with desire. It's more than that, far more, and if you'll only be honest with yourself for a moment you'll admit you know that very well. I don't just want your body. I want *you*!'

As he spoke the words, he realised it was no less than the truth. Oh, he wanted her, all right! He wanted her courage and her spirit and her sweetness, every bit as much as he wanted her full breasts and her rounded hips, her long slender legs and the secret places that lay between them. He wanted her – God help him – body and soul. He was fighting now not just for revenge but for something he had never for one moment imagined he could want so much. Her love.

And he had it. He saw it there in her eyes, burning brightly alongside the sparking fury, and exultation rose in him in a great wave before he remembered.

This was Andrew Mackenzie's daughter. He must not lose sight of that fact. He must not allow this welling of tenderness he felt for her to allow him to forget the vow he had sworn on his mother's grave for revenge on the man who had destroyed his family. At the present moment his twin desires were in harmony. But if ever they should part company it was to his dead parents that he owed his loyalty.

'You can't marry him, Regan,' he said. 'Not now.'

She covered her face with her hands for a moment. 'I know.' She whispered it more to herself than to Rolf. 'But I have to. I have to!'

'Why?' he demanded.

She shook her head helplessly. 'Oh, there are a hundred reasons!'

'Give me one.'

'Everyone expects it.'

He swore. 'Regan, that is no reason at all and you know it.'

'It is!' she argued. 'My father would be so disappointed . . .'

'Surely he wouldn't want a loveless marriage for you, no matter that his lands would be bound to the Dauntseys' to provide an empire that encompassed most of the Hawkesbury. Surely your happiness means more to him than that?'

'Perhaps. But I would be so ashamed . . .' She broke off, biting at her lip. 'Then there's David. He loves me so.'

'I love you,' he said roughly.

'But you've only known me a matter of days. You can't love me as David does. We were children together. We've always been close . . .'

'What has time to do with it?' he demanded.

She turned away, unable to bear the look in his eyes.

'David said he would take his own life if I refused to marry him,' she whispered.

'He said *what*?' Rolf thundered.

'The other evening. When he and his family were my father's guests for dinner. You remember I ran from the room and he came after me? I told him then that I couldn't marry him. And he said that if I did not he would take his own life.'

'Oh, Regan!' Rolf remonstrated. 'You can't allow him to blackmail you that way! He didn't mean it.'

'I can't take that chance,' she said despairingly. 'If he did – how could I live with myself, knowing I was responsible?'

'That's what he was counting on,' Rolf said, 'that he could frighten you into doing what he wants. Well, I didn't think much of Mr David Dauntsey before. Now, I think even less of him.'

Regan's eyes filled with tears once more. 'You mustn't blame him so.'

'Well, I do! What kind of man blackmails a woman into becoming his wife? A weak man, that's who, with no scruples and no pride.'

'You are being unfair to him,' she protested, but secretly she couldn't help agreeing with his evaluation.

David *was* weak. Perhaps that was why she found it impossible to love him in the way that he wanted. But equally it made her feel protective of him.

'And *you* are being unfair to all of us,' Rolf said. 'To yourself and to me, because you are denying us the love you know we share, and to David also. Do you really believe for one moment that you will make him happy, marrying him without love? Why, you are not even bothering to pretend you care for him – he knows already that the only reason you are going on with the proposed union is because you pity him and fear he may do something that will make you feel guilty for the rest of your life. How do you think he will feel about that when he has had time to think about it? And you won't even be the woman he thinks he is to wed for very long. Your sweet nature will suffer. You will become a bitter shrew, my dear, and that is not a recipe for happiness for anyone – much least the poor long-suffering husband.'

The tears filled her eyes again and spilled over. 'Oh, what am I to do?' she cried.

'Put an end to it, Regan, and quickly. The longer this charade goes on, the worse it will be. For both of you.'

'I don't know,' she wept. 'I am so afraid . . .'

'Afraid, Regan?' Rolf smiled. 'Not you, my dear. You are the bravest woman I have ever met.'

'I'm not!' she shot at him. 'I'm a coward! I may try to be brave, pretend to be even, but that's not the same thing at all! Inside, I'm just a frightened little girl!'

'Then I must look after you and help you.' The tenderness was there again in his voice; hearing it seemed to tear her apart.

117

'There's nothing to fear, Regan,' he said gently. 'I love you and you love me, and that's all that matters.' He was surprised to find he meant it.

'Oh, Rolf!'

She lay her head against his broad chest. Beneath his chin her hair felt soft and smelled of roses. He stroked it gently, from the crown of her head to where it lay in a tumbled wave over the bright silk of her wrap. Something twisted painfully deep within him and he drew her close, running his hand down her straight back and over the curve of her buttock.

He felt a tremor run through her at his touch and loved the soft yielding way her body felt against his. She was all woman, he thought – and what a woman! Desire for her burned in his loins, slow and insistent, but he knew that this time he must control it a while.

He continued gentling her without making the slightest move to assuage the passion that was flaring in him – and which he knew would flare in her again.

'End this torment, Regan, for both of us,' he murmured against her ear. 'Tell David tomorrow you cannot wed him and have done with it.'

She was silent for a moment longer, then he heard her breath come out on a sigh, felt it at the open neck of his shirt.

'Yes.' She raised her head, looking him straight in the eye. 'It's the only way, isn't it? It's the right thing to do.'

'It is, my love. For all of us.'

'I'll do it, Rolf. You have convinced me.'

Exultation rose in him. He had won! Just as long as that milksop David did not persuade her to change her mind again . . . And Rolf would make sure that he did not!

His hands found the bow of her girdle and tugged on it. As it gave the robe fell open and he slid his hands beneath the thin silk.

'Come to bed, my love,' he whispered.

And this time she made no protest as he lifted her in his arms and carried her to the bed.

Once in the night Regan woke to find herself nestled in his arms like a child.

She felt no guilt now, only a glow of happiness that seemed to encompass her. Something which felt so right couldn't possibly be wrong, she told herself. Rolf had convinced her with his arguments and sealed it with the most wonderful tender loving. And then he had held her whilst she drifted languorously into sleep.

She lay quite still, not wanting to disturb him or to relinquish the closeness of their embrace. She could hear the soft even rise and fall of his breath, feel it whispering on her face. She fancied she could hear the beat of his heart, too, thudding regularly against her own beneath the moist layers of skin which clung together.

It was wonderful – wonderful! Even the tiny aches in unaccustomed muscles and the low niggle deep in the pit of her stomach served only to draw her attention to remembered delights. Her legs were twined with his, the long muscles of his thighs hard against the softness of her own, his arm was about her, and she could feel the muscles in that too.

With the morrow, reality would return, with all its attendant problems and anxieties. But she wouldn't think about that now. For these few stolen hours Regan wanted only to relish the warmth and the closeness and the love.

For she did love him, she knew. This was no mere physical attraction, made the sharper and stronger because it was forbidden. This was something very real and very special. And it was more than she had ever dared dream it would be.

Regan closed her eyes and buried her face in his hard shoulder. Very gently, so as not to waken him, she parted her lips against the slight saltiness of his warm skin. Happiness, like a drug, made her languorous once more. Her lips pressed to his shoulder, her arm around the length of his back, Regan drifted once more into a deep and contented sleep.

She was still sleeping when the dawn light creeping in rosily through the undrawn drapes at the window woke Rolf.

His groin kicked as he became aware of her soft curves, naked, against him, and he controlled the flash of desire with an effort. He would have liked nothing better than to take her again, waking her with his caresses, but this wasn't the time. Ellen, the housekeeper, would come in soon from her quarters to begin making breakfast, and Jud, too, would rise with the dawn. Why, it was even possible that Elizabeth would come to the house early, knowing Regan was alone. She seemed to have a free run of the place and she was very close to Regan. The very last thing he wanted was for her to come bursting into the bedroom and discover him there.

He disentangled himself carefully and pushed himself up on to one elbow, pausing for a moment to look down at her. Red-gold hair lay in a tangled mane across the pillow and her small face was rosy and defenceless in sleep. His gut stirred again and he swung his legs over the side of the bed, levering himself up.

'Rolf . . .' she murmured drowsily, reaching for him.

He bent over to kiss her forehead, then moved swiftly out of reach of her searching arms. 'I have to go, love.'

'Don't . . . please . . .' She opened her eyes and raised a finger to wipe the sleep out of them.

'Regan, I must. For now. There'll be other times and plenty of them,' he promised.

'Mm,' she murmured. 'Very well.'

Then her lashes drooped once more on to those rosy cheeks and he knew she was drifting off to sleep again. Tenderness suffused him. Poor love, she was exhausted – and not surprisingly, considering the welter of emotion she had been through last night. And there would be more yet to come. She had her father to face, and David. Best let her sleep and regain her strength while she could.

For God's sake stop it! he warned himself. You are letting her get to you and you must not allow that! You have to remember who she is – Andrew Mackenzie's daughter. The means to your revenge. Thinking of it was a pain deep inside, a terrible, unbearable pain. But Rolf was used to pain. He had grown up with it. He knew how to handle it.

Hardening his heart, he gathered his clothing and boots from where they lay on the floor beside the bed and strode out, making for his own room.

'Regan, you look really happy,' Elizabeth said. 'Is it because you'll soon be David's wife?'

They were alone in the kitchen, lingering over the remains of their breakfast; the men had already left to go about their work.

Breath caught in Regan's throat. Of course, Elizabeth would have to be told too that the marriage was not after all going to take place. She was going to be confused – and desperately disappointed not to be able to stand at Regan's side whilst the ceremony took place, wearing her pretty new gown. But this was not the time. It wouldn't be right for Elizabeth to know before David or Andrew that Regan couldn't go through with it.

'Do I look happy?' Regan hedged.

'Yes, you do. You look like I felt when I got my very own pony,' Elizabeth said.

Regan smiled. The sharp edge of reality had begun creeping in, the disturbing prospect of what she had to do marring the pure, singing joy that had enveloped her since she had awoken and looked at Rolf through sleepy eyes that shone with excitement and new-found contentment. But nothing could touch the deep well of happiness within her. Not the thought of her father's anger, nor of David's distress, not a single worry about the future and what it may hold.

For the moment her body was replete with his lovemaking and her heart light with the joy of discovering that they meant so much to one another. She loved Rolf and he loved her. Nothing else really mattered. As long as that was true, all was right with the world.

It was mid-afternoon when the clatter of hooves on the cobbles announced Andrew's return.

Regan had spent the day giving Elizabeth some lessons, though keeping her mind on the books was not easy and in the end she had set Elizabeth a page of sums to work through and retired to her own private daydreams.

Rolf had come in from the farm for a midday meal and she had thought that her feelings for him must be written all over her face for any who cared to see. There had not been a single moment when they had been alone, but each time their eyes met the warmth which spiralled deep inside her was, she knew, reflected in the glow in her cheeks and the sparkle in her eyes. Once, leaning across to take a slice of bread, his hand had brushed her arm, and she laid her fingers on the place where his hand touched, as if they remained there and it was them she was caressing.

When she heard Andrew's horse come into the stable yard, Regan felt her heart begin to pound and nervousness made her feel slightly nauseous. She dreaded telling him her news, but there was no use putting it off. She had already decided to break it to him before facing David again, hoping that this time at least she might have his support for her decision, if not his approval. She went out to meet him. Andrew looked tired and dusty after his long ride, but elated.

'You're home then, Father,' she greeted him.

'I'm home.' He smiled broadly at her. There was nothing like the sight of his beloved daughter to make him forget his weariness.

'Did the visit go as you hoped?' she asked.

'It did. I've cut myself in on the plans Alistair and Colm Hillyard are formulating. We intend to buy another clipper and set up a chain of trading posts that will, if all goes according to plan, equal if not better the trading circle of the old days of the Corps. After all, there are more free settlers these days than there were then, all with money to spend. Unless we have to bear some disaster, such as losing the ship at sea, we should make a goodly profit.' He closed the stable door and laid an arm around Regan's shoulders. 'I'm laying up a fine inheritance for you, Regan. You and David and whatever children you may have should want for nothing as long as you live.'

A lump rose in Regan's throat.

She had planned to wait a little to give Andrew a chance to rest after his long ride before speaking to him of her change of heart. Now, this mention of her and David and their future gave her the opening she needed. Best, perhaps, to take the bull by the horns.

'I have to talk to you, Father,' she said.

He glanced at her sharply, surprised by the seriousness of her tone. 'Talk to me? You know you can always talk to me, Regan.'

'Yes, but this is . . . well, it's important, Father,' she said anxiously. 'And you're not going to be best pleased with what I have to say, either.'

Andrew frowned. There was something different about his Regan these last days. He had known it the night she had run from the dining room when the Dauntseys had come to visit, and he'd noticed the change in her since then, too, in a thousand little ways. But this afternoon it was more pronounced than ever. He felt his heart sink.

'Can't it at least wait until I've got my boots off?' he asked with mock jocularity.

'Yes – yes, of course. I'm sorry, Father. You must be so tired and here am I . . .' Her voice tailed away. The nerve was jumping in her throat again.

123

They went into the house. Andrew drew himself a long drink of ale, cold from the marble slab in the larder, and threw himself down in the most comfortable chair.

'What is it you want to say to me then, Regan?'

She swallowed at the lump of nerves. 'It can wait, Father, truly . . .'

'Regan.' He took a long pull of ale. 'We're alone for once and the house is quiet. Whatever it is you have to say, this is as good a time as any.'

She nodded, twisting her hands together in the folds of her gown. She had started this; there was now no way she could avoid finishing it. And she didn't want to avoid it. The sooner her father and David knew of her decision, the sooner she would be free – free to be with Rolf. But the thought of speaking the words terrified her so much that she was almost struck dumb, all the same.

Andrew regarded her fondly. The expression on her face reminded him of when, as a little girl, she had come to confess to some mischief or other. There had been plenty of such occasions, he remembered, and always her naughtiness had been followed by contrition. However much he had scolded her, he had never been able to be angry with her for long, and he certainly wouldn't be angry with her now, he told himself. No, whatever it was she had to confess to she must know she would be quickly forgiven. She was too dear to him for him to allow bad humour to come between them.

'Out with it, Regan,' he pressed her.

Her fingers tightened on one another in the folds of her gown and her chin came up, jutting defiance. 'I can't marry David, Father.'

Strangely, whatever he had been expecting, it was not this. He almost dropped his jug of ale as shock rendered his fingers useless. 'What?'

'I can't marry David,' she repeated, more slowly and with greater emphasis.

'In the name of God, why not?' he shouted, his voice a great bellow.

He saw her shrink, but her chin still jutted determinedly.

'Because I don't love him. Oh, Father, hear me out, please. I know it's what you want. And I know he's a good man. Why, I'm very fond of him myself. He's like a brother to me. But that's all. A brother. And I don't want to be his wife.'

Andrew sat stunned, digesting this outburst for a moment. Then he rose, crossing the room to lean heavily against the grand piano. 'Is this what the other evening was about?' he asked. 'Is this what was troubling you then?'

Regan nodded. 'Yes. I knew, all of a sudden, when we were discussing arrangements for the wedding, that I couldn't go through with it.'

'But the evening ended with the ceremony being brought forward,' he argued.

'Because I thought that marrying quickly was the only way I could marry David at all,' Regan said.

'And why would you do that?' Andrew asked, regarding her narrowly.

Regan bit her lip. 'You remember David followed me outside? When I told him I didn't want to be his wife he went crazy. He threatened to take his own life if I didn't wed him. I was afraid he might carry out his threat and that I'd have his death on my conscience for the rest of my life.'

'Dear God, Regan . . .' Andrew exclaimed in disgust. 'However distressed, however much he loves you, he should not have said that.'

'I know,' Regan said. 'If I'd had my doubts before, what happened that night confirmed them. I want a husband I can respect as well as love. I'm still fond of him, Father. I always will be. But the thought of becoming his wife repels me. The more I think of it, the more I know I cannot go through with it.'

Andrew nodded slowly. 'Yes – you are a woman of too

much fire and passion to be able to live like that,' he said. 'It pains me, of course. I had always hoped . . . But your happiness is my chief concern. You should not marry a man who repels you. It's against everything I would have for you.' He paused. 'Does David know yet?' he asked.

Regan shook her head. 'No. I wanted to tell you first. I'm afraid he will react badly again, and this time I hoped I might have your support.'

'You have it.' He sighed deeply. 'You are my daughter, Regan, and I love you more than anything in the world. If you want me to be with you when you break the news to David, then that's where I'll be. And I shall explain – as kindly as I can, of course – to Molly and Richard.'

'Oh Father, thank you!' Weak with relief she ran to him and hugged him. 'I knew you'd understand.'

He held her for a moment, sad but resigned. Then a thought occurred to him.

'There's just one thing, Regan. This Rolf Peterson hasn't anything to do with your change of heart, I hope?'

It was there in her face at once, the guilt she could not hide. 'Regan?' he said sternly. She made no reply and his quick temper rose like a summer storm. 'I warned you, my girl, he is not for you!' Andrew's voice was like thunder. 'I wouldn't force you into a loveless marriage with David Dauntsey. I want better for you than that. One day I hope you will meet a man you would wish to wed. A man who can make you happy as you deserve – as happy as your mother and I once were. But that man is not Rolf Peterson!'

She stared at him, frightened by his sudden fury, and he read the unspoken question in her eyes – *Why*?

'The man is a stranger to us,' he said harshly. 'A farm-hand, nothing more.'

Regan gathered her courage. 'That's not reason enough surely, Father?'

'It is for me!' Andrew gathered himself together. 'Now, I am going to my room to change out of these dusty clothes.

126

When I return we'll talk about how you are to break the news to David. But I do not want to hear Rolf Peterson's name mentioned, do you understand?'

Regan nodded. Tears brimmed in her emerald eyes.

'I will not have you marry him, Regan,' he told her flatly. 'Never, as long as I live, would I agree to such a thing.'

She was silent and as he climbed the stairs, Andrew found himself asking the same question Regan's eyes had asked. Why *was* he so against the thought of her and Rolf Peterson? It was, of course, as he had said. The man was a stranger and an itinerant farm-hand, totally unsuitable for the husband of Andrew Mackenzie's daughter.

But there was something else – some reason he could not identify.

And for the life of him, he did not know what it was.

Ten

Regan slept little that night. She was elated at having summoned up the courage to tell her father she was not, after all, going to marry David, and relieved that he had accepted it. But she was still nervous at the thought of facing her fiancé, even though Andrew had promised to accompany her to Glenbarr in a day or so, and his outburst against Rolf disturbed her.

She could understand, she supposed, that he was reluctant for her to marry a man he had described as an itinerant farm hand, but she couldn't help feeling there was more to it than that, though Andrew had refused to give any other reason.

There were far worse men in this wild country, she thought. Itinerant farm hand he might be, but Rolf was also honest and trustworthy, courageous and honourable, and he had proved himself to be a hard and willing worker too.

Well, she would just have to work on Andrew. Clearly at the moment he was shocked by her sudden decision to call off the wedding, but he had gone along with it for her sake. She couldn't imagine that he would deny her her heart's desire for long. He never had in the past and there was no good reason why he should do so now.

But it wasn't only her tumultuous thoughts that kept her from sleep. It was also the flickering fires of desire running through her veins and sensitising every nerve ending. Thinking of Rolf sleeping just along the corridor was almost more than she could bear. More than anything in the world she wanted to be in his arms again.

Restlessly Regan pushed aside the covers and swung her legs over the edge of the bed, crossing to the window and looking out. The moon was very bright, illuminating the drive and shining silver on the leaves of the rows of eucalypts and mimosa trees. In her state of heightened awareness it looked incredibly beautiful to her, a magic world of silver and black. How many times had she stood here before, looking out, and never once seen in quite this way! Regan pushed up the casement and leaned out, breathing in the soft still air and with it the sweet fragrant scents of the night.

It's because I'm in love that it all seems so wonderful! she thought, and again the desire to be with him stirred in her, the teasing ache of longing for the touch of his hands and his lips, the heady delight of feeling his body close to hers.

Oh Rolf . . . Rolf . . . His name was a mantra on her lips and the longing became almost too much to bear. Could she – dare she – go to him?

Regan crept across the room, her bare feet making no sound, and carefully opened her door. It creaked slightly on its hinges and she froze, scarcely daring to breathe, but the house was silent and sleeping. After a moment she eased the door open a little further, and a little further still, until the crack was wide enough to pass through.

Frightened and yet exhilarated by her own daring, she slipped out into the corridor and crept a few steps, silent as a shadow. To reach Rolf's room meant passing her father's bedroom door, but as she drew level with it, Regan heard the sound of his soft snores coming from within. Emboldened, she crept past.

Rolf's door was firmly closed. Regan hesitated before it, her heart beating a tattoo so loud that she fancied she could hear it in the silent house. Supposing his door, too, should squeak? She tried to remember if she had ever noticed such a thing and could not, but then, why should she? A creaking door in the middle of the day was not something to which one paid any regard.

She took the knob carefully in her hand, still wondering if she dared turn it, but her fingers seemed to have developed a will of their own. The knob turned easily. She pushed the door open a crack and to her relief it made no sound. A little more, a little more, and she was in his room and closing the door softly behind her once more.

She could hear Rolf's breathing now, deep and regular. She crossed to the bed and looked down at him, no more than a bulky shadow beneath the covers. His head was turned away from her; she reached out and touched his hair, thick and springy beneath her fingers.

He stirred in his sleep, turning over, and as the scent of him wafted up to her she could wait no longer. She turned back the sheet and carefully inched herself in beside him.

He slept naked. The warmth emanating from him seemed to burn through the thin cambric of her nightgown and she nestled into him, winding her arm around his long, hard back. He stirred again, pulling her close as if it were the most natural thing in the world. Then, as he surfaced through the layers of consciousness, she felt him stiffen.

'Regan?' His voice was a surprised whisper against her ear.

'Ssh!' She whispered back urgently. 'Don't make a sound!'

'Oh, Regan!' He moved against her; to her delight she discovered that he was already aroused, his manhood burrowing between her legs. She parted them to him, happiness and the excitement of the forbidden sweeping her quickly to a plateau of ecstasy.

'Make love to me, Rolf,' she whispered, and he needed no second bidding.

When it was over they lay warm, sticky and content in

one another's arms, and Regan felt drowsiness creeping up on her.

She must not go to sleep – and besides, she had so much to tell him! There had not been one single moment all day when they had been alone, and understandably Andrew had made no mention of the conversation he and Regan had shared. David must be told before the news became common gossip.

'I've told my father I'm not going to marry David,' she whispered now.

'You have?' There was jubilation as well as surprise in Rolf's answering whisper. 'How did he take it?'

'He agreed that it was wrong for me to wed a man I don't love. He's going to take me to Glenbarr tomorrow or the next day to break the news to the Dauntseys.'

'Thank God!' Rolf murmured. 'I feared that if it was left to you alone that devil might persuade you to change your mind again.'

'He couldn't have,' Regan murmured back. 'Not now. But I'm glad Father is coming with me all the same.'

Rolf's thumb stroked the soft skin of her throat, 'So we can be together, my love?'

She hesitated, unwilling to break the spell, but knowing she must.

'Not yet,' she said softly. 'Father was adamant that I must not take up with you.'

Rolf stiffened. 'Why?'

'Oh, I don't know. He thinks you're not good enough for me, I suppose. It's ridiculous, I know, but he has his ideas that I should marry someone with wealth, or land of their own.'

Rolf drew a deep breath. 'Regan, there is something I must tell you.'

But she seemed not to hear him; her mind was running firmly on its own track, afraid that Rolf would be hurt by the slight.

131

'*I* don't think that, of course. It doesn't matter a jot to me, how could it? And in any case, one day all this will be mine, and so my husband's. Though not for a very long time yet, I hope,' she added, shrinking from the thought that one day her father would leave her as her mother had. 'Anyway, I'm sure I can persuade Father to change his mind,' she went on. 'I can usually persuade him to almost anything.'

Rolf laughed softly. 'I'm sure you can! What man could deny you anything, Regan?'

'But we must give him time to get used to the idea,' she said softly. 'And there's David to think of too. He is going to be so hurt when I call the wedding off. I don't want to rub salt in the wound. And that's what it would be if he learned too soon that you and I . . .'

'That's true enough.' Rolf thought that he had been patient for so many years, it would be prudent to be patient for a little longer.

'We must just wait until a decent interval has passed,' Regan went on. 'Father will come around, you'll see. In the end, all he wants is my happiness.

'I'm sure you are right,' Rolf said softly. 'But it won't be easy, seeing one another every day and having to hide the way we feel.'

'I know.' Regan felt she could not agree more. She wanted to shout her love from the rooftops. 'But we can find the opportunity to be together sometimes like this. And when we can eventually be together properly, it will be all the sweeter for the waiting, won't it?'

He drew her close again, kissing her gently whilst his thumb and forefinger traced the line of her jaw and met on her small firm chin.

'You must go now, Regan,' he whispered. 'I don't want you to, but you must.'

'I know,' she whispered back regretfully.

She slid from his bed, leaned over and kissed him once more. Then, before she could weaken and climb in beside him once more, she turned and crept from the room, closing the door softly behind her. Back along the moonlit corridor she crept, past the door from behind which she could still hear her father's gentle snores.

In her own bed she curled up, wrapping her arms around herself and pretending they were Rolf's. How could she have fallen in love so completely and utterly – and so soon? But she had, and it was wonderful. Regan knew she would have no trouble sleeping now. Her body was satiated and her heart full of happiness. She closed her eyes, revelling in the glow of contentment, and within moments she was asleep.

Regan and Andrew did not make the visit to Glenbarr the next or the day after that. In fact, Regan learned, it would be at least a week before they would be able to talk to David and she burned with impatience at the delay. Now that her mind was made up she was anxious to put an end to the sham of her engagement.

But the following day Alistair and Sara returned from Cow Pastures with the news that they were to call at Glenbarr themselves, and David was to accompany them back to Sydney.

'The Dauntseys are apparently anxious to join us in our new venture,' Alistair said. 'David is to come with me and be a party to the initial manoeuverings. Then he can return and let you and Colm Hillyard know how it is proceeding.'

'David is coming in on the venture?' Andrew asked, surprised and, Regan thought, none too pleased.

'Why not?' Alistair asked. 'He's well suited to it, if you ask me. That boy was never cut out to be a farmer. Business will be more in his line – and Sydney life will suit him well, I'm sure.' He smiled at Regan. 'I hope you are not averse to living in a town, my dear. When you are married to David, you might well find yourself neighbours of ours!'

Regan flushed and caught her father's eye. He responded with an almost imperceptible shake of the head. Regan understood. She mustn't say anything yet, until David had been told, even though Alistair and Sara were family. But she longed to share her news with Sara, all the same, and not only because she herself was bursting with it. Knowing as she did how Sara felt about David, she longed to tell her that she may yet have her chance with him.

They would make a perfect couple, Regan thought, grasping at straws to ease her own guilt at breaking David's heart. Why, even the suggestion Alistair had made concerning the siting of their future home fitted perfectly. Regan thought she would hate to live in Sydney, whilst Sara – well, she had never known anything else, apart from the time spent with them at Mia-Mia, which had not suited Sara at all.

Dare I drop just a little hint? Regan wondered, and decided, regretfully, that she must not. It was unfair to burden Sara with her secret, which she might have great difficulty in keeping if she was to be in David's company over the next week or so.

She'll find out soon enough, Regan thought. And when she does, well, then it will be up to her what she does about it.

After Sara and Alistair had left once more the days fell into their familiar pattern, though for Regan nothing could ever be the same again. Her overriding mood was one of blissful happiness, punctuated by bouts of impatience and guilt.

She worked on her father's books as she had always done, breaking off sometimes to daydream. She played with Elizabeth and tutored her in her lessons. She played the piano a little. Once, when Rolf was there, she broke into *Drink to Me Only*, and when she lifted her eyes to his and saw the faint smile on his lips the colour rushed to her cheeks as the two of them secretly shared the memory of the night when he had sung it to her accompaniment. She rode too, but never far from the farm. Andrew was still anxious for her safety, though he was beginning to relax his watchfulness a little. But he would never allow her to ride with Rolf.

His objection was unspoken, but none the less obvious to her for all that. There was always work for Rolf to do that did not involve her, and she knew that Andrew was deliberately trying to prevent them from being alone together.

But they managed it. At night, when the house was still and silent, she would creep along the corridor to his room or he to hers, and they shared precious stolen moments lying in each other's arms, making wonderful passionate love and afterwards enjoying the delicious drowsy aftermath.

Familiarity was breeding confidence now. Regan now knew exactly which boards would creak beneath her tread and which were safe, and she had secretly managed to rub a little oil on the hinge of her bedroom door so that it no longed squeaked and threatened to give her away.

Then one night, cosy and contented in Rolf's arms after their passionate lovemaking, Regan drifted into slumber, and Rolf too fell asleep. When she surfaced once more, dawn light was creeping in rosily at the window. Oh dear God, it was morning!

Instantly Regan was wide awake, every nerve ending trembling with alarm. She sat bolt up right and the sudden movement woke Rolf too.

'What . . . ?' Then, as the situation hit him too between the eyes like buckshot: 'Sweet Jesus!'

'I must go!' Regan whispered urgently.

She leaped out of bed on to legs that were weak from both sleep and nervousness and stumbled, banging her shin hard against the iron frame.

'Oh!' she squealed before she could stop herself.

She scooped up her nightgown, laying discarded on the floor beside the bed and scrambled into it, her fingers clumsy and awkward on the fastenings. Oh, what had they done? Could she gain the safety of her own room before her father woke and discovered what had been going on? Regan wrenched open the door, scuttled into the corridor. And came face to face with Andrew.

'What the devil . . . ?'

Clad in his nightshirt, his iron-grey hair rumpled, Andrew was none the less a fearsome sight, and Regan quaked. 'Father . . .'

'Regan!' He stared at her, puzzled, then, almost instantaneously realisation dawned and his face darkened with fury. 'What do you think you are doing, Miss?'

Shock and guilt struck her dumb. In any event, what could she say? Nothing but a bare-faced lie could have concealed the truth, and Regan was no liar. And even if she had been, Regan doubted that her father would be taken in for one moment.

'Go to your room, Miss!' he blazed. 'And make yourself decent, if such a thing is possible!'

'Father . . .' It was still the only word she could manage to utter. Her mouth had gone dry and she felt like a child again caught in an act of extreme naughtiness.

'Get to your room, I said!'

At that precise moment Rolf appeared in the doorway behind her. Regan saw Andrew's furious eyes go to him and she looked around, terrified that he might still be stark naked, thus confirming what Andrew undoubtedly already knew. But thankfully he had stopped to pull on a pair of breeches. Above them, however, his chest was bare but for its feathering of coarse curling hair.

'As for you, Sir . . .' Words seemed to escape Andrew. He looked practically apoplectic, Regan thought fearfully. Then, with an effort, he regained the power of speech.

'I will see you downstairs, the pair of you!' he thundered. 'Just as soon as we have all had the chance to put on some clothes!'

He turned on his heel and stamped into his room, slamming the door behind him.

136

Regan turned, white-faced, to Rolf. His expression was almost as grim as her father's.

'Better do as he says,' he bade her curtly.

His thoughts whirling, Rolf found his shirt and put it on, then, cursing softly to himself, he pulled on his boots.

How could he and Regan have been so foolish as to allow themselves to be caught out this way? Never mind Regan, how could *he* have been so careless? Everything had been going so well. Now the game was up and he could very easily guess what Andrew's reaction would be.

He would send Rolf packing, not a doubt of it. Any father worth his salt would do the same. Why, it was what he himself would do under the same circumstances. And that would be the end of it. He might have achieved part of his objective for revenge by making a fool of Andrew Mackenzie, but it was not enough. He wanted Mia-Mia. More than ever, after these last days spent under the roof of his old home, he wanted that. And besides . . .

He wanted Regan. He admitted it now to himself. He wanted her more than he had thought it possible to want a woman, and the thought of never seeing her again was a pain in his heart as sharp as any he had felt before.

No, there was still all to play for in this game, and he still had a trump card up his sleeve. He was not, as Andrew believed, a itinerant farm-hand without a penny to his name. He owned his own flourishing farm in the rich pasture land beyond the mountains. If he could bring that into the equation without revealing his true identity there was a chance yet that Andrew would allow the match.

He might, in fact, demand that Rolf marry Regan to redeem her honour. Rolf's spirits rose a little, but he was unwilling to take the chance that things would work so conveniently in his favour. He must have another line of attack ready, another plan in case the forthcoming encounter failed to go his way.

Rolf thought for a moment, then crossed to the dressing chest. He had discovered writing paper, a quill and ink in one of the drawers, left there presumably for the convenience of any guest who used the room. He took a sheet, dipped the quill in the ink and wrote swiftly. Then he folded the paper, pocketed it, and went downstairs to face the man upon whom he had long ago sworn vengeance.

Andrew was already at the foot of the stairs, waiting.

'You took your time, Peterson,' he growled.

Rolf made no reply.

'Come into my study,' Andrew ordered. 'I don't wish to have this conversation where Ellen may overhear it if she comes in to make breakfast. I won't have my daughter's shame bandied about as idle gossip amongst the servants.'

Rolf followed him into the room, which was awash now with early morning sunshine. Regan was already there. She had dressed swiftly in a demure sprigged gown. She was very pale, with high spots of colour burning in her cheeks, but there was a determined jut to her chin now. His heart swelled with admiration. Regan was not about to let her father have it all his own way.

Andrew closed the door behind them and turned to Regan.

'I suppose, Miss, I have no need to ask what you were doing in Peterson's room, but I will ask all the same. I want to hear it from your own lips.'

Rolf bristled. He had never heard that Andrew Mackenzie had any experience as a lawyer, but at that moment he reminded Rolf more than anything of exactly that – a lawyer, or even a judge. Except that he would be not only judge, but jury too.

Regan, however, faced her father with dignity and spirit. 'I went to his room, Father, because these last days you have made it impossible for us to be alone together.'

'To chat, no doubt?' Andrew asked, heavily sarcastic. 'Is

that what you are to have me believe? Don't take me for a fool, Regan. No decent woman goes to a man's bedroom in the early hours of the morning wearing nothing but her nightgown.'

The colour flamed in Regan's cheeks. 'I have done nothing of which I am ashamed, Father,' she said fiercely.

'Then you are more of a hussy even than I had thought!' he roared. 'What would your poor mother have said if she were here? All these years never a day has gone by but I wished with all my heart that she was still alive. Now I find myself thanking merciful heaven that she is not. For to know that you could behave so shamelessly would surely break her heart.'

Hurt flared in Regan's eyes, but her chin remained high. 'I don't believe that, Father. Mama would have understood, I know. Any woman who loved as Mama loved you would understand.'

Andrew's face worked with rage. 'How dare you suggest your mother would have condoned such behaviour! She was the most honourable woman who ever drew breath.'

'And she loved you! That's why she would have understood. You two were lucky, I know. Mama's father approved the match and you had no need to meet in secret. But if it hadn't been so, I'll wager she would have done the same as I. That's why she wouldn't find it in her heart to blame me now.'

'Madam, you go too far!' Andrew raged. His hands had balled to fists. 'Go to your room and I will deal with you later when my temper has cooled. Otherwise I swear I will not be held responsible for my actions.' A muscle worked in his cheek. 'Go!'

Regan stood her ground, afraid, yet determined. 'No, Father, I'm staying to have this out. I am not a child now to be sent to my room when you think I have misbehaved.'

He took a step towards her, grasping her by the arm. His Regan had always fought back at him with spirit, but never before had she defied him with such resolution.

'Whilst you live under my roof, Miss, you will do as I bid you!' he thundered. 'Otherwise, child or not, I swear I will put you across my knee and spank you!'

Rolf stepped forward. His face now was as dark with anger as Andrew's. 'Unhand her, Sir!'

Andrew whirled, startled and enraged at the intervention.

'If you lay so much as a finger on her, then you will have me to answer to!' Rolf's voice was low but dangerous.

'And who are you to tell me how I should treat my own daughter?' Andrew demanded, but he released Regan's arm all the same.

'The man who loves her!' Rolf declared.

'The man to whom I gave shelter!' Andrew returned furiously. 'The man I took in to sleep under my own roof! I trusted you, Peterson, and this is how you betray my trust. Not content with persuading her to renege on her promises to the man she was to wed, you have seduced her too. You have stolen the honour of the woman you profess to love – and aye, her virginity too, if I am not much mistaken. I should have you horsewhipped, Peterson, for what you have done!'

'Father, stop this at once!' Regan intervened, catching at Andrew's sleeve, but he shook her off impatiently. This was between him and Rolf now.

'Who are you, Peterson, that you think you can come into my house and dishonour my daughter?' he demanded furiously. 'Just who do you suppose you are?'

For a dangerous moment the truth hovered on Rolf's lips. But he knew the time was not right. To reveal himself as Rolf Hannay now would gain him nothing but the satisfaction of seeing his arch enemy totally and utterly shaken. To achieve the ends he desired he must hide his true identity a while longer. For when she knew he had deceived her so, Regan too might turn against him and the game would be over.

There was yet, though, his trump card to play. 'Well there, Sir, I have to confess I have misled you somewhat,' he said. 'I am not without substance, as you believe. I own a farm and land of my own in the rich pasture on the other side of the mountains.'

Andrew's eyes widened with surprise and for a moment he was rendered speechless.

'I regret misrepresenting myself so,' Rolf continued, 'but I could think of no other way to remain at Regan's side long enough to win her love.' He looked at her, his jaw softening for a moment at the expression of wonder on her small pale face. 'From the moment I set eyes on her, Sir, I knew I could not bear to let her go. And so I pretended to be here, in this part of the world, seeking work. Now – well, the truth has to come out, and I'll lay my cards on the table. I want to marry her, Captain Mackenzie.'

Andrew was shaking his grizzled head in utter disbelief. 'You played out this charade in order to . . .' He broke off, unable to complete the sentence.

A spiral of triumph twisted in Rolf's gut. 'I did, Sir. Surely that should be proof enough – if proof is needed – that I love her. And you have my word that I will care for her and provide well for her if only you will agree this match.'

Regan's eyes were shining. She was trembling still, but from elation now as well as fear of her father's fury. Rolf loved her and wanted to marry her! To hear it spoken in words was the fulfilment of her wildest dreams. Moments later, however, they shattered.

'Your word, Sir!' Andrew exclaimed. 'And what, may I ask, is your word worth? If what you say is true, then you have lived here these last weeks under false pretences. If not, well, why should I believe you now? Lands on the other side of the mountain range? Balderdash! It's a pretty story, I admit, but a mighty far-fetched one.'

'It is the truth,' Rolf insisted.

'Then what are you doing so far from home?' Andrew demanded. 'And who is looking after your farm and your business interests whilst you absent yourself for – how long? How long did you intend to stay here? Would you really abandon all your responsibilities when no one at your farm knows where you are, for some indefinite period? I think not! You must take me for a fool, Peterson, that I would believe such an unlikely tale! No, you're a charlatan who likely saw an opportunity and seized it. Well, I'll see to it you do not profit from your treachery. You will pack your bags, Sir, and leave this house at once.'

'Father, please!' Regan gasped in horror. 'You cannot send Rolf away!'

'Indeed I can!' Andrew grated. 'Don't worry, I won't send him away penniless. He'll be paid what wages he has earned. But go he will, and within the hour!'

'Then I will go with him!' Regan cried fiercely.

'You will do no such thing,' Andrew informed her.

'And how will you stop me, pray?' she demanded.

'By force, if necessary.' Andrew crossed to his big roll-top desk, pulled open a drawer and extracted a pistol, levelling it at Rolf.

'Father!' Regan screamed. 'What are you doing?'

'What I should have done the moment I saw you leaving his room.' Andrew's voice was low and dangerous. 'Get your things together, Peterson, and leave my property. Or I swear I will put a bullet into your dastardly heart and take the greatest of pleasure in doing it.'

Rolf raised his hands in surrender. 'That won't be necessary, Mackenzie. I'll go, and quietly. For the moment. But don't think you have seen the last of me, for I promise you, you have not.'

He turned and left the room without a backward glance, and Regan, pressing trembling hands to her mouth, felt as though her heart would break.

Eleven

When Rolf had gone, setting Satan to a canter down
the drive, Regan rose from the chair into which she
had sunk when her trembling legs would no longer support
her. She had not watched him go – she didn't think she could
have borne it – and in any case she doubted Andrew would
have allowed her to do so. Never, in all her life, had she
seen her father quite so angry.

This must be how he had been in his days in the New
South Wales Corps, she thought. This must have been the
daunting presence that had quelled risings and controlled
his men and dangerous convicts alike in the time before her
mother's love and his own ageing had mellowed him. This
was the ruthlessness that had built an empire in an untamed
land. But never before had that powerful will been turned
against her. Never before had she had cause to fear him so.
For a terrible moment she had truly thought that he was
about to put a bullet into Rolf's heart, and the memory of
it, even now that he had safely gone, made her weak with
terror. If Rolf were dead, then she would have no reason to
live either. And yet . . .

He was dead to her now, in any case. He had ridden away,
back, no doubt, to wherever it was he had come from, or else
on to new adventures, and she would never see him again.
Tears filled her eyes and slid unchecked down her cheeks.

'For God's sake, Regan!' Andrew said roughly. 'Stop that
nonsense at once. He's not worth your tears.'

'He is too!' she flung at him. 'I thought you said it

143

was my happiness you wanted, but you don't give a fig for my happiness. If you did you would never have sent him away.'

'There are some times when a father knows what is best for his daughter,' he said, more gently now. The anger was subsiding and he hated to see her cry.

'How could you know whether he was bad for me or not?' Regan demanded. 'You don't know him.'

'And neither do you,' Andrew reminded her. 'Did he ever tell you this tale of a farm on the other side of the mountains?'

'No,' she admitted, 'but . . .'

'You see? Either he deceived you, or he is lying now. Whichever, is that the behaviour of an honourable man? I suspect, Regan, that he is an opportunist. He saw the wealth I have accumulated, the extent of our lands and the size of our herds, and decided he would like a share of it. By winning your affections and, hopefully, your hand.'

'You don't know that, Father,' she protested.

'I know that from the first there was something about him I did not trust. I tried to warn you, Regan.'

Her lip was trembling. She bit at it and tasted the salt of her tears.

'Why did you let him take you in?' Andrew asked hollowly. 'Oh, he's a handsome man, I grant you, but I thought you had more sense than to sell yourself so cheaply.'

'I didn't!' she protested. 'I love him!'

Andrew laughed bitterly. 'I fear you do not know the meaning of the word. If you think it excuses your creeping to his room in the middle of the night, then you are much mistaken.' He shook his head despairingly. 'I am very disappointed in you, Regan.'

'I love him!' she reiterated. 'How can it be wrong?'

He sighed. He had never for one moment suspected that Regan's good sense and the values he had instilled in her could be forgotten so easily. But he had reckoned without her tempestuous heart.

'Think, Regan!' he bade her. 'It is not only unseemly to give yourself to a man before marriage, but unwise. Many a bastard has been begotten so.'

Her eyes fell from his and hot colour flooded her cheeks.

'We can only pray no such misfortune will befall you, my dear daughter. Just the once – it may be all right. But even if it is not,' he brought his hand down with a thud on the oak top of his desk, 'I would sooner bear the shame and brazen it out than I would see you tied to an opportunist and blackguard such as he.'

'You're wrong about him, Father, I know it,' Regan said stubbornly. She crossed to the door. 'I'd like to be alone if you don't mind.'

'Don't you want breakfast?' he asked shortly.

Regan shook her head. 'I'm not hungry. I'll go to my room if it's all the same to you.'

Andrew sighed heavily. It hurt him to see her so upset but he was still convinced he had taken the right course of action. She would forget this Rolf Peterson – provided always of course that he had not sown his seed in her, and if he had, provided it did not take root – and in time she would come to be grateful that he had saved her from her own folly.

'You know, Regan, you are free to do as you like for the most part,' he said wearily. 'If you wish to go to your room, then do so. But for my sake, try to put that man out of your mind. For I do not want to hear his name spoken, ever again.'

The sheet of writing paper, folded, lay on her dressing chest.

At first, her eyes blurred with tears, Regan did not notice it. She moved about the room in a daze, touching familiar objects and finding no comfort in them. Beyond Rolf there was no reality. But Rolf had gone. Regan sank on to the bed and folded her arms around herself, weeping. The sobs wracked her body, great painful sobs that seemed to tear her apart, and the tears flooded her face and ran down her neck and into the hollow between her breasts.

When at last they were spent she lay shuddering from time to time with the intensity of her grief. She couldn't bear the thought that never again would she look into those slate-grey eyes and see the tenderness they concealed, never again taste his lips, feel his arms around her and his body filling hers.

I wish I could die! Regan thought wretchedly. I wish Father had turned his pistol on me and pulled the trigger, for without Rolf I don't want to live! She was only nineteen years old, and the future stretched before her, endless and empty.

At last, exhausted by her emotion, Regan drifted into an unhappy sleep, made restless and nightmarish by wild and vivid dreams when Rolf lay dead upon the study floor, riddled with the bullets from her father's pistol, and she wept, inconsolable, over his body.

When she woke again, she lay listless. Her face felt stiff from the tears that had dried upon it and her body ached from the intensity of her sobs. But it was the hollowness inside that she could not bear.

The sun was high now, flooding the room with bright harsh light. She rose, crossing to the dressing chest. From the looking glass her face gazed back at her, eyes red-rimmed in a face that was pinched with pain, and her hair tangled around it, red-gold and wild. Listlessly she reached for her tortoishell-backed brush.

And then she saw it – the sheet of folded writing paper inscribed with her name.

Breath caught in her throat; her heart missed a beat. She picked up the paper and unfolded it. Just a few words, the ink they were written in black and bold on the ivory parchment.

'I will wait for you, Regan, at the place where we discovered Elizabeth. Come to me, my love. Rolf.'

Her heart was beating wildly now, her grief forgotten in a surge of fierce joy. He was waiting for her! He hadn't simply ridden away, out of her life! And she would go to him. There was no decision to be made, none at all. She clapped her hand across her mouth, trying to marshal her racing thoughts.

How to do it without being apprehended? What to take with her? And then, most frightening of all, how long would he wait? The sun was high now; she must have slept for several hours. Supposing he thought she was not coming and left without her?

Trembling now with urgent haste Regan ran to the wardrobe, pulling out gowns and throwing them in a heap on the bed before realising. She couldn't take them, not any of them. If she was seen leaving the house with a saddlebag suspicion would instantly be aroused. She would have to go in the clothes she stood up in, or not at all.

Leaving the gowns where they lay she stripped to her corset and pulled on the shirt and breeches she wore for riding. Into the pocket she stuffed the note and one or two favourite pieces of the jewellery which had belonged to her mother.

'You'd approve, Mama, if you knew, wouldn't you?' she whispered, and felt strangely confident that Mama was, indeed, smiling on her. 'You'd have done the same for Father! I know you would!'

She glanced again at the tumble of gowns lying on the bed and took a moment to hang them up once more. She thought she could get away safely from the house – her father would likely be out now somewhere on the farm. But if someone should come into her room and see them lying there, then suspicions might be aroused. Regan wanted as good a start as she could get before anyone came looking for her.

She opened her bedroom door. The house was silent. She

147

went down the stairs, her heart pounding, and through to the kitchen. Ellen was there, preparing the vegetables for the evening meal. Somehow Regan managed a quick word with her. To her own ears her voice sounded tight and jumpy, but Ellen was her usual dour self, and, relieved, Regan knew that the housekeeper had not realised anything was amiss.

Dickon Stokes was in the stable yard, engaged in polishing some tack. He sat on an upturned barrel, the saddle held between his knees while he worked on it laboriously. He glanced up, his small piggy eyes screwed up against the glare of the sun, but Regan felt confident that he would have no reason to question her. Andrew would not have thought of making him party to family problems, unless it was simply to say that she was confined to the house, and even that, she felt, was unlikely.

'I'm going riding, Dickon,' she said, glad that in recent days Andrew had relaxed his ruling that she was not to ride out alone. 'Would you saddle Betsy for me, please?'

The man laid down the saddle he was working on a little resentfully. He was cross at being interrupted in his task, Regan guessed, but his years as a convict labourer had made him used to obeying the orders of her father and herself, and he made no comment.

'Hurry yourself!' Regan said sharply. 'I want to ride today, not tomorrow week!'

Another baleful glance, and he disappeared into the stable. Regan waited impatiently, terrified that Andrew might come home unexpectedly. If anything stopped her now . . . ! She thrust the thought aside. Nothing would stop her. She wouldn't let it.

After what seemed a lifetime, Dickon emerged, leading Betsy. He took her straight to the block, and Regan climbed on to it and mounted.

'Thank you, Dickon. You can get on with your work now.'

She touched her heels to Betsy's side and walked her

around the corner of the house. The drive stretched before her, dappled with shade, and mercifully empty of any living soul.

Regan urged Betsy to a trot. The sooner she was clean away from the house, the better. For one thing there would then be less likelihood of anyone seeing, and stopping, her; for another she was desperately anxious to be on her way.

At the end of the drive she turned just once to look back at the house that had been her home for all of her nineteen years. She loved Mia-Mia. But there was nothing here for her now. Her future lay on the other side of the mountains with Rolf.

Regan touched Betsy once more with her heels and turned the horse on to the road that led upriver.

Rolf sat on a fallen tree at the edge of the thicket which concealed the cave where they had found Elizabeth, his eyes constantly scanning the horizon. From this vantage point the countryside spread out beneath him as far as the eye could see – the pastureland which he and Regan had crossed together that day, and the road beyond it which led down river to Mia-Mia.

In the heavy heat of the day nothing stirred. Even the cattle had disappeared into the shady places beside the river, where they stood in groups, no doubt, with the cool water trickling over their hooves whilst their tails flicked ceaselessly against the flies.

Would she come? He had believed, without doubt, that she would. But now he was beginning to wonder if his optimism had been justified.

Andrew may have confined her to the house, locked her into her room even. Nothing would surprise him, given the other man's fury. Or perhaps she had not yet found the note he had left her. And if she had – well, perhaps she would decide against following him. She would be risking so much in doing so, giving up her secure comfortable life for she would know not what. But Regan was not one to pay much attention to security or comfort. She was a woman of passion and daring. Yes, he would wait a little longer.

As he watched and waited, Rolf set his mind to wondering how much of the truth he should tell her. She would have to know that he had assumed a false name during his time at Mia-Mia. There was no way he could continue with that deceit, for when they arrived back at Dunrae everyone would address him as Mr Hannay. But he doubted the name would mean anything to Regan. The Hannays had been dispossessed of Mia-Mia before she was born, and he didn't imagine Andrew had ever boasted to his daughter of how he had come by the property.

As to anyone else mentioning the hapless family to her, it was unlikely in the extreme. Why should they? They had doubtless long forgotten Peter Hannay and his wife and children, for who had they been? Just another family of failed settlers amongst so many.

No, if Regan had ever even heard the name, he would be surprised. And he could count on his sisters, Rosalie and Alison, to keep the secret. They didn't approve of what he was doing, he knew. Rosalie, in particular, had begged him to let the past be. But they wouldn't tell Regan the truth if he asked them not to.

One day she would have to know – but not yet. Before that he hoped to have her bound to him by ties that would not be easily broken, ties stronger even than her love for him. When she was the mother of his child, she could not up and leave him even if she wanted to do so. And even if she did, Mia-Mia would return to Peter Hannay's descendants, just as Rolf had sworn it would.

Be he hoped she would not leave him. He hoped it with all his heart.

If she came at all . . .

There was a cloud of dust on the road where it curled over the horizon. Rolf narrowed his eyes against the glare of the sun. Was it a mirage, conjured up by heat haze? He couldn't be sure. He stood up, shading his eyes with his hand, unable to prevent the hope which had begun to spiral within him.

The dust cloud was moving, coming closer. A horse and rider were approaching along the road. Still he told himself not to expect too much. It could be anyone. It might even be Andrew himself if he, not Regan, had found the note and he had forced out of her the location of the rendezvous.

Rolf waited with bated breath, every muscle tensed to the point of aching.

At the point where they had discovered the clump of the chestnut pony's hair on the boundary fence the dust cloud stopped. He could make out the figure of horse and rider now as they cleared the fence and began to cross the pastureland. Still he couldn't be sure. Regan – or Andrew? But only Regan would have known the exact spot where they had crossed, only Regan would be making for the virgin bush with the rise beyond in such a beeline. And the figure was too small to be Andrew, he felt sure.

Joy leaped in him; his heart began pounding in his breast. She was coming to him!

Rolf unlooped Satan's reins from the tree where he had tied him and with one leap was on the horse's back. Then he set off at a canter across the pastureland to meet her.

Happiness – and relief – welled in Regan as she saw Rolf come cantering towards her. She had been so afraid that she might have delayed too long and he would have left without her. As he neared her, tears pricked her eyes once more, and for a moment she could not speak. It seemed that Betsy, whinnying in delight at the unexpected meeting with Satan, spoke for her.

Rolf dismounted, and holding Satan by the reins, helped Regan down too.

'My love! You came!'

She melted into his arms, burying her face in his strong shoulder. He stroked her hair, tumbled from the ride, and kissed her gently.

'You waited,' she whispered. 'I was so afraid you would not wait.'

'What else would I do?' he demanded. 'But I must confess I was beginning to wonder if I must travel on without you. What kept you? Could you not get away?'

'I only just found the note you left me,' she explained. 'I left then at once. But I couldn't bring anything with me. I dared not pack a saddlebag in case I was discovered.'

His heart filled as he looked at her standing there in her boy's shirt and riding breeches. She had left everything for him – her home, her father, the safety of familiar surroundings, everything she possessed. And with the tenderness came a wash of guilt at how he had deceived her.

Determinedly he thrust it away. This was no time to become squeamish about his purpose. At long last he had Andrew Mackenzie where he wanted him. He must not weaken now.

'Did no one see you leave?' he asked.

'No one but Dickon Stokes, and I told him I was going riding.'

'And your father?'

'He's out somewhere on the farm. Likely it will be some hours yet before he comes home. And when he does, he may think I'm still in my room, sulking, unless Dickon disabuses him.' Her voice trembled. 'Oh Rolf, I thought I'd lost you! Hold me, please. I need to be held.'

'I'd like nothing better – except perhaps to take you into the cover of the bush and make love to you. But there'll be time for that later. Just now we must get on our way without delay. Your father may yet come looking for you and the greater the distance we can put between us and Mia-Mia the less chance he will have of finding you. Besides, we have a long journey ahead of us. It will

152

take us the best part of two days to reach Dunrae,' he told her.

'Dunrae – is that the name of your farm?' There was a look of wonder in her eyes.

'There's no time now for talking either,' he said flatly. He spread his hands, almost encircling her tiny waist. Beneath his strong fingers she felt so fragile that it was almost as if he could snap her in two. But he knew she was made of stronger stuff – and by God, she would need to be!

He kissed her once, lightly, his anxiety to be on their way overcoming any murmurings of passion. For just a moment his eyes met and held hers.

'You are sure, Regan, that this is what you want?'

She nodded. Her chin was lifted with determination, her eyes bright in her flushed face. 'I'm sure.'

'Then it's time to go.'

He handed her up into the saddle and mounted Satan, leading the way back towards the road.

Twelve

A ll day they rode, following the track which led through the mountains, only stopping occasionally to rest and water the horses. Dusk was falling, soft and swift, as the countryside on the other side of the mountains opened up beneath them, a dusk which seemed to hover like river mist over the wide expanse of pasture.

Regan had heard tell of it – the grass, knee-deep, stretching for hundreds of miles, the sheep that provided the fine merino wool for sending to the English mills, the soil, rich and sweet. Andrew had talked of it, but his pioneering days were over and he had been happy to settle for his own small empire on the Hawkesbury river. Now she gasped as her eyes took in the vast green expanse that looked more like a park than the wild country she had expected.

Rolf reined in, following her gaze with pride. 'It's a whole different world out here, Regan. But you'll want for nothing. I can well afford to keep you in the style to which you are accustomed.'

'I don't care about that!' she said spiritedly. 'I don't care about anything except being with you.'

Guilt twisted in his gut. 'We'll make camp here for the night,' he said, turning away so that she would not see the sudden darkening of his features. 'It would not be advisable to travel any further tonight, and the horses are tired.'

'Not only the horses!' Regan said. Though she was used to long hours in the saddle and though happy anticipation had kept her buoyed up as they rode, she realised now that she was weary and every muscle in her body ached.

'I'm hungry, too,' she added wistfully. 'But I don't suppose we're likely to get anything to eat.'

Rolf laughed. 'We'll feast like kings, if I'm not much mistaken. The river here is full of fish bigger and finer than any you've ever seen in your life.' He looked around, then pointed to a clearing in the trees. 'That looks a likely spot to make camp. Gather some sticks to make a fire while it's still light, and I'll go catch our supper.'

She did as he bid. It was easy to find kindling, and as she did so her thoughts went to Mia-Mia and what would be going on there. Her father would have found her missing by now. He would be furious – and hurt – and she was sorry for that. Would he come after her? He might, but she didn't think he would know where to begin looking. Rolf had said only that he farmed on the other side of the mountains, and the country was hundreds of square miles wide, spreading on and on to the interior of this vast continent. Besides, Andrew might be so angry he would decide to let her fend for herself, and she couldn't blame him if he disowned her. She could only hope that one day he would come to understand why she had done what she had done, and they would be reconciled. The thought of being at odds with her father was almost unbearable – but her heart had led, and she had followed.

After a while Rolf returned with an enormously fat fish.

'You see, Regan?' he said, showing it to her. 'I told you we wouldn't go hungry.'

'We certainly won't!' she laughed, and watched, impressed, as he took out his knife and gutted and cleaned it.

'I feel like an explorer!' she said as it cooked slowly over the fire she had made. 'It must have been like this for Blaxland and Lawson and Wentworth, mustn't it, when they first found a way through the mountains?'

He smiled at her enthusiasm. 'I expect it was. And you are an explorer, aren't you? We both are, following our hearts into uncharted country.'

Warmth shivered through her veins and a faint colour tinged her cheeks at his words.

'At least you're going home,' she said, drawing her knees up to her chin and cradling them with her arms. 'Tell me about it, Rolf. I want to know what to expect. What family do you have? When you first came to Mia-Mia you mentioned a brother.'

Rolf turned the fish on the makeshift griddle, not looking at her. 'I invented him, I'm afraid, as an excuse for leaving home. I am an only son. But I do have two sisters, Rosalie and Alison. Rosalie is married to Jack Wilson, my overseer, and they have two little boys and another baby on the way. Alison is as yet unwed, though not from lack of offers. She declares she hasn't yet met the right man, but I'm not sure she ever will. She enjoys her freedom too much – and she loves being a honeypot for every worker bee for miles around.'

'I'm sure it will be a different story when the right man does come along.' Regan smiled. 'She'll be happy to give it all up for him, just as I have.'

Rolf laughed. 'Maybe you're right.'

'And your mother and father?' Regan pressed him. 'Do they live at Dunrae too?'

He was still bending over the griddle, so she did not see the way his face closed in at her words. But she was aware of the stiffening of his back, and when he spoke his voice was hard and curt. 'My parents are both dead. They've been dead a long time.'

'Oh, I'm sorry . . . But they couldn't have been very old,' Regan faltered. 'How did they die?'

The moment the question left her lips she knew she should not have asked it. She felt the tension in the air between them, potent as the brewing of an electric storm.

'I don't want to talk about it,' he said curtly. 'The fish is ready. I think we should eat.'

He cut a portion with his knife, carefully lifting it from the bone, and passing it to her. The smell that rose to her nostrils was tempting, smoky and appetising, but Regan suddenly no longer felt hungry. The distance she had opened up between them by her innocent question was disquieting; it made her realise just how little she knew about this man for whom she had left everything she knew and held dear. But she loved him, she told herself, and he loved her. In time he would feel ready to open his heart to her and share his innermost secrets. For the moment she must be patient and simply trust him.

The first mouthful of fish restored her appetite. In all her life, Regan thought she had never tasted anything quite so delicious. They ate ravenously, and when they had finished and washed their hands and faces in a river shallow Rolf filled his flask with fresh cold water and they took it in turns to drink.

Back in the clearing Rolf arranged their saddle blankets to cover enough ground to make a bed with a fold to tuck over them when the night turned cool.

'Have you ever slept under the stars before, Regan?' he asked.

'Never. When I was a little girl I used to beg Father to let me, but he never would. He always said that when night fell he wanted me under his roof, where he knew I was safe.'

As she said it she felt another pang of guilt. Andrew had always been so protective of her.

'You'll love it,' Rolf was saying. 'The sky is so vast at night in the bush. And the stars so bright.'

He was right. Above them, the expanse of velvety blackness was studded with a myriad of stars, so many, and so bright, Regan felt if she reached out she could touch them.

'It's wonderful,' she said simply. 'How long have they been there, those stars? Since the world began?'

'In Dreamtime,' Rolf said. Regan glanced at him wonderingly. 'The aborigines believe the world began in Dreamtime,' he explained.

'Oh.' Regan had never met an aborigine.

'To them, Dreamtime is what the Garden of Eden is to those of us who call ourselves Christians. A time of perfection when the world was young.'

'Dreamtime,' Regan repeated, liking the sound of the word. 'I think I would like to believe in Dreamtime.'

His hand found hers. The touch shivered over her skin, as vibrant and exciting as the light of the stars, and a yearning began in the deepest parts of her.

'We have it, Rolf, haven't we?' she whispered. 'Dreamtime. It's how I feel when I'm with you. As if I were living in a dream.' She broke off, shy suddenly. She had never said such a thing to anyone before, never even thought it. 'Oh, don't take any notice of me!' she went on with a small embarrassed laugh. 'I don't usually go on this way. I'm just being a stupid romantic. I expect it comes from riding too long in the sun.'

His fingers curled around her wrist. 'You are far from stupid, Regan . . . As to whether you're a romantic, I wouldn't know. You don't act like one most of the time. But under all that fire, who knows? Perhaps you are. And that is what I mean to find out.'

She lifted her chin, challenging him with her eyes, though her heart was racing and her pulses beating a tattoo. 'And how do you intend to do that?'

His eyes returned her challenge. 'Will you love me under the stars?' he asked.

Happiness sang in her heart. This was the Rolf she had fallen in love with, the Rolf who could make her forget herself and her obligations to everyone who loved her.

'You know I will,' she said softly.

His face became serious. 'It may be the last time until we are wed. My sisters would not approve of us sharing a bed. And I have a duty to Alison. She must not think it's permissible for her to follow my example and make love with whichever of her beaux takes her fancy.'

'Oh I see!' Regan teased. 'You don't mind *me* being a fallen woman, but you don't wish your sister to follow in my footsteps.'

'The circumstances are quite different,' Rolf said. A sharp edge had crept back into his voice. 'Alison is in my care. I'm responsible for her.'

'And my father was responsible for me. You didn't let that stop you.'

'What man would?' Rolf demanded. 'Men are not known for stopping to worry about such things. And you, as I recall, were not unwilling.'

Once again Regan was aware of a pinprick of disquiet. She didn't like to hear him talk this way or to be reminded of the eagerness with which she had surrendered to him.

'Don't say such things!' she burst out, tearing her hand away from his.

'Why not?' He smiled at her fury. 'It's the truth. Now, enough of talk. Come here and let me find more interesting things for your mouth to do.'

He put his arm around her, drawing her to him, and much as she longed to prove to him that she was not the easy conquest he implied, she was unable to resist.

'Dear love,' he murmured into her ear. 'You see, as I said, the fire is there for all to witness. But I want to be the man who discovers what lies hidden beneath it.'

She turned her head and his mouth found hers. His kiss was gentle at first, soothing her doubts, quieting the fears that had suddenly encompassed her. Then his tongue parted her lips and instinctively she caressed it with her own. As he thrust deeper into her mouth she felt his body grow hard in the hollow between her legs and she moved closer to him with a tiny moan of desire as rivulets of fire ran through her veins.

159

He raised his head for a moment, looking down at her lovely face, soft and rounded with love, in the light of the moon which had risen over the clearing.

'You are no fallen woman, Regan,' he said softly. 'You are my Eve, and this is indeed the Garden of Eden.'

'Oh, Rolf . . .' She spread her hands across the taut muscles of his back, loving the feel of them, loving everything about him. 'It can't be wrong, can it, when it feels so right?'

'No, my love. It can't be wrong.' His fingers were on the fastenings of her shirt, undoing them slowly as if they had all the time in the world. 'Tonight we shall not rush at love. Tonight I'll show you how sweet the waiting can be, and I will make it a night to remember through all the other nights until we can sleep once again in each other's arms.'

'Oh, yes! Show me please!' Regan whispered.

He showed her. When it was over, Regan lay in the crook of his arm, blissfully staring up at the canopy of stars. Wonderful as their lovemaking had been before, tonight he had taken her to heights undreamed of, stroking and kissing every part of her until the delicious sensations became too much almost for her to bear. And still he delayed the moment of union, taking her with such long slow strokes that she thought she would die from the intensity of her mounting desire before the heavens exploded round her in a cacophony of brilliance.

Regan moved her hand now across Rolf's broad chest, lazily playing with the feathering of springy hair which lay there. Happiness filled her so that her whole body seemed to sing a soft song in harmony with the sounds of the night. She had never known it was possible to feel such love, so fulfilling, so complete.

She nestled her head against his shoulder, drowsiness overtaking her. How wonderful it was to be able to sleep in his arms, their hearts beating as one, their breath rising and falling in unison! Her lashes dropped like butterfly wings to her cheeks, warmth crept lazily through her veins, and before she knew it, Regan was asleep.

When she woke again it was daylight. Rosy rays of early sunshine crept through the canopy of leaves into the clearing and the bush was alive with the fluttering and chirruping of birds out in search of their breakfast.

Regan came slowly through the layers of sleep, reaching for Rolf and realising he no longer lay beside her. She stretched, opening her eyes, and heard his voice.

'You're awake, then. Good morning, my love.'

She turned her head towards the sound of his voice. He was standing a few feet away from their makeshift bed, already dressed in his shirt and breeches. The sight of him, so tall, lean and strong, stirred the love within her.

'Mm . . . I'm awake,' she murmured.

'Did you sleep well?' he asked.

'Like a baby,' she replied.

She pushed the blanket aside and sat up. Her neck was a little stiff and she was conscious of vague aches that came from lying all night on the hard ground, but otherwise she felt as refreshed as if she had spent the night on a mattress of finest feathers and down.

The delicious smell of fish cooking reached her nostrils and she wrinkled her nose, puzzled that the aroma should have remained so long before realising that it was not last night's supper she could smell, but this morning's breakfast.

'You've caught another fish!' she said, turning towards the fire where it lay baking on the hot stones.

'A strange diet, I know,' Rolf said, 'but it is the easiest food to catch and it will satisfy our hunger and fortify us for the day's ride ahead.'

'Oh, I don't mind!' Regan said, reaching for her breeches and wriggling into them. 'I should have thought to bring some food with me, I suppose, but eating was the last thing on my mind, and besides, I might have aroused Ellen's suspicions if she had caught me in her kitchen sneaking bread and meat into my pockets.'

'There'll be all the bread and meat you can eat when we reach Dunrae,' Rolf told her. 'Now, shall we break our fast? The sooner we can be on our way the better, for we still have many miles to cover.'

They ate as they had done the night before, holding the chunks of fish which Rolf cut off with his knife in their fingers, and then washing it down with fresh water from the river.

'There's something I have to tell you,' he said as they folded the saddle blankets and dowsed the fire. Regan glanced at him, struck by the sudden seriousness in his voice. 'Come here.' He took her hand. His eyes were shaded, distant somehow, and she felt an echo of the unease she had experienced the previous night.

'What is it?' she asked. 'Tell me quickly, Rolf. You're frightening me.'

'There's nothing to be frightened of,' he said, but his tone was short, impatient almost. 'It's just something you have to know before we arrive at Dunrae. When I first came to Mia-Mia I told you that my name was Rolf Peterson.'

'Yes.' Regan had enjoyed secretly linking her own name to his, listening to herself saying it and liking the sound it made. Regan Peterson. 'What about it?' she asked.

'My name is not Peterson,' he said. 'It's Hannay. Rolf Hannay.'

Her mouth fell open with surprise and her eyes narrowed. 'I don't understand,' she said. 'Rolf *Hannay*? But why did you tell us your name was Peterson if it is not?'

Rolf felt a wash of relief that at least she did not seem to have recognised the name of Hannay. But then, he hadn't thought she would. It was the deceit he had to explain now to her satisfaction.

'I had invented a new identity for myself,' he said uneasily. 'Just as I invented a brother to explain the reason for my leaving home.'

'I can understand that,' Regan said doubtfully. 'At least, I think I can. But your name – you didn't have to change that as well.'

He gesticulated impatiently. 'Talk travels freely in small communities. And my name is well known on this side of the mountains. If someone had happened to travel through and it was mentioned that your father had taken on a hand by the name of Hannay it's possible I might have been discovered. I didn't want to take the risk of such a thing happening.'

He crossed to where Satan was tethered, bending to pick up his saddle. Regan stared, perplexed, at his back. Last night they had been as close as two human beings could ever be. Now, in the twinkling of an eye, it seemed, he was a stranger again, a stranger with secrets that were beyond her comprehension. She simply could not understand the change that had come over him once more, any more than she could understand why he should have lied about his name. Perhaps it was as he said, that carried away by the fabricated story he had told her father, he had thought it best to hide his true identity too. But it made her uneasy. Was there some other reason why he had not wanted to own to being Rolf Hannay?

'You – you aren't a convict are you?' she asked before she could stop herself.

He glanced at her over his shoulder and his features seemed to be set in stone. 'No, Regan, I am not a convict.'

'Your father then?' she pressed on.

'My father neither. He and my mother came out from England, bringing us children with them, in the hope of finding a better life.' There was bitterness in his tone as he recalled the optimism that had driven his parents to make the long and arduous voyage – and the cruel way in which their dreams had been wrenched from them.

'Oh,' Regan said, ashamed of herself for asking, but still confused and uncertain.

Rolf looked at her standing there, small and lost suddenly, with her lip puckered by her teeth, and wanted to kiss it. But this was not the moment and there would be other times, as bad as this and worse, once the truth became known to her.

'You still want to come with me to Dunrae?' he asked abruptly. 'If the change in my name has affected you so, perhaps you'd rather go back to Mia-Mia and your father. If so, I'll see you safely back over the mountains. I wouldn't leave you out here alone, don't worry.'

Again the coldness of his tone was a knife thrust in Regan's heart. Again the thought worried at her: what else was Rolf hiding? And why did the name of Hannay sound vaguely familiar to her? There was something here she did not understand, something that, for all the blindness of her love, did not ring true.

But far worse than any of the nagging anxieties was the thought of riding back to Mia-Mia. It wasn't her father's wrath she feared. It wasn't even the lonely road and the dangers she might encounter upon it once he left her. No, it was the prospect of never seeing Rolf again that Regan could not face, the empty years ahead with nothing but the memory of his loving to comfort her. Whatever secrets she had yet to learn, whatever it was he was still keeping from her, nothing could be as bad as that.

Regan tucked her hair behind her ear with a hand that trembled slightly and lifted her chin to a determined jut.

'Don't think that you can rid yourself of me so easily,' she said defiantly. 'Of course I haven't changed my mind. I'm coming with you. Nothing on God's earth would stop me!'

The sun rose as they rode side by side along the road which was still, in places, little better than a track. It beat down mercilessly as midday approached and, fit as she was, Regan began to feel a little dizzy. Rolf had been mostly silent, riding with his eyes firmly fixed on the road ahead while she had been desperately trying to tease from her memory some recollection of where she had heard the name of Hannay before. But though at times she came tantalisingly close to grasping the memory, still it eluded her.

At noon they rested the horses for a while, then they pressed on again, further and further into the rich green pastureland, dotted white with thousands of sheep. Sometimes they passed a driveway leading to a farmhouse. Once they saw a man riding, and Rolf raised his hat in greeting before settling it once more low on his head and pressing on, ever on.

Still the sun beat down, far more fiercely, it seemed to Regan, than she had ever experienced it on the Hawkesbury. Her whole body felt sticky with perspiration and the dust that rose from the horses' hooves seemed to cling to her damp face and hands like a thick, filthy second skin.

The thought of arriving at Dunrae was unnerving, too.

What would Rolf's sisters be like, and how would they respond to the surprise of their brother bringing a perfect stranger into their home? It would have been one thing if she had been visiting only – every farm and homestead in this wild country was accustomed to their visitors staying for days, or even weeks, since the distances they had to travel were too vast to be undertaken for a meal and some conversation only, and in times of trouble the house would be opened up to any poor soul in need of shelter, a bed, and a roof over their head. But she was not a visitor. Rolf was bringing her to Dunrae to be his wife and, presumably, one day, its mistress. It sounded as if his younger sister, Alison, was mostly concerned with her beaux but the older one, Rosalie, was used to running the house and making all the decisions that entailed without reference to another woman. She might very well resent Regan's presence, and who could blame her? And there was still the nagging doubt that Rolf had not yet told her everything about himself. What was she going to discover when she came to Dunrae?

As the thoughts chased one another around inside her head and the sun beat mercilessly down, the dizziness worsened and Regan experienced a wave of nausea. The vast horizon, shimmering like a mirage, began to swim before her eyes. Desperately she sought some landmark to focus on, but there was nothing save the endless pasture, broken only by the occasional misshapen gum tree. She flexed her fingers on the reins as they turned first prickly, as if a thousand pins were being driven into them, then thick and woolly and useless.

Regan felt herself slipping from Betsy's back and could do nothing to save herself. Slowly, gracefully almost, she slid sideways and was dimly aware of the ground coming up to meet her. But she scarcely felt the jolt as her body connected with it.

For the first time in her life, Regan had fainted clean away.

As he realised what was happening, Rolf reined in, but there was nothing he could do to prevent Regan from falling. She hit the ground with a soft thud and he was off Satan's back in an instant, running around the horses to where she lay. He dropped to his knees beside her, gathering her into his arms, and at once he realised what had occurred. The ride had been too much for her; she had swooned.

He stroked the hair away from her face, cradling her against him, and saw the red rash angry on her pale cheek where it had grazed the ground. He brushed the dirt away from it gently and she stirred in his arms, moaning softly. Her lashes fluttered and her eyes opened to look up at him, green as emeralds in the pitiless glare of the sun.

'Rolf? I . . . What happened?'

'You fainted,' he said. 'I've pressed you too hard.'

'Oh, I'm sorry . . .' she murmured.

'Don't talk such foolishness!' he said roughly. 'It's I who should be sorry.'

'What must you think of me?' she asked thickly.

'That for all your daring and stubbornness, you are a woman who needs to be taken better care of than I have taken of you,' he said.

Gently he raised her to a sitting position, forcing her head down between her knees.

'Stay there for a moment,' he commanded. 'I'll fetch the water – what remains of it.'

He stood up and moved to the horses who waited patiently, flicking their ears and tails at the flies. He retrieved the flask from his saddlebag and rested Regan against his knee whilst he placed the flask to her lips. Then he poured a little over her forehead and used some more to clean the gravel from her cheek. He could have drunk the bottle dry himself – thirst was burning his throat – but Regan needed it more than he. After a few moments she flexed her arms and legs tentatively and gave a small shaky laugh.

'That's the first time I've fallen from a horse since I was twelve years old!'

'And very gracefully you did it too!' he complimented her. 'Have you hurt yourself, my love?'

'I don't think so. Apart from this, that is.' Her fingers went to her burning cheek, touching it exploringly and wincing. 'I broke my arm when I was twelve,' she added.

'God be praised you have not done so again! But I think you were unconscious when you hit the ground. Do you feel fit to go on?' he asked, knowing, even as he said it, that there was no choice to be made.

'Yes. I'll be all right. I have to be!' She struggled to her feet and he helped her.

'It's not much further now,' he said. 'But promise me you'll tell me if you begin to feel faint again.'

He helped her back into the saddle and mounted himself. Thank God she was not hurt! If she had been it would have been his fault. His, and his alone. Yes, she had followed him willingly, but it was because he had played her emotions like the strings of a violin – and all for his own ends.

A sudden thrust of disgust for himself and all that he stood for knifed through his heart. It wasn't Regan's fault that she was Andrew Mackenzie's daughter. It wasn't her fault her father had done what he had done. But now she was paying the price.

'And the sins of the father shall be visited upon the children,' Rolf thought, recalling the Biblical quotation from somewhere in his distant past. It was ever so, and always would be.

Yet knowing it did nothing to ease the rawness of his guilt, and though he touched Satan's sides gently, urging him to a steady walk only for the sake of the girl who rode at his side, it was Rolf's heartfelt wish that he could drive him to a headlong gallop and thus escape, perhaps, the black mood that had descended upon him.

Thirteen

'Look, my love, there's Dunrae.' Rolf turned to Regan as they breasted a small rise and a cluster of white buildings amidst the endless sweep of the pastureland came into view, a man-made oasis in the middle of the vast green desert.

Regan slumped a little with the relief of it. For the last hour she had thought of nothing but holding her weakness in check, and following the road she knew she must travel. Now, however, her doubts and fears began creeping back, together with nervousness at the prospect of meeting Rosalie and Alison, and shame that she had been unable to make the journey without being overcome by heat and exhaustion.

'You won't tell them, will you?' she begged.

'Tell them what?' he asked, puzzled.

'That I swooned. Don't tell them, please.'

He laughed aloud. What a woman she was! After all she had been through, he was telling her the end was in sight, and all she could think of was her pride!

'I won't tell them if you don't want me to,' he agreed. 'How will you explain the graze to your face, though? I wouldn't like my sisters to think I was the cause of it!'

'Oh . . .' Her fingers flew to her cheek. 'Oh – I'll think of something.'

'I'm sure you will. You are nothing if not resourceful.' He smiled. 'But for my sake, Regan, make it good!'

As they approached the farm Regan looked around curiously. Though much newer than Mia-Mia the layout was almost the same. Why, it could almost have been built

169

as a copy, Regan thought as they turned off the road into a tree-lined drive and the house with its surrounding veranda came into view. A horse and foal grazed in a small paddock, hens clucked and ducks waddled in their enclosure, but otherwise there was no sign of life.

They rounded the house, clattering into the stable yard, and a small wiry man came running to meet them. 'Mr Hannay! You're home!'

The unfamiliar name jarred on Regan, but she was too tired to give it much thought.

Rolf dismounted and tossed the reins to the man before going to help Regan down. As her feet touched the ground she swayed slightly, leaning unsteadily against him for a moment.

'Uncle Rolf! Uncle Rolf!'

The excited cry of a child made Regan turn round and she saw a little boy of five or six come racing around the house and into the stable yard. Behind him, trying desperately to keep up, and failing, came another boy, perhaps two years younger, his round baby face red with the effort, chubby legs moving as fast as they would go.

Rolf turned towards them. 'Philip! James! Steady now steady!'

But they hurled themselves at him anyway and he swung the pair of them into his arms, one on each shoulder. For a moment Regan looked on, feeling quite left out as they hugged him with obvious delight. Then, over Rolf's shoulder, the older boy spied her and wriggling an arm free pointed to her.

'Who's that, Uncle Rolf?'

'This is Regan.' Rolf set him down, though he still held the smaller boy, whose chubby arms wound tightly round his neck. 'Say hullo to her, Philip.'

Philip's small freckled face was frowning, but he approached Regan obediently, holding out his hand. 'Hullo, Regan. I'm Philip.'

Regan took the outstretched hand solemnly. 'Hullo, Philip.'

'Where's your mother?' Rolf asked him.

'In the house. Doing her sewing.'

'We'd better go and find her then, hadn't we?' Rolf said.

Regan bit her lip. The moment had come when she must meet Rolf's sister. Then a voice from behind her said: 'There's no need for that, Rolf. I'm here.'

Regan turned and came face to face for the first time with Rosalie Wilson.

Even at first glance, there was no doubting that Rosalie was Rolf's sister. She had the same dark hair, escaping from a knot at the nape of her neck, and the same grey eyes. She was tall and her build suggested she was usually slender. Now, however, not even the loose folds of the sprigged muslin gown she wore could disguise the swell beneath it.

Philip had returned to Rolf, tugging at his breeches and begging to be picked up again.

'Leave your Uncle Rolf alone, Philip! He has had a long ride. He must be tired.' She brushed a strand of dark hair behind her ear, her eyes, narrowed against the sun, going to Regan. 'You're not alone, I see. Who is this, Rolf?'

'It's Regan, Mama!' Philip cried, proud to display his superior knowledge. 'I know because Uncle Rolf told me. And I've shaken her by the hand!' he added importantly.

Under the scrutiny of those sharp grey eyes, Regan was all too aware of what a fright she must look – dirty and dishevelled, and with that angry graze still livid on her cheek.

'It's been a long ride,' she murmured apologetically.

'I can see that!' Rosalie smiled faintly. 'How far have you come with Rolf?'

Rolf stepped towards Regan, slipping his free arm around her waist.

'All the way from Mia-Mia,' he said. 'Rosalie, this is Regan Mackenzie.'

'Regan *Mackenzie*!' There was shock in Rosalie's tone and her glance at Rolf was quick and almost accusing. 'Do you mean this is *Andrew* Mackenzie's . . .' Her voice tailed away.

'His daughter, yes,' Rolf finished for her.

'You know my father?' Regan asked, surprised.

'Everyone in Australia has heard of your father,' Rolf said swiftly. 'He's a legend, isn't he?' Over Regan's head his eyes met Rosalie's, warning her to silence. 'Shall we go into the house, Rosalie? There's water for a hot tub for both of us, I hope? Then the two of you will have all the time in the world to get to know one another.'

'Yes – yes, of course.' Rosalie glanced at Betsy, who was drinking noisily from the water trough which stood close by the stable door. 'Have you no baggage?' she asked wonderingly. 'Did you bring nothing with you?'

'Nothing.' For the first time since she had fled from her father's house, Regan realised just how completely she was to be forced to rely upon the hospitality of the Hannays. 'I left in rather a hurry,' she added apologetically.

'I'll have to find you some clothes then,' Rosalie said. 'You can't dirty my best brocaded chairs sitting in them like that!'

But beneath the sharpness, Regan detected a note of sympathy. Rolf's sister was like him in more than looks alone, she decided. Brusque she may appear, practical she certainly was, but there was humanity beneath the somewhat daunting exterior.

Rosalie led the way into the kitchen and produced a pottery jug covered with a small beaded cloth from a marble slab in an alcove.

'Lucky for you both I've freshly-made lemonade,' she said tartly.

'I could drink the jug dry,' Rolf agreed. 'And I'm sure Regan could too. The ride has been hard on her.'

'But he allowed me to have the last of our water,' Regan said loyally.

'He would.' Rosalie set the tumbler in front of Regan. 'My brother, at least, is a gentleman.'

Again the sharpness of her tone and her choice of words puzzled Regan, but she was too exhausted to give it much thought.

'Where's Alison?' Rolf enquired, lowering his glass.

Rosalie snorted. 'Over at the Poole's place. Roderick Poole came to visit and took her back with him. She's been gone three days now.'

'So Roderick Poole is her latest beau, is he?' Rolf said, with a thin smile. 'Well, I only hope she's been behaving herself in my absence.'

'At least she hasn't run away from home with nothing but the clothes she stands up in!' Rosalie retorted tartly, and Regan felt her face flame. It was as she had feared. What must Rolf's sister think of her!

'I know it seems a strange thing to do,' she said before she could stop herself. 'But I couldn't bear the thought of Rolf leaving without me. I love him, Rosalie. That's the truth – and you might as well know it from the outset.'

'Well, at least you're honest and straightforward,' Rosalie said with the ghost of a smile. 'Now, let's see about getting a tub of water so that you can have a bath. Then I think it's time my brother and I had a serious talk.'

'What in heaven's name are you playing at?' Rosalie demanded.

She had shown Regan to the guest room and Rolf had carried up the hot water to fill the tub before returning to the kitchen to wait for the copper to heat enough water for his own bath. The moment he was through the door Rosalie had banished the children to play outside and confronted

173

him, arms folded about the swell of her belly, grey eyes fixed on him with piercing intensity.

'She told you the truth, Rosalie,' he said wearily.

'The truth it may be, but it's only half a story!' Rosalie returned tartly. 'You leave here with the intention of gaining your revenge on Andrew Mackenzie and repossessing Mia-Mia, and you return with his daughter! What I want to know is what has gone on in the meantime, and exactly what she is doing here now. And how did she come by that graze on her cheek, I'd like to know?'

'She fainted and fell from her horse,' Rolf said. 'She made me promise not to tell you, so I'll be grateful if you don't mention it again. As for what she's doing here, don't you see that through Regan I can achieve everything I swore to achieve? And without so much as a single drop of blood being spilled. Through Regan, Mia-Mia will once more pass to the descendants of Peter Hannay.'

Rosalie stared at him, slowly shaking her head as if suddenly she did not know him at all. For as long as she could remember Rolf had been obsessed with revenge, and try as she might, she had never been able to talk him out of it. But always he had still been the brother who had protected her and Alison, who had worked day and night to keep the family together and build a new – and good – life for them. She had been terribly afraid of what might happen when he had left to journey to Mia-Mia. She had foreseen bloodshed and strife; she had feared, in the long quiet of the night, that his hatred of Andrew Mackenzie would do for him, just as it had done for his father before him, and he might never return alive. But this . . . Never in a million years had she imagined that he would stoop to something like this.

'You can't mean it, Rolf!' she said harshly. 'You made this poor girl fall in love with you in order to satisfy your need for revenge! Is that how you fight your battles?'

'I fight with whatever weapon I have to hand,' Rolf returned, his voice dangerously low. 'Have you forgotten how that fiend caused the death of our father? Aye, and our mother, too, for she had to sell herself to keep us when she had nothing left but her own poor body.'

'No, Rolf, I haven't forgotten.' Rosalie's eyes clouded as she recalled that terrible day when her father had ridden out, never to return. Small as she had been, it still haunted her dreams. As for their mother, now she was a woman herself with children to protect, she could bleed for the indignities Jessica had put herself through to keep bread in their mouths and a roof over their heads. 'I haven't forgotten. How could I? But you can't right a wrong by making another one. It's not that poor girl's fault that she is Andrew Mackenzie's daughter. Breaking her heart won't bring our parents back, and I won't be a party to it.'

Suddenly, though he could not understand why, Rolf was furiously angry.

'Regan will know the truth when I'm ready to tell her and not before. Until then, you will keep silent about what you know, and so will Alison. If you do not . . .'

She held his gaze. 'Yes, Rolf? If I do not, what will you do?'

His hands fell to his sides, the anger dying as swiftly as it had come.

'You know very well I would do nothing to harm you, Rosalie. You are my sister, and I would fight for your well-being with my life. But I'm asking you, begging you, say nothing yet. Leave it to my judgement how, and when, Regan learns the truth.'

For a long moment she was silent, then she sighed deeply. 'Very well, Rolf. But I warn you, think very carefully, for what you are doing is every bit as bad as condemning that poor girl to a living hell. She loves you and you will damn her to purgatory.'

'We are all damned,' Rolf said in a voice so low she could barely make out the words.

'Forget about revenge, Rolf,' Rosalie begged. 'Let the past lie where it belongs.'

Rolf's eyes met hers, and she saw the raw pain in them. 'I am not talking about the past. I am talking about the here and now. I am damned also, because, God help me, I love her too. I love Andrew Mackenzie's daughter. And if that is not a living hell, pray tell me what is!'

The moment the door of the guest room had closed behind Rolf, Regan had stripped herself of her filthy clothes and, barely hesitating to test the temperature of the water with her toe, plunged into the tub.

It was pure bliss to immerse herself in the warm water. Regan relaxed luxuriously for a moment before soaping herself vigorously. Then she relaxed again, letting the water ease away some of the aches of the long ride from her sore muscles, and thinking about the dubious welcome she had received. Though Rosalie had said not a word out of place, yet Regan had gained the distinct impression she was none too pleased by her unexpected arrival.

Well, that was hardly to be wondered at. At the best of times an unexpected visitor might be unwelcome. Now, heavily pregnant, Rosalie would have less energy and less patience than usual. But it wasn't just that. There was something else. Regan thought again of Rosalie's shock when she had heard that Regan was a Mackenzie, and the instantaneous recognition of the name. Oh, it was probably just as Rolf had said, that her father's name was well known to all and sundry. But all the same . . .

Regan stood up abruptly, reaching for the towel which was laid out ready for her use. She dried herself and slipped on the robe Rosalie had draped over a chair. What was expected of her now? Had Rosalie intended her to return downstairs wearing the robe, or would she think Regan immodest if she appeared in front of Rolf wearing so little? Regan realised that Rosalie's good opinion was very important to her.

She opened the door of the guest room and made for the head of the stairs, her bare feet making no sound on the carpet runner which covered the polished boards.

The rise and fall of voices in the kitchen below floated up to her. Though she could not make out what they were saying, she could tell from their tones that some sort of argument was taking place. Well, the last thing she wanted to do was walk in on something like that, particularly if it was about her, as she was very afraid it might be.

Regan retraced the steps to her room. The warm tub had made her languorous and the big bed, with its patchwork counterpane, looked inviting. She sat on the edge of the bed, then lay back against the lavender-scented pillows. Her eyelids felt heavy. She let them droop. A moment later, without any of the usual drifting down through the layers of consciousness, Regan was asleep.

It was light when Regan opened her eyes again, but a different light than before, soft and rosy. At first she thought it must be sunset, then she heard the crow of a cock and when she moved her limbs they felt heavy, as if a very long time had passed since she last stretched them.

She got up and crossed to the window. Someone had drawn the chintz curtains almost together whilst she slept. She pushed them fully open and saw the sun was rising, not setting, over the roofs of the outbuildings.

Dear God, it was morning! She had slept a full fourteen or fifteen hours!

Horrified, she began to make for the door, and it was then that she noticed the gowns, stacked neatly on the dressing stool, plain grey calico intermingled with sprigged muslins. There was a pile of underwear, too, all freshly laundered and, like the pillow cases, scented with lavender, and Regan guessed that Rosalie had left them there for her.

Regan selected a gown sprigged in green and blue. It was rather on the large side and several inches too long, but it would have to do. Regan could not help thinking longingly of her own gowns, hanging in her wardrobe at Mia-Mia – the tartans and the stripes, the bold colours and the silks, and most of all the new emerald gown she had collected from Broken Hill on the day she had first met Rolf.

How long ago it seemed now – yet it was only a few short weeks. A few short weeks that had changed her life forever!

Regan crossed to the dressing chest, taking the brush that lay there and brushing her thick tumbled hair vigorously until she was able to exert some control over it. The face that looked back at her from the glass was still pale, but the graze on her cheek had turned darker and less livid and there were no longer dark shadows under her eyes.

Oh, how I wish I had one of my own gowns! Regan thought again, as she examined her reflection. But the wistfulness was not for what she had left behind, but rather because she wanted to look her best for Rolf, and knew she did not.

Her eye fell on a length of brilliant blue sash cord which was clearly used to loop back the curtains when they were fully open. Regan took it, tying it around her waist as tightly as she could and finishing with a flourishing bow at the back. Yes, that was better! The gown puckered madly around the tie, but at least her small waist was back on view! At last Regan felt ready to face the day and whatever it held for her.

With her head held high, she left the room and made her way down the stairs.

Early as it was, Rosalie, Rolf, the two little boys and a man who Regan guessed must be Rosalie's husband were already in the kitchen and seated around the big pine table which was spread with bread, butter and a platter of cold ham. Regan felt all eyes on her as she entered the room – the children's wide and curious, their parents' serious and unfathomable.

Rolf rose, pulling out a chair for her. 'You're awake then.'

'I'm so sorry!' Regan apologised. 'After my bath I just lay down on the bed for a little rest and . . . well . . . I fell asleep!'

'You needed the rest more than you needed supper!' Rosalie said with a wry smile. 'You must be hungry now.'

'I am,' Regan agreed. And she was, ravenously so.

'This is Jack, Rolf's overseer and my husband,' Rosalie went on, cutting a slice of ham and loading Regan's plate.

Regan nodded at him across the table. He was a big handsome man with thick fair hair bleached almost white by the sun and eyes of brilliant blue in a bronzed face. Already there were long deep lines etched there, but they were kind lines that spoke of a good-natured disposition. Instinctively Regan liked him, and warmed to him. She could well understand why Rolf had been content to leave the running of the farm in those big capable hands during his absence.

'You found the gowns I looked out for you, I see, Regan,' Rosalie said, returning to her own breakfast. 'They are a little too big for you, I expect, but later on, when the men are at work, I'll see how much they need to be taken in and shortened.'

'Oh, you mustn't do that!' Regan protested. 'It's kind of you to lend them to me, but you mustn't spoil them by alterations.'

'Nonsense!' Rosalie said roundly. 'I can't wear them in my condition and won't be able to for some time, even after the baby comes if what happened after James was born is anything to go by. Having babies does nothing for the waistline, I'm afraid, as you'll discover one day. And we can't have you tripping over the hem and hurting yourself.'

'But I can have some of my own made,' Regan said. 'I could ride into town and . . .'

Rosalie laughed, and Rolf answered for her.

'The nearest town is thirty miles away, Regan, and the nearest seamstress fifty, or maybe even more. Rosalie orders what fabric she needs and has it delivered by bullocky.'

'I wouldn't trust another woman to stitch my gowns in any case,' Rosalie added. 'I make everything that I and the children need. There are many things you learn to do for yourself out here, so far from civilisation.'

She did not ask how long Regan would be staying and Regan guessed that she and Rolf had talked long and hard last night whilst Regan slept.

She glanced towards him, longing for him to smile at her or make some small loving gesture, but his expression was inscrutable and he continued with his breakfast almost as if she were not there. His hands, strong and sun-tanned, held his knife and fork with the same sure steady touch that he held the reins when he rode, and for a mad moment she remembered how good they felt on her body. Oh, if only he would touch her now! Sharp sweetness spiralled within her as she thought of it, and she felt the colour rising in her cheeks.

Useless to think that way. Rolf was too private a man to allow public displays of affection. A feeling of insecurity washed over Regan. She glanced around the table. Rolf's family – every one of them secure in their own home and their daily routine, perfectly at ease with one another. Where did she fit in as an outsider? If she and Rolf were wed, then she would be a part of this close-knit circle, but for the present she was simply a visitor – Andrew Mackenzie's daughter who had run away from home to be with Rolf.

'Right then, Jack, let's get to it.' Rolf scraped back his chair and rose. 'I've been gone too long and I'm anxious to see how things have fared in my absence.'

He looked so tall and handsome standing there, legs

splayed, hands on hips, the master of his own house! Regan felt a swell of love and pride. But hard on its heels came a shaft of something like panic. Rolf would likely be gone all day. Need of him coursed through her and before she could stop herself she said: 'Can I come with you?'

The instant the words were out she regretted them. Lord, she sounded like a child begging for a treat! And Rolf's response shamed her still further.

'I don't think that would be wise. I'm sure you are still tired after our long journey and we shall be riding hard – and far. I wouldn't be able to make any allowances for you.'

Regan's cheeks flamed at the pointed reminder of how she had swooned yesterday. *'That wasn't like me at all!'* she wanted to say. But to do so would be to have to explain to Rosalie and Jack, and besides, truth to tell, she did still feel a little odd. There was an ache low in her stomach that she supposed must have been caused by the long ride or the fall or even the night spent on the hard ground, but somehow didn't quite feel like any of them, and if she turned her head too quickly the world seemed to spin about her.

'Farming here is man's work,' Rolf went on. 'And in any case, you and Rosalie need the chance to get to know one another.'

He took his hat from its peg by the door then went to each of the boys in turn, rumpling their hair as they gazed up at him adoringly. Then, with scarcely a glance at Regan, let alone a kiss or touch, he strode out.

Regan's heart seemed to sink to her boots and for a moment she wished she could allow herself the luxury of bursting into tears. Instead she concentrated hard on watching the two little boys, who were clamouring impatiently for permission to get down from the table.

'Yes, go on, the pair of you!' Rosalie said, smiling and pretending to be exasperated.

They scampered out and she turned to Regan, brisk and no-nonsense as ever.

'When we've cleared the breakfast away I'll get my sewing basket and we'll see what we can do about that gown,' she said.

Regan nodded, trying to be grateful. But all the same, the hours she must spend alone with this woman stretched endlessly ahead of her.

For the first time in her life that she could remember, Regan felt loneliness.

Fourteen

Loneliness was a feeling that Regan was to become accustomed to in the days that followed. Each morning, as soon as he had eaten breakfast, Rolf left the house to go about his business on the farm and she was left alone with Rosalie and the children.

They, at least, were a delight, small bundles of energy and mischief, and Regan took pleasure in entertaining them. But Rosalie seemed as distant as ever. Her manner remained brusque, something seemed to hang unsaid in the air between them, and at times Regan caught Rosalie looking at her with an expression that might almost have been pity.

Would it be different with Alison? she wondered. The girl was still away, visiting at the Pooles' farm, and was likely to be for the foreseeable future.

The days passed slowly, but Regan thought she would have minded them less if only she could spend some time alone with Rolf in the evenings – or at night. But always after the evening meal the hours until bed were spent in the company of Rosalie and Jack, the two men often discussing business until Regan thought she would weep with frustration. Then, when it was time to retire, they would each go to their separate rooms. Sometimes it seemed to Regan that he was deliberately avoiding being alone with her at all.

Added to that, she still did not feel well. Often in the mornings she woke as heavy and weary as though she had not slept at all, and sometimes she felt quite nauseous. The

183

ache remained too, low in her belly, so constant that she had become quite used to it. And it was nothing compared to the ache in her heart! Once, she had thought it would be enough simply to be with Rolf. Now she knew it was not. She needed to touch him, to hold him and to be in his arms. But there was something different about him, here on his own property, with his own family. He was like a stranger to her, and Regan felt she could not bear it.

One night when they had all retired to bed and the house was silent, Regan decided she had waited long enough. For an hour or more she had laid sleepless and miserable, her body aching for his touch, the loneliness pressing in around her. I'll go to him as I used to at home, she thought. At least we can talk without the others to overhear every word we say.

Pushing aside the covers she slipped out of bed. The moon was bright, illuminating every corner of the room which, although now familiar to her, had begun to feel like a prison.

Rolf's room was just across the passage and here she was not intimidated by the thought of her father, snoring in the next room to her own. Stealthily she opened the door and crept on bare feet across the landing.

The moment she opened his door the scent of him reached her nostrils, the warm intimate scent of a man sleeping. Her heart leaped, every sense awakened and singing. Dear God, how she loved him! Then, as she listened to the even rise and fall of his breath, she found herself wondering how he could sleep so when they had not embraced once since arriving here at Dunrae? If he loved her, why wasn't he awake and yearning as she was?

For a moment shyness and nervousness almost overcame her, then the determination returned. She had to talk to him if nothing else, ask him about his plans for them and what the future held. She started towards the bed and a board creaked. Instantly he was awake.

'What the devil . . . ?'

'It's me, Rolf,' she whispered. 'Regan.'

'Regan!' Even half-asleep he sounded angry. 'What are you doing?'

'Rolf, please . . . I had to be alone with you.'

As she said it she felt ashamed of herself. What had she come to that she pleaded with a man – any man, even Rolf. But she couldn't help herself. When love had come in at the door pride had flown out of the window.

'You shouldn't have come!' He sat up, pushing aside the covers and throwing his legs over the side of the bed. The moonlight shone on his finely honed body for a moment, naked and gloriously, inescapably, masculine, and Regan's pulses beat fast with desire for him. But he did not reach for her and pull her down on to the mattress as she longed for him to do. Instead he reached for a robe and pulled it on. Disappointment and frustration as his body was hidden from her made her want to weep.

'I only wanted to talk to you!' she said, denying her own impulsive longing. 'We haven't talked since we arrived here.'

'And we can't talk now,' he returned harshly. 'At least, not here. Do you want to wake the entire household?'

'We need not . . .' She began to plead, hurt that what had been good enough for him at Mia-Mia was not good enough for him here, at Dunrae.

'Hush!' He motioned her to silence, taking her by the arm and leading her to the door. For a dreadful moment Regan thought he was about to return her unceremoniously to her own room. But instead he led her down the stairs, through the kichen and out into the garden.

A wind had sprung up and there was a chill in the night air that spoke of the approach of autumn. As it whistled through her thin robe Regan shivered. Rolf led her to a shady arbour where she had whiled away a few lonely hours in the heat of the days.

'We can talk here for a little while, but not too long,' he said. 'I've a busy day ahead of me tomorrow and I need my sleep.'

Again hurt flared in her. How could he think only of the rest he was missing when it was so long since they had been alone together? She simply could not understand the change that had come over him. He had never complained about being kept awake when they had lain making love at Mia-Mia – but then of course Mia-Mia was not his farm, the working of it not his concern.

'Have you no time at all for me?' she flared. 'I know you've been away and there is much to do, but surely you could find a few minutes to be with me? I've left everything for you, Rolf, and you act mostly as if I'm not even here! Don't you want me any more?'

He turned to look at her, slender and proud and, yes, angry and hurt, standing there in the moonlight holding her robe around her like a suit of armour. Oh yes, he wanted her! His gut clenched with the wanting, his body growing hot and hard as he thought of her sweetly yielding flesh and the way it felt beneath his touch.

Yet something kept him from reaching for her as he longed to do, the same something that had made him keep her at arm's length these past days. Since his talk with Rosalie he had felt unwilling to be alone with Regan, and though every time he looked at her he wanted her, yet something stronger had made him deny the urge.

Now, for the first time, her words made him recognise that something. The emotion that was blackening his mood, making him turn from her, was shame. Shame at what he had done to her. And something else besides. Dread of what her reaction would be when she learned the truth of why he had sought out her father and the ruthlessness which had driven him to take what she had offered. He loved her, but how could they ever be happy? When she knew the truth she would despise him. He would have achieved the end he had sworn to achieve all those years ago. But at what cost to both of them?

He thrust his despair aside, taking refuge once more in short-tempered irritability.

'I've been busy, Regan. You must know that.'

She turned away helplessly and he saw a shiver run through her.

'You're cold,' he said. 'We'd better get back inside.'

He made to take her arm, to take her into the house and end this encounter that was fast becoming more than flesh and blood could stand. But as he did so she turned to him with a soft sob, burying her face in his chest, and he was lost. For a moment longer he held on to his iron control, holding her stiffly against him, then, as her softness and warmth called to him, his flesh rose to her and the surge of need became almost too much to bear.

'Don't leave me, Rolf,' she whispered. 'You want me! I know you do!'

Her sweet body moulded itself to his, her arms were around him, holding him fast. She raised her face, eyes glinting with tears, lips parted invitingly.

'Oh, Regan . . .' he groaned.

He covered her lips with his own and the taste of her stole the last of his resolve.

As one they sank to the sweet soft bank of the arbour and there, in the moonlight, all doubts and guilt were forgotten as they melted together. In spite of his burning desire, Rolf kept it in check until he felt Regan tighten around him, felt her body arch and heard her muffled cry. Then and only then did he allow himself free rein, and with just a few glorious thrusts reached his own pinnacle with a shout of triumph.

For a moment or two he lay, easing his weight on his elbows, whilst happy satisfaction kept all his previous misgivings at bay. Then, as he sank slowly back from the heights towards reality, he moved abruptly, not looking at her as he fastened his robe.

'Rolf?' Her voice was soft, satiated and mellow with love. 'Oh Rolf, you do love me, don't you?'

He could not bring himself to answer. Oh yes, he loved her! But much good would it do either of them.

'We will be wed, won't we?' she whispered urgently.

'Yes, we'll be wed,' he said roughly, and cursed himself that the circumstances could not be different. 'After shearing.'

'Not until then?' she asked, disappointed.

He hesitated. Perhaps, given all the circumstances, it would be wise to make her his wife and bind her to him irrevocably without delay. But once again something was holding him back.

'You're impetuous, Regan, and impatient. Only a few short weeks ago you were planning your wedding to David Dauntsey.'

'No, *I* wasn't planning it,' she returned. 'Not really. Everyone else was planning it for me. This is quite different.'

'Maybe.' Pain was making him angry again. Little did she realise just how different! 'But I doubt there will be time to make the arrangements before then. This isn't the Hawkesbury. And in any case, it's only right that we give my family time to get used to the idea.' He motioned abruptly towards the house. 'It's time we were going back in.'

Regan bestirred herself as the cold wind whispered again over her bare flesh, making her shiver. She pulled her own robe around her and stood up.

Once more, for those few brief minutes, she had felt that she and Rolf were close again. Now, so soon afterwards, she felt he had gone away from her. The happiness drained out of her. Puzzled and with a heavy heart she followed him back into the house.

'Regan! Regan, where are you?' Philip's piping voice carried into the stable where Regan was unsaddling Betsy.

It was a fine bright day but the wind that heralded autumn had cooled some of the sun's heat and Regan had decided that morning to go out riding. Since the day she had arrived she had scarcely been in the saddle, fearful that she might swoon again out there alone in the bush, and Betsy had begun to be restless from lack of exercise. Regan too had been missing the freedom and the joy of the wind in her hair, and with the weather cooler she had decided to risk it. A ride was just what she needed to clear the cobwebs of confusion that were addling her brain and her emotions.

Except that it hadn't. Oh, she'd enjoyed cantering over the rich pastureland with the sheep scattering at the thunder of approaching hooves. But when it was over all her anxieties and misgivings were still there, making her feel as woolly as the sheep.

She would have to talk to Rolf again, she decided. But there would be no chance tonight. Rolf and Jack had ridden out to the farthest-flung boundaries and were not expected back until tomorrow.

'Regan!' she heard Philip call again, and a small smile touched her lips. In the time she had been at Dunrae she had become very fond of the two little boys.

'In here, Philip!' she called. 'I'm in the stable!' He came bursting in and she laughed. 'You're in a mighty rush! Steady up, Philip! You'll frighten the horses!'

She turned towards him and the smile died on her lips. Philip was not his usual boisterous self, looking for a game. The expression on his small face looked more like panic.

'Whatever is the matter?' Regan asked sharply.

'Oh, Regan, come quick! It's Mama!'

Regan's heart seemed to miss a beat. 'What's wrong with Mama?'

'I don't know. But she fell off the stool and hurt herself! Oh, Regan, I was so frightened. I didn't know what to do and I couldn't find you!'

'I'm here now,' Regan said soothingly. 'Where are the

189

convict women who help in the house? Weren't they able
to help?'

Philip shook his head, drawing his sleeve across his nose
to wipe away his tears of panic. 'No. Mama sent them to the
orchard to help harvest the apples.' He grabbed at Regan's
sleeve. 'Come on, Regan! Hurry!'

Pausing only to secure the stable door, Regan ran towards
the house and into the kitchen.

'Regan! Thank goodness!'

Rosalie was half-sitting, half-lying on the floor, her
back resting against the tall wooden cabinet. Her hair was
dishevelled, as though she had been running her fingers
through it, and her face contorted with pain. Regan's foot
crunched on broken earthenware; she glanced down and saw
the smashed crock, the floor swimming with liquid, and the
overturned stool.

'Rosalie! What happened?' she cried.

'I've made pickles. I was storing them away and I fell.'
She broke off, biting her lip against another wave of pain.

'Oh, you shouldn't have!' Regan scolded. 'You shouldn't
have been climbing up on stools! Not in your condition!'

'I thought I could manage. And now . . . Oh Regan, I
think the baby's coming.'

Panic washed over Regan. '*Now*?' she gasped stupidly.

'Yes, I think so. You'll have to help me, Regan.'

'But I don't know anything about birthing babies!' Regan
cried, the panic growing. 'Where are the women? One of
them must know . . .' She turned to Philip, who was lurking,
round-eyed, in the doorway, together with James, who had
appeared like a shadow out of nowhere. 'Run to the orchard,
Philip! Fetch them at once!'

'No!' Rosalie's voice, though strangled with pain, was
decisive as always. 'I don't want them here. You can do it,
Regan. There's nothing to it . . .' Her voice tailed off and
her breathing became heavy and ragged as a fresh wave of
pain gripped her.

Regan fought to get a grip on herself. She'd seen Betsy foal and it was true she had seemed to manage it with very little assistance. But Rosalie wasn't a mare. She was a woman. The thought of helping her bring her baby into the world filled Regan with terror. But what choice did she have? Well, the first thing was to make Rosalie more comfortable. She couldn't give birth here on the kitchen floor in a sea of vinegar, button onions and broken pottery. And the children shouldn't be here to see, either.

'Off you go, boys, and play outside,' she instructed them 'Can I trust you to be good? I hope I can. And stay there until I come and find you. Do you understand?'

They nodded, their small faces still solemn and frightened, and they stole one last look at their mother before trotting out.

'Now, let's get you to a sofa,' Regan said to Rosalie. 'I don't suppose you can manage the stairs, can you?'

'I can try, if you'll help me,' Rosalie said stoutly. 'I'd rather give birth in bed if I can.'

Regan bent over Rosalie, ignoring a wave of nausea that suddenly threatened. She wedged her shoulder beneath Rosalie's arm and helped her to her feet. With Rosalie leaning heavily on Regan the two women made the slow and tortuous journey up the stairs. Regan turned back the covers and Rosalie plopped down heavily with a huge sigh of relief.

'Oh, that's better! I just couldn't seem to find the strength to get up on my own!'

'Perhaps the pains will stop again now you're lying down,' Regan said hopefully, but a moment later her uncertain optimism was crushed as she saw Rosalie's face contort again.

'I don't think so,' Rosalie managed as the spasm passed. 'They've been coming ever since I fell. And closer together, too.'

'How long?' Regan questioned her.

'Oh, about an hour.' Rosalie wiped the beading sweat from her forehead with a trembling hand. 'I was in labour with Philip for two days. But James took only six hours.'

Regan swallowed hard. Six hours. And this baby might make its appearance in even less. There was nothing for it, she would have to act as midwife. What would she need? Hot water, towels, scissors. Again her stomach clenched with fear, again she pushed the fear away.

'Will you be all right on your own whilst I go and light the copper?' she asked anxiously.

'I'll be all right.' Rosalie was bravely trying to appear her normal, practical self. 'And Regan, you'll find a stack of old bed linen in the chest on the landing. I've been saving it up in readiness. All you need do is tear it up.'

Regan nodded. 'I won't be long. Just don't have the baby until I get back!'

Regan ran downstairs and set the water to boil. Then she swept up the broken pottery and went out to check on the two boys. They were playing, very quietly for them, with a wooden horse on wheels, pushing it listlessly from one to the other, and two pairs of anxious eyes fastened on Regan, silently questioning her.

'Your mama is going to be just fine,' she reassured them. 'But you have to be good children for a while longer yet.'

James screwed up his small face. 'I'm hungry!'

Philip dug him in the ribs for daring to raise such a mundane subject at such a time, and he scowled, close to tears. 'Well, I am!'

'I'll get you something to eat,' Regan promised. 'What would you like?'

James' face brightened. 'Can we have pork?'

'I don't know,' Regan said. 'I'll see what there is.'

She went back into the house, found pork, pickles and fresh bread, and set it out on the table.

'The food is on the table, boys,' she called to them. 'Come

and have it whenever you're ready. Then go out to play again until I come and call you.'

They came, so subdued that Regan felt confident she need not worry about their behaviour today.

The water had begun to sing. Regan pulled it to the edge of the heat where it could continue to simmer until it was needed.

'I'm going back upstairs now,' she told the boys, and paused to rumple their hair as she had seen Rolf do. 'Don't look so glum, now! Behave yourselves, and you'll likely have a new brother or sister before this day is out.'

Back upstairs, she checked on Rosalie, who was tossing and turning in discomfort, the sweat now running unchecked down her face.

'I think it will be a while yet,' she said fretfully. 'But Regan, I'm so hot.'

Regan fetched a wash cloth, moistening it with some of the water in the jug that stood on the dressing table and mopping Rosalie's burning face and neck. Then she collected one of the old sheets from the chest on the landing and ripped it into lengths.

She felt calmer now, but still anxious. It was going to be a long afternoon, and at the end of it . . . Regan clenched her jaw. She only hoped she would be equal to what was going to be required of her.

As the day wore on Rosalie's pains grew harder and closer together. Regan hovered around the bed, frustrated by her inability to do anything to help ease her suffering. Oh, why should women have to endure this? Regan wondered, and found herself thinking suddenly of her own mother, who had died giving her life.

She began to tremble. Supposing Rosalie should die? Regan thought of the two little boys downstairs who would be motherless, imagined herself having to break the news to Jack and to Rolf on their return on the morrow. Then, with an effort, she pushed the nightmare thoughts to the back of her mind. Rosalie had already given birth to two healthy children. She wasn't going to die with this one.

Late in the afternoon Regan heard voices floating in through the open window. It was the convict women, Maude and Elsa, on their way back from the orchard to their own quarters. Regan longed to ask for their help but mindful of Rosalie's request, she merely leaned from the window and asked them to prepare something from the larder for the children's supper.

The sun had begun to set over the eucalypts, and Rosalie's strength was almost exhausted, when Regan caught her first glimpse of the baby's head, dark and glistening.

'You're almost there, Rosalie!' she cried, excitement overwhelming her anxiety. 'One last push now! Push!'

And there was the baby – tiny, red and wrinkled, with a thatch of thick dark hair, a small perfect body and little arms and legs that flailed indignantly with the outrage of being thrust into the world! Her first cry was indignant too, but Regan thought it was the most beautiful sound she had ever heard. She cradled the child for a moment in her arms, tears of joy and wonder welling in her eyes and aching in her throat, before gently wrapping her in one of the pieces of torn-up sheet and placing her on Rosalie's breast.

'It's a little girl,' she said, her voice full of awe.

'Oh, my darling!' Rosalie's eyes were bright with joyful tears, the agony of the last hours already forgotten. 'Hullo, little one!'

'What are you going to call her?' Regan asked. 'Have you and Jack decided yet upon a name?'

'Oh, yes,' Rosalie said softly. 'She's going to be named Jessica, after my mother.'

Rosalie's mother – and Rolf's too. Jessica. The mother he had clearly loved so much, but of whom he refused to speak. Suddenly Regan found herself remembering the doll he had bought for Elizabeth. He had suggested the name Jessica for her, too, and Regan had thought then that it had belonged to someone very special to him. Now she knew she had been right.

'I only hope,' Rosalie said softly, 'that I am not cursing her with that name. I only hope she will have a happier life than our poor mother did. But I do so want my daughter to be called after her. It shows we haven't forgotten her – and it's like a fresh chance, too, for us to do for her all the things we were too young to do for my mother then.'

Regan, busy with tidying the room, turned to the bed, hoping to learn more in this moment of shared confidences.

But it was not to be. Exhausted by her labours, Rosalie had fallen asleep, the baby in her arms.

Gently Regan lifted her, placing her in the crib that stood ready beside the bed and tucking the sheet around her. Once again, wonder overwhelmed her.

This, she thought, had been a day she would remember for the rest of her life.

Fifteen

By the time the menfolk returned late the following afternoon Regan was exhausted. Single-handed she had nursed Rosalie and the baby, running up and down stairs a thousand times in between looking after the boys and preparing food for all of them. Added to which she had managed little sleep last night. Every time she dropped off, it seemed, she was woken by Jessica's thin complaining wails and though Rosalie assured her all was well Regan could not contain her anxiety sufficiently to rest easy. But at least she felt she had achieved a new rapport with Rosalie.

'I don't know how I would have managed without you,' she said as Regan plumped the pillows behind her head. 'I can never thank you enough, Regan, for what you did.'

When she heard the clatter of hooves on the drive, Regan ran out eagerly, anxious to break the news to the men, but the two boys beat her to it. They raced out with such abandon that the men had to rein the horses in to avoid riding them down.

'We've got a baby sister!' Philip yelled breathlessly. 'Regan brought her!'

'Baby sister!' James echoed, determined not to be left out.

Jack's face was a mixture of joyful surprise and alarm. He was off his horse in an instant and racing towards the house. The boys followed, trotting eagerly along in an effort to keep up with their father, and Regan and Rolf were left alone.

'You delivered Rosalie's baby?' Rolf asked. There was

respect in his eyes – and tenderness, too, Regan fancied. She shrugged, trying to make little of it, though the pride warmed her once more, along with a happiness she could not contain, just to see him again.

'There was no one else to do it,' she said.

'Then for my sister's sake, I thank you.' There was love in his voice.

As he dismounted from Satan his arm brushed hers and she felt the contact send small rivers of awareness tingling over the bare flesh. He leaned across, slipping one arm around her waist and pulling her to him. For a moment his lips touched hers and the taste of them warmed her heart and sent her pulses racing.

'You're home, Mr Hannay!' It was one of the convict labourers, emerging from one of the outbuildings. Rolf released Regan and the moment passed. But as she made her way back to the house, Regan felt a great deal happier than she had at any time since arriving at Dunrae.

That evening when supper was over and the boys put to bed, Jack went to Rosalie's room and Rolf and Regan were left alone. The soft light of the candles cast an intimate glow over the table and for a while they sat in companionable silence.

Mellowed by the wine they had drunk to celebrate the baby's birth, Rolf glanced across at Regan and felt the love well up in him. Dear God, but he had never felt this way about a woman before, had never imagined himself capable of such passion and such tenderness. That it should be for this woman, whom he had set out so cold-bloodedly to seduce was beyond belief. Yet it had happened. He loved her, and longed only to care for her. She looked so tired and yet so radiant sitting there with the candlelight playing softly on her face, with love and trust shining in her eyes. And he was deceiving her, betraying her trust instead of protecting her from hurt and harm as every one of his instincts longed to do.

197

Brave, vulnerable Regan. His love. And his despair. 'Come here,' he said softly.

She pulled her chair closer to his and he took her hand, stroking it gently with finger and thumb before lifting it and pressing it to his lips.

The scent of her skin was wonderful, the faint bouquet of the lavender-scented soap she used more arousing than any exotic perfume from the East. He longed to scoop her into his lap, feel the soft fullness of her breasts against his chest, slide his hand up her long shapely legs beneath the voluminous folds of Rosalie's homespun gown and find the warm secret places that lay between them.

But he refused to allow himself to do so. He had already taken too much advantage of her. He had promised himself he would not do so again until she knew the truth. If then she still offered herself to him willingly, he would praise the Lord for blessings he did not deserve and take her with joy and love. If not . . .

An iron fist clamped around Rolf's heart. He had spoken the truth when he had told Rosalie that he too would be in purgatory. And he had only himself to blame. Himself – and a vow sworn by an adolescent boy on the grave of his beloved mother.

'Rolf?' As if she felt the turmoil within him, Regan looked at him questioningly.

He smiled at her with lips that felt stiff. 'Regan.'

She hesitated. 'Did Rosalie tell you that she plans to name the baby Jessica after your mother?' she asked tentatively.

A jagged edge of pain knifed into him, followed by a yearning ache of admiration and envy. Such a gesture was typical of Rosalie. Like him, she refused to wear her heart on her sleeve, yet she had planned a living memorial to the mother who had given so much for their well-being. It was a gesture of love and hope, born from a sadness and anger as deep as his own. But whilst she had created in their mother's memory, he had thought only of revenge.

And it wasn't only Andrew Mackenzie, the author of all their troubles who would be destroyed in the process. It would be himself and the woman he loved too.

'I haven't treated you very well, have I, Regan?' he said raggedly.

'You've been busy,' she said. 'I understand that.'

'But you have been hurt by my neglect and for that I am truly sorry,' he said. 'You've given up everything, Regan, to be with me, and this is how I repay you.'

'It's all right, truly.' She gave a small shake of her head. 'And after all, I came of my own free will. You didn't steal me away in the night, did you?'

Guilt choked him. *I might as well have done*, he thought.

'Just as long as you love me,' Regan went on. 'That is the only thing that matters.'

'Oh, I love you!' he said with feeling. 'More than life itself.'

'That's all right then.' She sighed with contentment.

His gut stirred. Once more he fought the temptation to take her in his arms. First, he had to tell her the truth. He took her hand between his, looking directly into her face.

'Regan, there is something I have to tell you. Something I should have told you a long time ago.'

Her brow wrinkled into a puzzled frown. Then she giggled suddenly and the giggle quickly became a peal of laughter.

'What's so funny?' he demanded, vaguely affronted.

Regan covered her mouth with her free hand to stop the giggles, but over it her eyes still laughed at him. 'You look so serious!' She laughed again.

'I am serious.' He was thinking that what he had to say would put a stop to her laughter. Perhaps for a very long time. His gut clenched. 'Regan, there is much you don't know about me.'

'I know all I need to know,' she said warmly. 'I know that you are brave and kind – and clever too. If you built this farm up from nothing then you must be clever. And

resourceful. And hard-working.' She raised an eyebrow at
him. 'Need I go on?'

'Oh, my love.' She was making this harder for him by
the minute. 'I am not all the things you say I am. Not by
a mile.'

'Modest too!' she teased.

'Not even that. Regan, you must stop giggling and listen
to me.'

The sound of footsteps on the stairs. He broke off,
glancing towards the door.

Jack entered the kitchen, blissfully unaware that he was
intruding.

'She's sleeping.' He threw himself down into his chair,
the picture of contentment. 'Another night's sleep, and she'll
be well on the road to recovery. Thank God you were here,
Regan – though that minx Alison should have been here too.
She shirks her responsibilities, that one! I dread to think what
might have happened if Rosalie had been alone.'

'Jack . . .' Rolf began, then bit off the words.

It was too late now. The moment had passed, his resolve
to tell Regan the truth had weakened. Rolf did not know
whether to be exasperated or relieved.

Regan sat in the bathtub soaping herself and enjoying
the luxury.

A week had gone by since baby Jessica had been born,
a busy, happy week. Because Rosalie was still confined to
bed Regan had carried out all the duties that were usually
Rosalie's responsibility, and though she still felt a little
unwell at times she had enjoyed every full moment. Caring
for the two little boys was a joy – they were so full of fun
and so affectionate now that they had grown more used to
her, and the warmth that had been born between her and
Rosalie remained. There were still the times when she caught
a thoughtful, almost worried, expression on Rosalie's face
as they talked, and she could still be sharp and brusque, but

Regan had come to accept that this was her way and even to like her for it. As for the baby, Regan could not see her without feeling a glow of pride. She had played her part in bringing her into the world and Jessica was a constant wonder to her.

Today had been as busy as always, but Rolf had returned early for once, and she had asked him to watch the boys for a while. 'If I don't have bath I swear I'll expire!' she said, and was warmed by the look of love she saw in his eyes.

Now, she reached for the soap, lathering it over her skin, then letting the warm water rinse it away. As her fingers reached her breasts, she winced slightly. My, but they were tender! Never could she remember them feeling so sore, not since the days when they were sprouting. Regan smiled to herself as she remembered how unwelcome that development had been! And the first time she had experienced her monthly courses . . .

The smile faded suddenly on her lips. Her monthly courses – she had not endured once since coming to Dunrae! Horrified, Regan's fingers returned to her breasts, and glancing down she saw that they were heavier and fuller than usual, the tips, usually rose pink, darker and more clearly defined. Little waves of shock ran through her veins – veins which she could now see clearly against the creamy white of her breasts.

Oh dear God, I believe I am with child! Regan thought.

Why hadn't it occurred to her before? It explained every-thing – the sickness, the tiredness, even the day she had fainted. Regan sat motionless as the water cooled around her. She was carrying Rolf's child. The enormity of it was such that she could scarcely take it in, and she did not know whether she was pleased or dismayed. But whichever, now there could be no going back.

'Rolf, you have to tell Regan the truth.' Rosalie eased herself against the pillows. She knew Regan was safely out of earshot, taking a bath in the privacy of her room, and when Rolf brought her a welcome drink she had seized the opportunity to speak to him alone.

Rolf averted his eyes from hers, crossing to the window and looking out.

'She deserves to be told the truth,' Rosalie persisted. 'When I think what she did for me I am ashamed to think of how we are deceiving her.'

'And you think I am not?' Rolf ground out. 'I loathe myself every moment of every day for what I have done to her.'

'Then tell her!' Rosalie urged. 'I've seen the way you feel about each other, but what future can there be for you whilst this secrecy lies between you?'

'And what future can there be when she knows how I deceived her?' Rolf swung round, his anguish clearly written in every line of his face.

'You must tell her how it was for us,' Rosalie said urgently. 'She may understand.'

'And she may not. God alone knows I'm not sure I would if the positions were reversed.' He was silent for a moment. 'You're right, though, I know,' he said after a moment. 'I was about to tell her the night after the baby was born. Then Jack came in and the moment was lost. Since then the opportunity has not arisen.'

'Then you must make it. I can't live with this much longer, Rolf.'

'You'll wait for me to break the news to her though?' he asked.

'It's best it comes from you. Truth will out, Rolf, and heaven alone knows how she will take it if she hears it from another.'

Rolf turned sharply. 'Then keep Jack with you for an hour or so after supper. I'll tell her then.'

Rosalie nodded, satisfied. 'I'll pray for you, Rolf.'

His lips twisted ironically. 'It's a long while now, Rosalie, since I believed there was a God in heaven to listen. But at this moment, I hope with all my heart there is, and that He will answer your prayers.'

Throughout supper Regan felt as if she were bursting with her news. The excitement of her discovery had robbed her of her appetite and it was as much as she could do to force down even a few mouthfuls of the food she had prepared.

Her baby, hers and Rolf's! Surely he would be as happy as she was! Surely this would mean they would be married at once rather than waiting until after shearing!

When the meal was over she put the boys to bed, delighting more than ever in the sight of their small rosy faces peeping out from beneath the covers before she blew out the candle. 'Goodnight, boys. Sleep tight,' she said softly, and their piping voices, sleepy already, chorused in return: 'Goodnight, Regan.'

On her way back downstairs she looked in on Rosalie on the pretext of asking if there was anything she needed, but in reality to take the opportunity of peeping at little Jessica.

'Would you ask Jack to come up and see me?' Rosalie said. 'There's something I want to talk to him about.'

Regan was surprised to catch a note of strain in Rosalie's voice.

'Is everything all right?' she asked. 'You're not in any discomfort?'

'No, I'm fine,' Rosalie assured her. Then she caught at Regan's sleeve. 'You do know, don't you, how fond we've become of you, Regan? How glad we are you are here?'

'I'm glad I'm here too,' Regan said, puzzled. It was so unlike Rosalie to say such things. 'I do miss my father, though.'

It was true. She did miss him, now more than ever. If only he were here to share the news that he was to be a grandfather! Well, God willing, when she and Rolf were married they could visit him at Mia-Mia and make him understand – and forgive.

In the kitchen Rolf and Jack were busying themselves clearing away the remains of supper. It was a surprising scene – the men never usually lowered themselves to such mundane tasks – but it was a heart-warming one.

'Rosalie wants to talk to you, Jack,' Regan said. 'Will you go up?'

'Aye, when I've finished this.' Jack was drying a pot which Rolf had washed. He set it on its shelf and draped the drying cloth neatly over the rack beside the fire to dry. Then he left the room and Regan and Rolf were alone.

'Rolf . . .' she began eagerly, but as he turned towards her it was as if he had some agenda of his own and had not even heard her. Something in his face frightened her. Then he took her hand, leading her over to the chair and pulling it out for her to sit down.

'Regan, we must talk.'

'Yes, we must!' she agreed. 'We never seem to have the chance these days. And there's so much . . .'

'There is indeed.' But he was not smiling.

Had he guessed? she wondered. And if so, why did he look so serious? Could it be that he wouldn't be pleased to hear her confirm what he suspected?

Unnerved, she could bear the suspense no longer. 'I am with child, Rolf,' she said.

His head jerked up, his eyes wide with surprise, and she knew that whatever he had been going to talk to her about it had not been this.

'I am with child,' she repeated. 'I'm sure I am. I am going to have your baby, Rolf. Please – oh please! – say that it makes you as happy as it makes me!'

Dumbfounded he stared at her, a million thoughts chasing one another round and round inside his head.

Just why he should be so surprised he could not imagine.

Was it not what he had planned from the moment he had realised she was Andrew Mackenzie's daughter? Yet surprised he was – and shocked.

'You're sure?' he asked.

'I said so, didn't I? Isn't it wonderful? Oh, say you're happy, please! The moment I realised I couldn't wait to tell you!'

'Yes, of course I'm happy, Regan.'

But he didn't feel happy. He felt suddenly totally trapped by the web of his own deceit. He had what he had wanted, planned for. An heir to Mia-Mia in whose veins ran Hannay blood. But there was no sense of triumph, only fear that by his own actions he would lose them both, his beloved Regan and his unborn child.

And once again the moment of truth had been snatched away from him. He couldn't tell her now, spoil her joy in this shared moment. Besides, God alone knew what effect the news would have on her and their baby. The shock might cause her to miscarry. Strong she might be, but was she strong enough for that?

With a silent groan of agony for all of them, Rolf did the only thing he felt he could do. He took her in his arms.

'You didn't tell her, did you?' Rosalie said accusingly. She had called to Rolf as she heard him passing her room.

'I couldn't,' he said. 'I tried to, but before I could she had some news for me. She is with child, Rosalie.'

Rosalie closed her eyes briefly. Little Jessica suckled contentedly at her breast.

'Oh, Rolf, what have you done?' she asked softly. He said nothing, and she crossed herself, her face a study in sadness.

'If she is with child, Rolf, then God help us all.'

Sixteen

Regan was happy as a lark. She sang to herself as she went about the daily chores, a little tunelessly, for although she loved to play the piano she had no ear for holding a melody. But that didn't matter. There was no one to hear her but the convict women. Rolf and Jack had left early, Rosalie was still confined to bed, and Philip and James were with her. When Regan had taken her a jug of the ale that was supposed to help her provide plenty of good breast milk, they had been curled up one on each side of her whilst she read to them, and Regan's heart had warmed at the homely scene. One day soon she, like Rosalie, would have a family of her own. And Rolf would share it with her.

He must be happy about the baby, Regan thought contentedly, for he had wasted no time in breaking the news that he was to be a father to Rosalie.

'I hear you are with child,' she had said to Regan.

'Yes, Rosalie, I am,' Regan confirmed. 'I'm delighted and so is Rolf. Oh, I know that we should have waited until we were man and wife, but I love him so much.'

'And he loves you,' Rosalie said. 'Never forget that, Regan.'

If it was a strange thing to say, Regan was too happy to notice.

'We'll take care of you, never fear,' Rosalie went on. 'You're not afraid, are you?'

Regan shook her head. 'No, I'm not afraid.'

And it was true. Once, not so long ago, the thought of

childbirth had terrified her. But that was in the past now. Rosalie's confinement had allayed her fears.

A clatter of hooves on the cobbles caught her attention. Might it be Rolf returning early? He had kissed her a tender goodbye when he had left this morning and she had seen concern for her in his eyes.

'Take care of yourself, Regan, do you hear?' he had urged her. 'Don't do anything to overtax yourself. If there's heavy work to be done, get one of the convict women to do it. That's what I keep them in food and lodging for.'

Now Regan crossed to the window and saw a horse and buggy heading towards the house. A young woman was driving, a young woman with flowing brown hair fastened in a knot at the nape of her neck. Regan's eyes widened. Knowing how far Dunrae was from the nearest town she knew this was unlikely to be a social visit. Could it be that this was Alison, returned from the Poole place?

Regan took off her apron and hurried out on to the veranda. One of the convict labourers had appeared from nowhere to take the reins, and as she watched, the girl climbed down from the buggy, brushing the dust from her skirts and settling them into place.

When she saw Regan her eyebrows lifted into two perfect arcs of surprise.

'Alison?' Regan asked tentatively.

'Yes.' Eyes, blue as her bonnet, stared at Regan haughtily. 'I'm Alison Hannay. And who, may I ask, are you?'

'I'm Regan. Regan Mackenzie.'

The blue eyes narrowed. 'Did you say *Mackenzie*?'

Abruptly Regan was reminded of the greeting she had received from Rosalie when Rolf had first brought her to Dunrae. 'Yes, that's right,' she affirmed, lifting her chin. 'I'm here with Rolf. He brought me here from my home, Mia-Mia.'

'My God!' Alison's eyes flashed. 'Are you related to Andrew Mackenzie?'

'I am his daughter,' Regan said proudly. 'It seems my father is well known in these parts.'

'To us he is, certainly!' Alison said coldly. 'The name of Mackenzie is not one that we Hannays are likely to forget.'

Regan frowned. 'What do you mean by that?'

'You mean you don't know?' Alison's features were tight with hatred.

Regan held herself tall and erect, though inwardly she was quivering like a jelly.

'If I knew I'd hardly be asking. But I think perhaps there's something you should know. Rolf and I are to be married. I'm sorry that you have to hear it this way, but it seems you are questioning my right to be here, and so I feel I have no option but to explain.'

Alison laughed harshly. 'Rolf would never marry a Mackenzie. He'd die first!'

Uncertainly stirred in Regan's gut but she stood her ground, determined not to be cowed by this arrogant young woman.

'I'm afraid you are wrong, Alison,' she said. 'Rolf loves me and I love him.'

'That I certainly don't believe!' Alison snapped. 'Rolf may have his own reasons for marrying you – and now that I come to think of it, I suppose I can guess what they are. But love . . . huh! My brother would never love a Mackenzie. Not after what your father did to us.'

Regan had begun to tremble from head to foot, but somehow she kept her head high.

'I think you had better explain yourself, Alison,' she said shortly. 'I don't like these continual references to my family as if we were some kind of monsters.'

'The truth hurts, does it?' Alison spat. 'You *are* monsters!' Her fingers tightened around the whip she still held as if she would like to lash Regan with it.

Regan turned away. She was shaking violently and the

questions were chasing round and round inside her head. But they were achieving nothing, nothing but an enmity which was the last thing she wanted, given that soon she would be Alison's sister-in-law.

'Don't dare to turn away from me, you harlot!' Alison spat out. 'You want to know why the name of Mackenzie is hated in this household? Very well, I'll tell you. Your father ruined us. You call Mia-Mia your home? Well, so it may be – now. But before it was yours it was ours. Our home! Built by the sweat of my father. He cleared the ground Mia-Mia stands on. He laid the foundation stone with his own hands. He stocked the meadows and planted the fields. He worked from dawn till dusk so that we children scarcely saw him. But he was nothing but a poor settler, as despised almost as the convicted criminals who are sent here to serve out their time. When times became hard he had nothing to fall back on. And that was when your father saw his opportunity.'

She broke off for a moment, closing her eyes against the memory.

'What do you mean?' Regan whispered.

'He ruined us to get his hands on Mia-Mia,' Alison ground out. 'Your father was an officer in the Corps. He had money, he had power, he had the backing of the Governor even. And of course he had his place in the Rum Ring. What did a poor man like my father have? Nothing. Nothing to help him through the bad times save a noggin of rum. And your father traded on that. He encouraged my father to drink to drown his sorrows, running up accounts he had no hope of paying. Then, when the debts had mounted, he took Mia-Mia from us in payment. He ordered us to vacate the property and leave everything my father had worked for. We were to be homeless, with no means of supporting ourselves.'

Regan's lips felt stiff. She was remembering, against her will, Rolf's refusal to discuss the fate of his parents and the strange dark mood that descended on him whenever she asked.

'I was only a tot,' Alison went on, and it was almost as if she had forgotten Regan was there now. 'But that day is imprinted in my memory and will be until I die. Mackenzie rode away in the sure knowledge that before long Mia-Mia would be his. He left us destitute. My poor father was distraught. He rode out – drunk, I suppose, but who could blame him? – and half crazy. He never came back. He fell from his horse and broke his neck.'

'Oh, dear Lord!' Regan was horrified. 'But surely my father helped you then? He would have regretted his actions, I know he would! Ambitious he might have been, but he would never have been so heartless . . .'

'That's all you know!' Alison laughed harshly. 'Heartless? That's too soft a word for him! He still demanded what was rightfully his. We had to leave Mia-Mia, though Mama was beside herself with grief and fearful for the future. She managed to keep the family together – at a price. Do you know how she did it, Regan? She sold herself, along with jugs of ale and tipples of rum and brandy at an alehouse up the river.'

'Oh, dear God!' Regan whispered.

'For our sake, she became a common prostitute. My dear mother! But she had more honour in her little finger than your father has in the whole of his body, and don't you forget it!' Alison said fiercely.

'Oh . . . I'm so sorry . . .' Regan was too shocked to think straight, but not for one moment did it occur to her to disbelieve Alison's story. Terrible as it was, little as it fitted her image of the loving father who had raised her, yet that story had the ring of truth. And it explained so much about Rolf and Rosalie which she had found puzzling.

'It's a little late to be sorry, wouldn't you say?' Alison asked harshly. 'Twenty and more years too late.'

'What can I say?' Regan whispered. 'What can I do?'

Alison smiled mirthlessly. 'I think you've already done exactly what Rolf intended. You're pregnant, aren't you?'

Regan grasped the veranda rail. 'How did you know?'
'I guessed.' Alison's smile was a grimace of hatred now.
'Rolf swore revenge on our mother's grave. He swore that
one day he would get Mia-Mia back for the descendants
of the Hannay family. And what better way to do it than
through his own child? Once again, a Hannay will be heir
to the house my father gave his life for!'

The air, hot with autumn sunshine, suffocated Regan. She
tightened her grip on the veranda rail, but it seemed to be
swimming away from her, merging into the cloud of dust
blown by a sudden gust of wind. Her legs turned to rubber
beneath her. Regan felt herself falling, falling. And then she
knew no more.

'Alison, what in heaven's name have you done?' Rosalie's
voice came at Regan through a thick mist. 'You shouldn't
have told her like that! She is with child!'

'I wasn't to know,' Alison said. She sounded indignant
and a little frightened.

'You never think before you speak, Alison!' Rosalie said
crossly. 'Regan, Regan, can you hear me? Come back to us,
please, Regan!'

Regan felt a cold pressure on her forehead. She opened
her eyes to see Rosalie bending over her holding a wet wash
cloth against her brow.

'What are you doing down here, Rosalie?' she asked
shakily. 'You should be in bed!'

'How could I stay in my bed with all that shouting going
on?' Rosalie demanded.

'Why are you in bed, Rosalie?' Alison's voice tailed away
as realisation dawned. 'Oh, you've had the baby!' she said
guiltily.

'Yes. Over a week ago now, as you'd know if you'd been
here instead of at King's Cross, mooning over Roderick
Poole!' Rosalie said sharply. 'Well, make yourself useful
now that you are here. Go and fetch the brandy.'

'You shouldn't even have your feet to the ground yet, Rosalie!' Regan made a valiant effort to sit up and the world did another slow spin around her.

'Don't try to talk,' Rosalie ordered.

Alison returned with the brandy and pushed it unceremoniously beneath Regan's nose. The smell of it turned her stomach, but under Rosalie's urging she sipped obediently and as it trickled into her veins, spreading warmth, she realised she did indeed feel a little better.

Alison helped her to her feet and though the ground felt unsteady beneath her she made it safely to the kitchen, where Philip and James lurked, looking frightened. A thin wail came from upstairs. Alison looked wide-eyed towards the stair well.

'Go up and fetch Jessica,' Rosalie ordered her. 'I'm not going back to bed until I'm sure Regan has recovered.'

Alison looked from one to the other of them, exasperated and not a little dismayed to find she had not one, but two, patients on her hands. 'Oh, I wish to goodness I'd stayed at King's Cross!' she exclaimed, flouncing out.

'I think we all wish that, Alison!' Rosalie said sharply to her retreating back. Then she turned to Regan. 'You mustn't take too much notice of Alison. She hasn't a thought in her head beyond flirting with her latest beau.'

'She seemed to know what she was talking about though,' Regan said dully. 'Are you going to tell me what she said isn't true?'

Rosalie grimaced. 'I'm not going to tell you anything. It's Rolf's place to do that.'

'He's left it a little late though, hasn't he?' Regan said bitterly. 'Oh, I can hardly believe it! That my father should do those things – and that you all knew while I did not. But worst of all . . .' Weak tears gathered in her eyes. 'He doesn't love me at all, Alison said. He is just using me as a way to get revenge on my father . . .'

'He does love you, believe me, Regan!' Rosalie said

urgently. 'It's true your father ruined us and Rolf set out to gain revenge, but something changed when he met you. He fell in love. I know because he's told me so, and even if he hadn't I'd know it just by looking at him – and the way he looks at you. He's tried to tell you the truth more than once and . . .'

'Well he hasn't tried very hard!' Regan retorted, stung afresh that Rolf had discussed all this with his sister behind her back. 'And anyway, surely the time for telling me was long ago before I ran away from home to be with him. That was the time, surely!'

Her eye fell on Alison, standing in the doorway with little Jessica in her arms and she felt she could bear it no longer. She had been so happy, so confident about the future. But it had all been nothing but a sham.

'I don't want to see him ever again!' she burst out. 'I'm going home! I'll saddle up Betsy and leave at once!'

'Don't talk such foolishness, Regan!' Rosalie protested, alarmed. 'You can't ride off all that way on your own! Don't you remember what the journey was like, how poorly it made you? And that was when Rolf was there to look after you.'

'I don't need him!' Regan blazed.

'Of course you do. If you try to cross the mountains alone you'll kill yourself and your baby too. Listen to me! You can't do it, Regan!'

And Regan knew, with a sinking heart, that it was true. She couldn't do it alone. In fact, in her condition, she doubted she could do it at all. She had come to Dunrae willingly, but now the hundreds of miles of wild country had made a prisoner of her.

'Oh, fiddle-de-dee!' she spat out. 'I suppose you're right. But you can tell that brother of yours that I hate him. And I'll never forgive him as long as I live!'

She ran upstairs, her eyes so misted by tears she could scarcely see where she was going. In her room she flung herself down on the bed and wept uncontrollably. It wasn't good for her to cry like this in her condition, she supposed, but she couldn't help it. And what did it matter, in any case? Nothing mattered. Her life was ruined, and Regan thought she no longer cared if she lived or died.

Seventeen

It was growing dusk when Regan heard the hoof beats that told of Rolf's return. All day she had remained in her room, heedless of Rosalie's pleadings with her to go downstairs for something to eat. Eat! She thought that food would choke her. And she couldn't bear to be in their company, either, knowing that all along they had known what she had not.

As for Rolf, she certainly didn't want to see him. How was it possible to hate someone so much and yet still love them? How was it possible to feel so much pain? Regan threw herself down on the bed once more and buried her face in the pillow.

Rolf strode into the kitchen and tossed his hat on to the table. He had seen the buggy in the stable yard and knew that Alison must be home, so it was no surprise to find her there. But he was surprised to see Rosalie downstairs and surprised too that the boys, who were playing quietly, building a tower of wooden bricks, did not rush forward to greet him as they usually did. Instead they seemed subdued, looking solemnly at him from behind their construction.

'What a day we've had!' Rosalie greeted him.

'Where's Regan?' he asked, alarmed.

'In her room,' Rosalie said shortly. 'She's refusing to come down.'

'Why? What's happened?' Rolf looked from one to

the other of his sisters and saw guilt written all over Alison's face.

'I didn't know, Rolf! It wasn't my fault!' she said sulkily. 'I didn't know she didn't know what her father did to us. I don't see why I should take the blame!'

'You'd better sit down and we'll tell you all that's happened,' Rosalie said tightly.

But Rolf was already heading for the stairs. He wasn't going to discuss this with his sisters. All that mattered was going to Regan. The rest of them could go hang for all he cared! Fired by urgency and filled with dread, he took the stairs two at a time.

As the door burst open Regan raised her head. He had stopped short in the doorway and the sight of him, so tall and handsome, made her heart turn over. But it was also a stark reminder of what she had lost. 'Leave me alone!' she flung at him.

She heard the click of the door as he closed it behind him and the tears welled in her eyes once more. She squeezed them tight shut. She didn't want him to know she was crying.

'Regan, I know what you must think.' His voice was rough. 'But that isn't the way it is. Regan, talk to me, please!'

'There's nothing to talk about.' She turned over abruptly, pulling herself up. 'You've lied to me and deceived me, Rolf. You've made a complete fool of me. I only hope you're satisfied. And now I just want to go home and forget I ever met you.'

He spread his hands helplessly. 'At least let me explain . . .'

'You don't need to do that!' she threw at him. 'Alison did it for you. My father used your family ill, I understand – and for that I'm sorry. But did you have to go to such lengths for your revenge? What have I done that I should be treated so?'

'Regan, you don't understand . . .' he began.

She lifted her chin, her eyes blazing now with all the pain, all the humiliation he had inflicted on her. 'I understand very well! I've had all day to think about it, Rolf. You sought me out because at last you'd found a way to make the Mackenzies pay. Oh! What a gift it must have been for you when you found me in trouble! You could play the hero and give yourself a head start in making me fall in love with you.'

'It wasn't like that, Regan,' Rolf protested. 'I never even knew Andrew Mackenzie had a daughter and the moment I saw you . . .'

'You set out deliberately to seduce me,' she said. 'And what an easy catch I was! What a foolish innocent that I believed you felt as I did! I hate myself for giving you what you wanted so easily. But believe me, I hate you more. And if you think you will get Mia-Mia back through our child, then you are much mistaken. I will die before I ever give you the satisfaction of setting foot on our land again.'

Rolf winced beneath her onslaught. He deserved it, he knew. Oh, why had he not told himself of the circumstances that had brought him to the Hawkesbury? He could at least have broken it with gentleness and love. But he had prevaricated and now it was too late. Alison had enlightened Regan in her own inimitable fashion. Damn her!

But blaming Alison was no way out. Rolf knew he had no one to blame but himself.

'Regan, I no longer care about Mia-Mia,' he said urgently. 'I no longer care about revenge. Oh, it drove me in the beginning, I admit it. It was the only thing that kept me going in the dark days as I cared for my sisters and built a home for them, and a business to sustain us. I don't expect you to understand that. You have never been hungry, not knowing where your next meal is coming from, or whether you would have to sleep without a roof over your head. But that is how it was for us and I swore a vow on my mother's grave that one day Mia-Mia would be ours once more.'

'Would she be proud of you now?' Regan flashed. 'Proud of what you've done?'

'No, she would not,' he admitted. 'I know now I was wrong to live with such hatred in my heart. Nothing matters now but you, Regan. You and our child. I love you, Regan.'

She hesitated, almost swayed by his passionate words and the anguish she thought she saw in his face. She wanted to believe him so much. But how could she?

'You deceived me shamefully,' she said, 'and even now you're trying to turn things around. Well, it won't work. I hate you, Rolf. Oh, how I hate you!'

He balled his hands helplessly, wanting only to take her in his arms; make her see that he loved her. But as he took a step towards her she recoiled, beating out at him with her hands.

'Don't dare to touch me! Haven't you done enough? I want you to take me home! I would have left today without ever having to look on you again, but I'm in no fit condition to ride. Will you drive me? If you love me as you say you do, will you at least do that for me?'

He hesitated, on the point of agreeing to her request. It was over. She hated him, and who could blame her? But the thought of letting her go like this was more than he could bear. And besides, there was the child to think of now.

'I will not!' he said harshly. 'I won't let you throw away all we mean to one another, Regan. You will stay here until you come to your senses and listen to me.'

'And you think you can make me do that by keeping me a prisoner?' she demanded.

'I can at least try!' he said grimly.

The eyes that had so recently looked at him with love now blazed with hatred.

'Then you are even more of a monster than I thought!'
Regan cried.

How she got through the days that followed Regan never
knew. She could not look at Rolf without loving and hating
him both at the same time. Her every nerve cried out for his
touch, yet her despair at knowing how he had treated her
would not allow her to acknowledge it.

She was tormented too by terrible guilt for the madness
that had overtaken her. She had betrayed poor David, given
herself to a man she scarcely knew, defied her father . . .
Whenever Regan thought of her father, the turmoil within
her grew worse. She could hardly believe the things Rolf
and Rosalie said he had done. But of course in the old days
things had been different. Men had done hard and ruthless
deeds in order to survive.

Lying awake, night after night, Regan tried to make
excuses for him and cringed with shame as she thought
of the Hannays. But none of that altered what Rolf had
done. If he had come to Mia-Mia and challenged her father
to a duel she could have understood it. If he had come with
hired men to take back the land by force, she could have
understood it. But to pretend he loved her and father a child
by her! That she could never understand – or forgive!

On the third day of her incarceration the madness took
hold once more. She couldn't allow him to do this to her.
If it killed her and the child both she had to at least make
the attempt to escape! As the first rosy light of dawn began
to streak the sky Regan dressed in her own breeches and
shirt, crept out of her room and down to the stables. At
her approach Betsy whickered softly with pleasure. Regan
found her saddle and bridle and led her outside, glancing
up anxiously at the windows as her hooves clacked on the
cobbles.

'We're going home,' she whispered to the horse.

Betsy pawed and shifted, restless from lack of exercise,

and Regan's fingers were trembling so that fixing the buckles seemed to take forever. But at last the final one was in place. Regan heaved a sigh of relief. She pulled on the girths to check all was secure – and heard a voice behind her.

'Are you thinking of going somewhere, my love?'

She whirled round, her heart thundering in her breast. Rolf was on the veranda, leaning idly against the rail. How long had he stood there watching her? she wondered.

'It's very early to be riding out,' Rolf said in a drawl that sounded almost amused. 'You weren't intending to go too far, I hope?'

She found her voice. 'As a matter of fact I was!' she flung at him. 'You can't keep me a prisoner here for ever.'

He came down the steps, standing hands on hips, facing her. 'You are in no fit condition to ride so far – even if you could find the way.'

'Oh, I'd find it!' she retorted. 'If it took me a week, I'd find it!'

'By which time you would likely have lost our child – if you had not killed yourself first,' Rolf said lightly. 'Oh Regan, Regan, I thought you had more sense.'

'And I thought you had more honour!' she retorted. 'It's you who have forced me to such extreme measures, keeping me here against my will. Well, it won't work. You'll prevent me from going now, I suppose. But you can't watch me every hour of every day. You have work to do and I'll find my chance.'

'Then I shall have to make sure Betsy's tack – if not Betsy herself – is unavailable to you,' he said harshly.

Tears, always so ready these days, sprung to her eyes. She brushed them away.

'You're mad if you think you can get away with this!' she flung at him. 'Sooner or later my father will find out where I am and come after me. Then you'll be sorry. He'll have you horsewhipped for what you have done!'

220

Rolf's lips tightened. 'I dare say he would if he had the chance,' he said bitterly. 'But you forget, Regan, I am no longer a mere youth, the son of a family to be ground underfoot, and your father is no longer an officer of the Corps. Besides, if he intended coming after you, why hasn't he already done so?'

She bit her lip. She had no answer to that. Was it that he had not yet been able to discover her whereabouts in the vast countryside? Or that he had washed his hands of her?

'Oh, I hate you!' she burst out.

'You don't mean that, Regan,' he said, his voice low and urgent. 'Have you forgotten so soon how it was with us? If so, I mean to remind you.'

Before she could so much as protest he drew her towards him, his lips seeking hers. In vain she struggled against his iron grip. Her heart was pounding, her pulses racing.

How dare he assault her like this? And yet, within her, small sharp shards of desire were flicking and dancing and against her will her lips softened beneath his. Oh, dear God, she wanted him still! One touch, one kiss, and her treacherous body was weakening.

As if he sensed her imminent capitulation, his hard mouth became gentler and his iron grip on her arms relaxed a little. Regan moved swiftly, like a cat, wriggling and at the same time pushing at him with all her strength. 'How dare you!' she flung at him.

He grasped her again and this time try as she might she could not struggle free.

'I dare because I love you, Regan!' he ground out. 'And because in spite of what you say, I know you love me. I know what I did was unforgivable, but I swear it was unplanned.'

She managed a little laugh. 'Give me one good reason why I should believe you.'

His face darkened. 'Give *me* one good reason why I should fall in love with the daughter of a blackguard such as Andrew Mackenzie!

Her mouth fell open. 'Oh!' she squeaked indignantly.

'Oh, indeed. The last thing I intended was that. But it is what has occurred, and I swear to you no one regrets it more than I.'

'Then let me go!' Regan said fiercely. 'If you love me, let me go!'

'Will it make you happy never to see me again?' he demanded. 'And what of our unborn child?'

'Oh – I don't know . . .' Regan sobbed. The sound of footsteps on the cobbles made her break off. They both turned to see Johnson, one of the convict labourers, approaching.

'Johnson, see to it that Betsy is unsaddled and returned to her stable,' Rolf said curtly. 'Lock her tack safely away and bring the key to me. And you, Madam,' he added softly, 'come into the house and put this nonsense about running away out of your head.'

His hand firm beneath her elbow, he led Regan into the house.

'You can't go on with this madness, Rolf,' Rosalie said. She was sitting in the big comfortable chair in the kitchen where she had spent most of her days since Alison had come home. 'You are achieving nothing by keeping Regan here against her will. Take her home.'

Rolf sighed. 'If I let her go, Rosalie, I'll never see her again.'

'If she loves you as I think she does then when she's had the chance to think things over perhaps she'll come back to you,' Rosalie argued.

Rolf snorted. 'You really think Andrew Mackenzie would allow such a thing – even given that she can ever bring herself to forgive me? He'd see me in hell first.'

'Regan has a mind of her own,' Rosalie said. 'And perhaps age has mellowed Mackenzie. If he loves Regan her happiness will be his first consideration.'

Rolf raised an eyebrow. There had been precious little

consideration for Regan's happiness when Andrew had ordered him to leave Mia-Mia. But then, he supposed, any father would have done the same. And Andrew adored Regan without doubt.

'Take her home, Rolf,' Rosalie urged again. Rolf stood, stony as a statue, and she threw her arms into the air in exasperation. 'Oh, you're as stubborn as she is! Can't you see, you're only painting yourself as black as she believes you to be! And don't you realise she'll only try to run away again the first opportunity she gets. Could you live with yourself if something happened to her?'

Rolf's shoulders slumped. Rosalie was right, he knew. And what future was there for them now? She hated him, and he could hardly blame her for that. Though the thought of her leaving was unbearable, perhaps his only hope lay in setting her free.

'If I lose her, Rosalie, I shall lay the blame at your door,' he said heavily.

'If you lose her, you'll have no one to blame but yourself,' she returned tartly.

'I know it.' He stood motionless whilst the anticipated pain seemed to tear his heart in two. He had set out to hurt Andrew Mackenzie and ended up hurting Regan – and himself – more. The revenge he had lived for was no longer worth the candle. If nothing else, Regan had taught him that love was far stronger than hate. But what had the lesson cost him?

'Take the wagon and drive her home,' Rosalie urged. 'We can manage here without you for a few days. We've managed without you often enough before.'

He nodded, sighing deeply, as if the decision was a sword thrust in his heart. At the door he looked back over his shoulder. As ever, his face gave nothing away. Only his eyes betrayed his pain.

'I'll tell her,' he said, and Rosalie sank back into her chair, weak with relief.

* * *

Regan stood by the window staring out. As the door opened she turned and saw Rolf standing there.

'Go away and leave me alone!' she spat.

Rolf's hands went to his hips so that his stance betrayed nothing of the heartache he was feeling. The time for pleading was over. Now he had nothing left but what little of his dignity he could muster.

'I thought you wanted to go home,' he said brusquely.

Something that might almost have been dismay flared in her eyes and hope flared briefly. Had he called her bluff? Then she lifted her chin.

'You mean you are offering to take me?'

'Yes,' Rolf said. 'Get together whatever you want to take with you and we'll leave as soon as the horses can be harnessed to the wagon.'

'I came with nothing, I'll leave with nothing,' she said proudly and he had no way of knowing what she was thinking that the most precious things she had brought with her to Dunrae – love and hope for the future – had already been lost.

'Make ready, then,' he said and turning on his heel, left the room.

The wagon stood ready with Betsy tied to it so that she could trot alongside. It had been packed with everything they would need for the journey and there was no longer any reason for delay. Now the decision had been made, Rolf was clearly impatient to be off.

'Oh, Regan, I'm so sorry it has come to this,' Rosalie said. 'I shall miss you.'

'And I'll miss you,' Regan returned. 'But I have no place here now, Rosalie.'

'You will always have a place here!' Rosalie said fiercely. 'If you change your mind and decide to return, I shall be the first to welcome you.'

The two women embraced briefly and Rolf rumpled the two little boys' hair.

'Cheer up! Let's have a smile from you two imps!'

Their faces remained solemn and Philip spoke for both of them. 'We don't want Regan to go!'

Amen to that! Rolf thought. Aloud, he said, 'Regan wants to go home. To her father and everything she knows. You must understand that.'

They thought about it and after a moment Philip said, 'It's true. We wouldn't want to leave Mama and Father and all our toys, would we, James?'

'No,' James echoed in his piping voice. 'We wouldn't like that.'

Regan managed a small stiff smile at them, then she went down the veranda steps and Rolf handed her up into the wagon. As they moved off Regan cast one last look at the little group who she had thought were to become her family. Then, turning away from Rolf so that he would not see that her eyes were shining with tears, she looked towards the mountains beyond which lay her home.

Eighteen

The journey was as different as could be from the one which had brought her here. For one thing it was a good deal slower, for no wagon could make the pace that Satan and Betsy had made. But it was the difference in spirit that was most marked. On the tortuous journey to Dunrae, love and happiness had sped the miles for both of them. Now the road stretched before them, endless and empty, with nothing at the end of it but parting and heartache.

In mid-afternoon they stopped to rest and water the horses, and when the sun began to sink over the horizon, a ball of ruby flame that promised a fine day for the morrow, Rolf selected a suitable clearing to make camp for the night.

As she picked without much appetite at the salt pork and bread Rosalie had packed for them Regan found herself recalling the fresh fish Rolf had caught and cooked for them, and how it had tasted like the nectar of the gods. Such a short time ago! Yet already it seemed to belong to another life. Sadly she watched Rolf arrange the blankets for their bed and remembered how wonderful it had been to sleep in his arms. Tonight there would be no such joy. Though Rolf had placed the two makeshift beds close together for warmth and safety they were unmistakeably that – two beds, not one.

Regan slid between the blankets and lay staring blindly up at the stars. It was a very long time before she fell asleep.

Beneath the blanket, Regan stirred blissfully. She was in Rolf's arms and everything was well with them. She

226

couldn't remember why it had not been, couldn't understand why recently she had been so unhappy. He was her love, and she was his. What else could possibly matter?

She could feel her body coming alive beneath his touch, her breasts tingling deliciously as he stroked them. The baby was pressed between them, protected by their bodies and their love and his fingers slid down to the firm mound, caressing it before moving on downwards to slip into the secret place between her thighs. Desire stirred deep within her, first tiny flickers, then an urgent spiral of need. She pressed her mouth against his neck, tasting the salt tang of his flesh, and arching her back to accommodate those probing fingers.

Oh, she loved him, she needed him, and he was coming to her . . . She twisted her arms about his neck, loving the feel of the tendons beneath her fingers, her whole body crying out with the need to be at one with him. But there was something between them, muffling the delicious sensations. Something stifling her, yet at the same time drawing her towards a place she did not want to be . . . Regan screwed up her eyes, resisting. But it was useless. The wonderful aura of love and happiness was fading, harsh reality creeping in. With a sinking sensation Regan surfaced through layer upon layer of consciousness.

A dream. It had only been a dream. She wanted to weep with frustration and misery.

From the even rise and fall of his breath she knew Rolf was sleeping. Yet somehow in her dream she had managed to roll closer to him so that they nestled together, separated only by the rough blankets.

Regan lay motionless, hardly daring to breathe. Oh, it felt so good to be so close to him again! To smell the faint masculine odour of his skin, to press her mouth against his flesh and taste the salt as she had tasted it in her dream! She lay, loving him as he slept, relishing this stolen moment when she could pretend to herself that everything was as it had been, that he had not lied to her and deceived her, that they were simply two people in love.

Around them the bush was silent and sleeping, the stillness broken only by the occasional sharp cry of a night bird and the shifting of the horses.

Oh, would that this could last forever – or that she could turn back the clock so they could start afresh with all the circumstances different! Regan nestled her head into the hollow between his chin and shoulder and suddenly he stirred, reaching for her in his sleep. Drowsily Regan wriggled closer. The blankets were rucking down; the top halves of their bodies were in contact now, and it was wonderful.

'Oh Rolf!' she whispered. 'Oh Rolf, my love . . .'

Her voice came to him in a dream. As he surfaced slowly from the deepest of sleeps he was aware only of Regan's head against his shoulder, her arms about his neck. Awake or asleep his body responded at once to her touch, his groin becoming hot, his flesh hard. Still scarcely knowing what he did Rolf pulled aside the blankets, allowing his hand to run the length of her spine, pressing her to him.

'Dear love,' he whispered, making to roll on top of her. And felt her stiffen beneath him.

'No!' Her voice was like the crack of a pistol shot, and the arms that had lately held him so tenderly became flailing weapons of defence. 'Stop it! Stop it this instant!'

Bewildered he looked down at her. The light of the moon showed him pursed-up lips, tight-shut eyes. A face he loved and desired more than life itself, a face he knew he would love and desire to the end of time. But a face that was now denying him what she had so recently offered.

'Regan, don't do this to me!' he ground out. 'I want you!'

'Oh, so you're going to rape me now, are you?' she flung at him.

In an instant his urgent passion was quenched, his longing for her buried by outrage.

'I have never taken you against your will, Regan, and I never would!' he yelled. 'It was you who instigated this intimacy. I was asleep and you woke me with your kisses. How dare you call my response rape?'

'I was half asleep too,' she said, a little petulantly. 'I didn't know what I was doing.'

'But why did you do it at all?' he demanded.

She pursed her lips. 'I don't know what you mean.'

'Why turn to me in your sleep if you don't love me? Ask yourself that, Regan!'

She already was, but the answer her heart was clamouring to give was not one that her head could accept. Not after the way he had used her, lying his way into her life and stealing it for his own ends. The tears ached in her throat once more; determinedly she swallowed them.

'*Love* you, Rolf?' she whispered, her tone heavy with sarcasm. 'No, I don't love you. You made me *want* you, yes. I admit it. And for that I hate you with all my heart.'

He tried to ignore the last sentiment. Somehow he had to get through to her before it was too late. Tomorrow they would reach Mia-Mia and he would lose her forever.

'You admit you wanted me then,' he persisted. 'Enough to creep into my arms while we both slept.'

The memory of how her body had yearned for him wrenched at her so that she felt she was being torn apart. But she couldn't give him the satisfaction of knowing that.

'No!' she cried. 'I don't even want you any more!'

'I see,' Rolf said heavily. 'So you thought merely to torment me?'

'If you like, yes.' It was as good an explanation as any.

'Very well, if that's the way you want it, Regan, then that's the way it will be.'

He stood up, towering over her as he folded the blankets afresh to remake his tumbled bed. Gazing up at him, so

229

tall and strong in the moonlight, Regan felt her resolve wavering.

Oh, she did want him! She did! But that was just the treacherous response of her body's addiction to his love-making. If she gave in now, as it was urging her to do, she would only be handing him the power to hurt her again and again.

Rolf remade his bed in silence but did nothing to right hers. Regan pulled the blanket back over her as best she could without standing up as he had done. She didn't think her legs would support her. Rolf clambered between the folds and she noticed there was now a good foot of clear ground between them.

'Tomorrow we shall reach Mia-Mia,' he said. 'Then, Regan, we shall have no need to look on one another ever again.'

With that he turned his back on her and in a frighteningly short time the depth of his breathing told her he was asleep.

They rose with the dawn. Rolf was already up and moving about when Regan surfaced mistily from her disturbed and troubled slumbers. His blankets were already folded and stacked away in the wagon and he was drying his face and hands after washing in the river.

'You're awake, then.' There was no tenderness in his tone. 'We'll get on our way as soon as we can. Do you want breakfast?'

She shook her head. Nausea was coming at her in waves but she thought she would die before she would let him know it.

'I won't bother then,' he said coldly. 'I'll eat when I've deposited you at Mia-Mia.'

As if I were a parcel! she thought furiously.

By the time the sun was fully risen they were on their way and by noon the road was leading them downwards towards the Hawkesbury valley.

almost incoherent with overwhelming relief. 'Oh, I thought you were both dead!'

'Hush, Regan!' Rolf said impatiently. 'Hush, for the love of God, and help me get your father to the house!'

For Regan, the next hours passed in a blur. Afterwards she recalled it only as fragments, separate pieces in a puzzle which had somehow fit together but the whole shape of which she could not, for the life of her, remember.

As if looking at a panorama of events which had happened to someone else, she saw herself helping to support her father into the house; saw herself checking on Elizabeth, who had miraculously slept through the whole nightmare, recalled her enormous relief when help arrived from Broken Hill – John Bray had ridden there to raise the alarm when the convict band had first launched the attack. The fire had burned itself out, and she remembered her fierce joy when she had taken a jug of ale to the stable yard to refresh the exhausted volunteers and felt a warm rough nose nudge her arm. It was Betsy. She must have bolted in fear from the convict band and found her own way home. And hopefully the other horses would be returned in a day or two when the military had quelled the rising, as they would surely do.

But most of all she would never forget the look on Andrew's face when he recovered enough to thank Rolf for his bravery.

'I misjudged you, Peterson,' he said, calling Rolf still by the name by which he had known him. 'You risked your own life to save me out there. For that I will be forever in your debt.'

Rolf had shrugged. ''Twas nothing. I did what any man would do.'

'I think not,' Andrew said gruffly. 'And I have to tell you I can think of no more fitting husband for my daughter. If she wants you, that is,' he added with a short laugh.

If she wanted him! All Regan's doubts had disappeared

now. The grief and despair she had felt when she had thought he was lost in the blazing stable had proved to her that she did indeed love him. And as for Rolf – how could she continue to doubt his love for her when he had risked his life not once, but twice, this night? Not only for her, but also for the man he had professed to hate? To do what Rolf had done would have been a heroic act no matter who he was attempting to rescue from the inferno. To have done it for the man upon whom he had sought to wreak revenge was a testimonial to Rolf's selfless bravery and to his love.

The one piece of the puzzle that was missing was what had brought Rolf to Mia-Mia.

When at last Regan collapsed exhausted on to her bed and felt the mattress dip as Rolf lay down beside her the question sprang to her lips.

'What are you doing here, Rolf? You should be halfway back to Dunrae!'

'You want me to go, then?' he asked teasingly.

'No!' Her hand found his in the grey dawn light. 'No, I don't! I just want to know what made you turn around and come back.'

He was silent, stroking her hand with his thumb. Impossible to explain, even to himself, the compulsion which had overcome him as he stopped to make camp for the night. From the moment he had left her his heart had been urging him to go back and make her listen to him. But he had resisted, certain it would do no good and only cause more heartache for both of them. But as he made to unharness the horses he had suddenly experienced a rush of foreboding so strong it had stopped him in his tracks. Something terrible was going to happen. It was as if it was happening already. And it had to do with Regan.

Rolf had never been a man to believe in premonition. He was, above all, practical and not a little cynical. But now he simply could not escape from the overwhelming feeling that Regan was somehow in danger.

He had to go back. Even as he refastened the harness, his fingers clumsy with barely controlled urgency, he had scoffed at himself. It was just a trick his mind was playing on him because the thought of not seeing her ever again was more than he could bear. And yet still he had returned, driving along the darkening road as fast as he dared and still feeling he was not making enough speed.

And thank God he had! For as he had drawn up outside Mia-Mia he had heard her scream.

'Why did you come back?' Regan pressed him, but her voice was drowsy now.

'Because I love you,' he said.

It was the simplest explanation, and the only one that mattered.

'And I love you,' she murmured.

She nestled her head against his shoulder and in an instant was fast asleep.

Epilogue

'Here it is, my love. This is where my mother lies,' Rolf said. His voice was husky with emotion.

As he had walked up the rise to the rough grave the memories had come flooding in and for a few moments it had seemed almost as if he had become once again the boy he had once been.

The grave was covered now with fresh green grass but the wooden cross he had fashioned remained. It was weathered now, but the name upon it was still legible. Jessica Hannay.

His eyes misted as he thought of her, of her love and her courage, the legacy of which had followed him down the years. He wished with all his heart that he could turn back the clock and make things right for her. And he hoped that perhaps by some miracle she was looking down on him now. He would like to think she could see the man he had become and what he had made of the life she had given him by the dint of her suffering.

'Oh, Rolf, she must have loved you very much,' Regan said, slipping her hand into his.

He could not answer. His throat was too full.

Regan knelt, laying the simple posy of wild flowers that she had brought on the grassy mound.

'I love him too, Jessica,' she said softly. 'And I promise you I always will.'

She stood up again, smiling sadly at Rolf through tear-filled eyes.

He put an arm around her waist and she laid her head against his shoulder. In the crook of his other arm his little son wriggled contentedly, jamming a small thumb in his baby mouth.

Rolf experienced a rush of warmth and gratitude as they stood there together, a family, the new generation of Hannays. He had found happiness he had never dreamed of in those far-off days, happiness he felt he had done nothing to deserve, and he thanked the fates with all his heart that it was so.

He had kept the vow he had sworn on this very spot all those years ago. One day there would once again be a Hannay at Mia-Mia. But it had not been accomplished by bitterness and hatred. It had been accomplished by love.

Rolf and Regan's eyes met over the head of their baby son and the sun, which had been hidden behind a cloud, chose that moment to emerge. It lit the wooden cross and the faces of the little family, bathing them in golden light.

It was as if Jessica were smiling on them, an omen for all the years to come.

The nausea had eased now but Regan's heart felt heavy as lead and beneath it was a great gaping hollow where her stomach should have been.

Almost home. Soon he would set her down and drive away. The thought was so terrible it ached in every nerve and muscle.

Regan glanced at Rolf, sitting stony-faced beside her, and the words that could put a stop to this nightmare hovered on her lips. She had only to tell him how she truly felt and he would turn around and take her back to Dunrae. But she couldn't bring herself to do it. And what was the point? How could she ever trust him again or believe a single word he said? No, better to make an end of it, go home and try to forget him and the tumultuous love they had shared. Better to face her father's fury and the shame of being an unwed mother, better to live her life without him, the man who had made such a complete and utter fool of her.

But with every mile Regan's heart sank still further, and again and again she had to force herself to refrain from admitting that, yes! – whatever he had done she loved him still.

The road was dry and rutted now, running arrow-straight as far as the eye could see. There was a cloud of dust on the horizon. Regan strained her eyes beneath the bonnet Rosalie had insisted on loaning her. For a long while the dust cloud shimmered like a mirage on the hot road, then gradually it took shape. Two men, galloping this way.

Rolf's hand went to the pistol he wore strapped at his hip. In this wild country men on galloping horses could mean many things, and it was better to be safe than sorry. Then, as they neared, Regan recognised one of them – Amos Friend, who lived in Broken Hill.

'It's all right, Rolf, it's Mr Friend,' she said.

The approaching horses slowed so as to pass the wagon safely on the narrow road.

'Why, it's Regan!' Amos called out as he came close. 'Good day, Regan!'

'Good day, Mr Friend . . .'

The words died suddenly on her lips as her eyes went to his companion, and her heart fluttered in her breast like a trapped bird.

Oh, dear God, the second man! She knew him too! Well, she'd seen him before, at least, and that face was burned for ever in her memory. For the first time since that day when she had come upon the murdered man lying on the road, his attacker beside him, Regan found herself looking into the face of the bushwhacker!

Regan's mouth had gone dry. For endless moments they gazed at one another, Regan's eyes wide with horror, the man's narrowed and dangerous. Had he recognised her? She felt sure he had. Those eyes were challenging her to speak out and accuse him.

She knew she dare not. Rolf's hand no longer hovered over his pistol. One word from her and the man would shoot them both dead. Regan sat, mute with terror, as the men rode past and trotted into the distance. And still she sat, unable to move a muscle.

'Regan?' Rolf was looking at her with concern. 'Are you ill? You're pale as death.'

Her breath came out on a long shuddering sigh. 'That man. The one with Amos Friend. It was him, the bushwhacker! And he recognised me too, I know he did!'

'Why did you not say something?' Rolf asked, but he already knew the answer.

'And get us both killed?' Regan retorted. 'If he'd thought I was going to give him away he would have put a bullet in me without a second thought – and you, too, if he'd seen you go for your gun. But what was he doing with Mister Friend?'

'Is he of doubtful character too?' Rolf asked.

'Oh no, he's as solid a citizen as could be imagined! If he had known the company he was keeping . . .' Regan broke off, biting at her lip. 'The bushwhacker must be worming his way into honest society. He knows I can point the finger at him, and now he knows who I am. Just a few innocent questions to Mister Friend and he'll also know where to find me!'

'Then you must tell your father all this the moment you get home and leave it to him to decide what's best to do,' Rolf said, smarting with the knowledge that he would be far away and unable to do anything to protect Regan.

He flicked the whip to urge the horses forward. The sooner he reached Mia-Mia and deposited Regan into her father's keeping, the sooner he started back for Dunrae, the better. Then and only then would he be able to begin picking up the threads of his life and put behind him this woman who had found her way into his heart and torn it apart.

At the end of the drive to Mia-Mia Rolf halted the wagon. 'I'll leave you here, Regan. You are in sight of the house and I'll watch until you reach it.'

'Won't you come in for refreshment, then?' she asked, desperate to delay the moment of his departure.

A corner of his mouth tightened and his voice was heavy with irony. 'I don't think I'd be welcome, Regan. There would likely be a scene such as a lady should not have to witness. Your father promised to have me horsewhipped, and no doubt he'd try. But I would not take such punishment lying down. The result could be ugly indeed.'

Regan nodded. He was right, of course. She was nervous enough as it was of facing her father; if Rolf was there too it would be a thousand times worse. But oh! – nothing could be as bad as watching him ride away, knowing she would never see him again.

Once more the words to beg him not to leave her thus hovered on her lips; once more she bit them back. Her fierce pride simply would not allow her to speak them. She clambered down from the wagon. Everything in her was crying out for one last embrace, one last kiss. But resolutely she denied herself them. If she threw herself into his arms now she would never find the strength to walk away.

'Goodbye, Rolf.' Her voice was tight with unshed tears.

'Goodbye, Regan.' His face was a mask of granite.

She tugged on Betsy's reins and started down the drive. For a while she could not bring herself to look back, but when she did he was still there watching her.

The tears overflowed from her brimming eyes and began to slide unchecked down her cheeks. The tall, handsome figure at the end of the drive was blurred now, seen through a veil of moisture. Resolutely Regan turned and walked Betsy towards the house.

'Regan, Regan!' It was Elizabeth, racing towards her down the veranda steps.

She threw herself at Regan, burying her face in the dust-stained breeches, and Regan dropped the reins, stroking the little girl's hair and holding her close. Then she became aware of another figure standing on the veranda. Her father. Gently she disentangled herself from Elizabeth's clinging arms and went towards him.

At first glance, his face was like thunder. Then she saw that his eyes were bright with tears and he held his arms open to her.

'Oh, Regan, my Regan! Thank God you're home!'

She ran to him, burying her face in his chest. 'Father! Oh, Father, I'm so sorry.'

For a moment he simply held her whilst the tears escaped and rolled down his weathered cheeks. He had thought he had lost her, as surely as he had lost his beloved Anne. Now, praise be, she was home again, safe and sound. Andrew Mackenzie sent up a prayer of thanks to a God he had long since ceased to believe in.

'Father, please let me try to explain,' she whispered.

And still he held her. 'Don't say a word, Regan, and neither will I. I am only glad, my dear, that you have come back to me.'

Nineteen

Regan and Andrew ate supper alone. Jud was away down river and Elizabeth had been put to bed, and at last they were able to talk. Andrew explained that he had not come to seek her out since he had believed that if she had been driven to such desperate measures he must allow her to follow the dictates of her heart, and Regan was able to tell him of Rolf's true identity and the reason he had come to Mia-Mia.

Andrew was astounded – and furiously angry.

'How dare he use you so?' he exclaimed. 'And all over some imagined wrong!'

'It wasn't imagined,' Regan said quietly. 'Mr Hannay rode his horse to his death because you were turning him out of his farm. You can't blame Rolf for wanting revenge.'

'The man was drunk,' Andrew returned curtly. 'If he killed himself falling from his horse he had no one to blame but himself.'

But through the bluster Regan thought she caught a gleam of guilt.

'You shouldn't have done it, Father,' she said.

He sighed deeply. 'You don't know what it was like in those days, Regan. It was a harsh world, and every man for himself. But perhaps you're right. There were deeds done then that shouldn't have been. And now, I suppose, they've come back to haunt me.'

'They have, Father. For I love him still, and . . .' On the point of telling him about her condition, she broke off. She couldn't face that yet. 'How is David?' she asked changing tack.

'He's well. He was dreadfully upset at first, of course, but I think he has found someone to help mend his broken heart. He and Sara have been seeing a good deal of each other and they seem very happy together.' His eyes met hers in the candlelight. 'You're not thinking of taking up with him again, are you? I don't think it would be wise – or fair.'

Regan shook her head. 'I couldn't, Father. I knew even before Rolf came along that David was not the one for me. Even if I can't have Rolf, I could never settle now for anything less than the love we shared.'

'And it was wrong of me to press you to the match,' Andrew said heavily. 'I have a good deal to answer for, don't I, Regan?'

She reached across and touched his hand. 'You thought it was for the best. Now, there is something else I have to tell you, Father. You remember the bushwhacker I came across on the day Rolf rescued me? I saw him today, with Amos Friend.'

As she explained, Andrew's face darkened. 'Dear God, it must be the man he's taken on to help run his business! I saw them together the other day, and I didn't care for the look of him. Tomorrow, first thing, I'll ride for the military and expose him. Once he's in custody you'll have no more to fear.'

Regan nodded, grateful to think the monster would soon be behind bars.

'I'm very tired, Father,' she said. 'Would you mind very much if I went to bed?'

He smiled at her. 'Regan, nothing will make me happier than to know you are sleeping in your own bed again. You are home. That's all that matters to me.'

The moment she relaxed in her own comfortable bed Regan

was asleep. Several hours passed, with not so much as a dream to disturb them, when suddenly she was roughly awakened. She opened her eyes to find her father leaning over the bed, shaking her.

'Regan!' His voice was low but urgent. 'Wake up! There's someone in the yard outside. I'm going to investigate. Fetch Elizabeth and look after her. There could be trouble.'

Instantly Regan was wide awake and trembling.

'Remember, stay in the house for your own safety!' Andrew cautioned her again, and then he was gone.

Regan threw back the covers and got up, pulling on a robe. She crossed to the window and looked out. The stable yard, bathed in moonlight, appeared deserted. Then, to her horror, she saw something moving in the shadows and a gaggle of men with torches emerged, making for the convict quarters. Regan could see they were armed with pitchforks and reaping hooks. Her heart came into her throat with a sickening thud.

A convict break-out! It was one of the settlers' greatest fears. A band of desperate men would rampage from farm to farm, stealing horses, looting, burning and killing, and all the while freeing more convicts to swell their number. They were here, at Mia-Mia, and her father had gone out alone to confront them!

As he emerged from the house, pistol in hand, Andrew could see nothing untoward. Then a flicker of light drew his eye to the stable door. Two shadows slipped inside and Andrew erupted with blazing fury. Someone was trying to steal his horses! He dashed forward, his pistol cocked. 'Damn you!' he grated, kicking the door wide open and stepping inside.

Something hard and heavy caught him on the back of the neck. He had one moment in which to experience utter shock and a blinding pain before the pistol fell from his hand and he dropped like a stone, unconscious, to the rough stable floor.

*   *   *

She had to fetch Elizabeth. She had to make sure the little girl came to no harm. Regan ran across the room and into the corridor. Then she drew up short. Someone was there, a big burly figure coming towards her. Regan's hands flew to her throat as a shaft of moonlight illuminated his face.

It was him, the bushwhacker! With a stab of utter terror, Regan realised that he had come for her.

He saw her at the same moment that she saw him; the same shaft of moonlight told him he had found his quarry. Oh, his plan had worked and nicely! He could never have hoped to get to Regan without causing some kind of diversion, and by tomorrow it could well have been too late. So he had freed a few convicts and sent them on the rampage to Mia-Mia to occupy the menfolk whilst he slipped unnoticed into the house. And here she was, the woman who could expose him for the criminal he was and put an end to all his efforts to break into the society that had long rejected him.

'So!' he grated. 'We meet again.'

A scream burst from Regan's throat. She dived in at the nearest open doorway – the guest room which had been Rolf's – but before she could slam it behind her the man was there, his foot jamming it open, his bulk filling the gap. Then, with a shove that sent her reeling, he was in the room with her, cutting off any hope of further escape.

As she recovered her balance Regan braced herself, expecting the man to shoot at any second, but he did not. Instead he stood there looking at her and grinning unpleasantly.

'What do you want with me?' she squeaked.

'I'm going to kill you, of course.' She could hear from his tone he was enjoying this.

'Then kill me and have done with it!' she threw at him.

'Oh, there's no hurry.' Again he seemed to be laughing at her. 'Your father has his hands full outside – more than full.

I think he's been taken care of. I think we should have a little fun first, you and I. You're a bonny one and no mistake.'

He reached out and touched one of her curls. Regan pulled away, outraged and disgusted. 'How dare you?'

His hand caught her arm in an iron grip. His laugh had become a snarl now.

'Not good enough for you, am I? Well, we'll see about that! I'll take my pleasure with you, Miss, if I like – and I do like! Then, when they find you in the morning, they'll think 'twas the convicts who raped and murdered you.'

He pulled her towards him. Regan screamed again as his hand grasped at her breast and the thin fabric of her wrap gave. Dear God, he meant to rape her before he murdered her!

She began to hit out wildly with her hands, screaming all the while, but he was too strong for her. Step by step he forced her back towards the bed. The back of her knees cracked against the iron frame and she collapsed on to it, conscious only of this monster towering over her.

'Leave her, you blackguard!' The shout was like a thunderclap in the room.

Rolf's voice? No, it wasn't possible!

As startled as she, the man relaxed his hold on her, straightening for a moment, and in that instant a shot rang out. The man swayed on his feet, clutching at himself, then, like a great felled tree, he crashed down beside her.

Regan screamed again as she felt his blood, hot and sticky, on her bare arm. She barely knew what was happening. Then strong arms were lifting her.

'Regan, my love! Did he harm you?'

It *was* Rolf! Still she could not believe it. Yet, by some miracle, he was here!

'Oh Rolf, Rolf!' she sobbed. 'What are you doing here?'

240

'Did he harm you?' Rolf asked again roughly, not answering her question.

'No, I'm all right. But the convicts are rising. Didn't you see them in the stable yard?'

'I came in at the front. I heard you scream and . . .' he stared at her. 'What convicts?'

'I don't know. There was a rabble and Father is out there alone. We must go to him!'

The terror in her tone convinced him she was telling the truth.

'Stay here!' He released her, making for the door, but she followed him anyway.

There was a strange flickering light in the landing and a smell of acrid smoke. A new wave of terror possessed Regan. Fire! The devils had started a fire! She ran after Rolf down the stairs, almost tumbling in her haste, then, as they ran through the kitchen she gasped with horror. The stables were ablaze.

'Rolf, the horses!' she cried, racing out down the veranda steps.

There was no sign now of the convict band, and no screams of terrified horses either. In an instant Regan realised what had happened – the convicts had stolen the horses and then fired the stables. But where was her father?

'Oh, Miss Regan!' A figure came running towards her and she recognised Dickon Stokes. So he, at least, had not taken off the join the motley band, though they had clearly unlocked him from his quarters. Dickon was almost beside himself. 'Your father's in there!' He indicated the blazing stable. 'The blackguards knocked him out, so they told me. And he's still in there!'

'Oh, dear God!' Regan clapped her hands over her mouth at this new horror.

'I'll find him, Regan, never fear!' Quick as a flash Rolf turned to Dickon. 'Give me your shirt, man. Hurry now!'

Practically tearing the shirt from the startled Dickon's

back, he dunked it in the water trough and wound it around his face. Then, without another word, he raced towards the blazing stables.

'Rolf!' Regan was petrified as she saw him illuminated for a moment against the flames before he dived to his knees to escape the worst of the smoke.

Dickon was shaking his head in disbelief at what he had just witnessed. 'He shouldn't have gone in there!' he muttered distractedly. 'No man can survive in there!'

Hardly were his words out than there was a loud crash as a timber fell inside the stables and then another, and the flames shot out reaching for the sky.

'Rolf!' Regan sobbed again. Her heart was hammering a tattoo of fear, and dread seemed to have drained every bit of strength from her limbs.

They were in that inferno, the two men she loved. Rolf had raced into danger without a second thought to save the man who was his sworn enemy. And now perhaps she had lost them both. Her stomach knotted, her breath came in ragged gasps.

'Come away, Miss Regan,' Dickon urged her, but nothing on heaven or earth would have torn her away though the heat of the fire was scorching her skin even at this distance. Another beam crashed down and showers of sparks chased the flames into the night sky. Regan covered her face with her hands, immobilised by the horror.

'Glory be!' Dickon's shout made her drop her hands from her face.

From the blazing doorway Rolf was emerging and he was not alone. He was half-supporting, half-dragging Andrew Mackenzie.

Dickon and Regan dashed forward to assist – and not a moment too soon. Scarcely were the two men clear of the stable when, with an almighty crash, the entire roof caved in.

'Oh, Rolf – oh, thank God! Father, Father!' Regan was